Free Spirit

I dedicate this book to my wonderful family – I could not have better
To my three daughters, Cheryl, Wendy and Joanne
And of course my husband – Austin

Free Spirit

Coral Leend

ROBERT HALE · LONDON

ISBN 0 7090 7975 3

Robert Hale Limited
Clerkenwell House
Clerkenwell Green
London EC1R 0HT

2 4 6 8 10 9 7 5 3 1

Typeset in 10½/13pt Plantin
by Derek Doyle & Associates, Shaw Heath.
Printed in Great Britain by St Edmundsbury Press,
Bury St Edmunds, Suffolk.
Bound by Woolnough Bookbinding Ltd.

CHAPTER ONE

'Y OU big cheat! You gave Lucy a kitten. You knew I was going to give her one. You know I was!' Incensed, eleven-year-old Madoc Morgan threw himself from his pony straight at Robert.

Caught off guard, his elder brother fell from his mount, hitting his head on a stone edging the road. Madoc, agile as a cat, landed on his feet, then saw the carriage bowling towards them at speed.

'Rob! Quick! Get up!' Madoc yelled, bending down and tugging at his brother, who was slumped on the road. 'Get up!'

Horrified, the boy stared at the two horses racing straight at them. Struggling to pull Robert out of their path, he saw their tensed muscles straining. He heard their snorting breath, their hoofs ringing on the stones, saw the whites of their eyes as they bore down on them. With another desperate tug he managed to move Robert slightly as the Morgan family's groom, Liam, who had been some distance behind, raced his mount immediately across the path of the oncoming horses. Startled, the carriage horses faltered and Liam caught the harness of the outside animal, hanging on with both hands. Guiding his own mount with his knees, he attempted to swerve them away from the boys. Still at a fair pace the horses veered slightly away from the children on the ground, not avoiding them completely as the inside horse stumbled slightly over them, but the carriage flew past, missing them by inches.

Liam flung himself off his horse alongside the boys.

'Are you hurt?

Speechless, panting in shaking breaths, Madoc shook his head, though blood was streaming down his face from a kick by a flying hoof.

Then he gasped: 'Rob. Rob's hurt.' He looked down at his brother, mangled and still. 'He's not dead, is he?'

Liam said nothing as he examined Robert. He was putting his fingers to the boy's throat to feel for his pulse when the driver of the carriage came racing back to them, his face ashen.

'Oh, my God! Are they killed? I didn't see them, they just came from nowhere.' As Madoc was up on his knees, he turned his attention to Liam with Robert. 'Is he dead?' he gasped. 'I didn't see them.'

'He's not dead.' Liam's voice was low. 'And it wasn't your fault.'

'It was my fault,' Madoc's voice was trembling. Shivering, he chewed at his lip, afraid he was going to cry, something he hadn't done since he was a baby. 'Will he be all right, Liam?' he choked out, staring at his inert brother.

The occupants of the carriage also came hurrying back, just as the driver spoke to Liam.

'You saved their lives,' he said. He looked at Liam with respect. 'When I saw you race across in front of us I thought *you* were a goner too. You risked your life to save those two boys' lives.'

Autumn 1860

The copper-ore barque heeled steeply to starboard, rolling Madoc Morgan, mate on the *Gower Girl*, on to his back as he slept in his bunk. A drop of water dripped down on to his face and he stirred, twitching his nose, rubbing his face against the rough blanket covering him. As the ship lurched back into another trough he grunted a protest at his cramped position, in a bunk too narrow and too short for his broad shoulders and height, and opened his eyes, his thoughts still full of Lucy.

So often he pictured her lying next to him, their bodies close, as he fantasized about her. He imagined his hands touching the softness of her white skin, wandering down over her body. She was so delicate and lovely, so unattainable; but in his dreams she welcomed his caresses, returned them.

She's married! His eyes flicked open, and savagely he smothered her image as his eyes caught sight of a cockroach making its way across the wooden beams above him. The dark beauty of the Chilean girls at Valparaiso was always attractive. He found their bold eyes inviting, their bronzed arms appealing – they certainly knew how to make a man feel good. Is that why the woman in my dreams so often has black hair instead of gold? he wondered, not for the first time. He stretched, then pulled on his sea-boots as the bell sounded the end of the watch.

Taking over command from the second mate, his eyes narrowed against the driving rain, Madoc peered up at the sails, shielding his eyes with his hand. His keen gaze travelled quickly across the rigging and the yards above, then, satisfied that all was well, his gaze returned to the horizon. They were approaching the coast of Britain, making for the Bristol Channel, and would soon see land. Their navigational calculations had to be exact as, once leaving the coast of South America, it was quite normal not to sight land for thousands of miles until they reached the channel. In the distance, on parallel courses, Madoc could see two other copper-barques of the fleet keeping pace with them.

Although his father owned the prosperous Morgan Shipping Company, at sixteen Madoc had requested to start as an apprentice on one of the company's ships.

'Are you sure that is what you wish to do?' his father had questioned when Madoc had approached him in the library at home. 'Wouldn't you rather serve as a midshipman in the Royal Navy?'

Madoc shook his head. 'I have considered that. But I want to sail on one of the family ships.'

'The RN is an excellent service. You could do well there, then return to our own fleet once you have experience as an officer . . . or captain?'

'No, sir. You know I've long held an ambition to sail around the Horn on a copper-barque?'

'Hmm!' David Morgan's expression was grim. 'I was afraid you might bring that up.' He was a big man: the chair creaked as he leaned back, rubbing a hand over his chin.

Though Morgan Shipping owned several copper-barques, twice rounding Cape Horn on a return trip to Chile, on the west coast of South America, Madoc realized that his father was not anxious to have one of his sons sailing the icy southernmost oceans. Madoc had heard often enough about the notorious conditions around Cape Horn. Sailing those waters was exhausting work, hard and dangerous, with snow, icebergs and mountainous waves to cope with, apart from the ever-present wind which necessitated raising heavier sails simply to withstand the strain of rounding Cape Horn. David's gaze came back to Madoc.

'To tell the truth, I was hoping you had forgotten about it. I don't think your mother will be too enthusiastic,' he added sardonically.

Madoc pulled a face, giving his father a hard stare, knowing he would empathize with his ambition.

'So? Can I?'

'Hmm.' David picked up the paperweight on his desk, turning it thoughtfully in his hands. He looked up and sighed. 'Very well. Though I would rather you took your first few trips on one of our eastern-going merchant vessels. One not navigating the Horn.'

Madoc beamed. 'But I can leave school?'

'This is not about leaving school, Madoc. This is a big step and very different from being a midshipman in the RN ... which is a gentleman's occupation.'

'I do realize that, sir.'

'And even being a master on a Cape Horn copper-barque is not a comfortable calling. It is harsh, dangerous and . . .'

'But I want some adventure ... sorry, sir!' he added, realizing he had interrupted his father.

'You'll get that all right.' David let out a barking laugh. 'And it will be damned hard work. No one goes along for the ride, not even the owner's son.'

'It's what I want, sir. To be one of the best.'

Because of the appalling weather that the small vessels encountered, Swansea Cape Horners were renowned amongst seafaring men as being some of the most capable and toughest sailors in the world.

David studied Madoc.

'Rob is thinking of going to university for a few years,' he said, mentioning Madoc's elder brother. 'You wouldn't like to do that? He may do a tour of Europe too.'

'But he doesn't have the choice of going to sea because of his arm.' Madoc's voice was bleak, as it always was when he considered Robert's disabled arm, which he had caused.

'I don't think Rob would wish to.' David knew which way Madoc's thoughts were veering.

'Which ship would you suggest I served on, sir?' Madoc was anxious to get back to the subject.

So at sixteen he had served his first trip as an apprentice on a merchant ship travelling to India. And then, in the face of his mother's violent opposition, Madoc had joined the crew of the *Gower Girl* and, at seventeen, realized his ambition to sail around Cape Horn.

Now, a veteran of many trips, he was approaching their home port of Swansea once more and looking forward to seeing the family again . . . but not Lucy. She was miles away. Three years ago she had chosen to marry an army officer and was now living with him in India.

'Land ahoy,' the look-out called from above, raising a smile on Madoc's face and a cheer from the men working on deck and the yards above. Madoc acknowledged the look-out with a wave and ducked below to tell Captain Davies, horny hands either side of the ladder as he half-slid down it to reach his quarters in the stern.

'Landfall, Skipper,' Madoc said. He rubbed a hand over his black curly beard. 'I suppose I'd better get myself a shave before we reach port.'

'You had that, Madoc. Otherwise your mother will think she has Blackbeard the pirate coming home.'

Excited, Nia lay in her bed, staring at the ceiling, sleep evading her. Amy, her friend, curled up in the next bed, murmured in her sleep and turned over.

My last night in college, Nia thought. I'm going home, to Wales. My last essay written, my last lesson in decorum completed, my last sum finished, my last French translation . . . but that's not all. I was sent here to learn, to absorb, but mostly to become a lady.

And to any observer she had achieved that objective – on the outside at least!

But I am still me, I haven't changed. I am just the same person. And Madoc is still the son of a gentleman, and I the daughter of their gypsy groom and a maid. She sighed, unsettled and restless.

Nia's mother was no longer a maid, her father no longer a groom. Encouraged by Madoc's father, who was forever grateful to him for saving his sons' lives, Liam had built up a thriving business for himself as a horse-trainer and breeder. Now he was an employer himself, his advice constantly sought, the animals from his stables coveted and in great demand by the wealthy. So much so that he had difficulty in supplying enough animals for the ever-lengthening string of waiting purchasers. Nia thumped her pillow again, and turned over on her side. She was beginning to drift off to sleep, when an image flashed into her mind: a girl's delicately boned features, framed with hair as bright as the sun. Lucy! What if Madoc has married Lucy?

But Lucy had always been Robert's girl, never had time for Madoc. Lucy, the girl whom Madoc had idolized – and Nia hated. Nia scowled, recalling that first time they all met. Lucy had seemed unbelievably lovely, like a picture painted to hang on the wall. The two girls took an instant dislike to one another – but Madoc had been captivated.

I still hate her!

At the railway station the following day Nia hugged her friend, kissing her cheek.

'How shall I manage without you,' Amy sobbed, tears pouring down her face.

'You'll have holidays and can visit me,' Nia comforted her.

Amy gave a gasp as the guard blew his whistle.

'Hurry! You'll have to get on the train.'

Nia kissed Amy's cheek, then mounted the metal steps, lifting her skirt in both hands, a porter supporting her arm as she manoeuvred its wire-hooped fullness through the doorway. Her trunk was housed in the luggage section of the train and the porter had already installed her hand-luggage in her compartment. She turned, pressing a coin into his hand.

'Thanks, lady.' He beamed touching his cap and walked away tossing the coin in the air.

She looked through the window at Amy, who was suddenly enveloped in sulphurous fumes from the engine's fire.

'I'll write to you as soon as I get home.' Nia's voice rose to a shout to make herself heard above the hiss of steam that suddenly split the air.

Amy nodded, saying something, but Nia could only see her mouth moving not hearing any words. An official at the end of the train waved a flag and the train gave an ear-piercing shriek, causing Amy to clap both hands over her ears. With a squeal of metal the train lurched into life, juddering forward in sharp jerks as it left the train-shed.

'Goodbye.' Both girls waved lace handkerchiefs as the train pulled away.

As Nia peered through the window clouds puffed from the funnel, leaving a trail of acrid smoke, filling Nia's nostrils, and she drew back, pressing her handkerchief to her nose. She sank into a corner seat, or as near to the corner as her wide skirt would allow as it covered the cushions as far as the centre of the bench seat. Mrs Larch, a middle-aged widow employed by the college to chaperon their young ladies home on train journeys, had already settled herself further up in the other corner and was searching in her reticule for her book.

'Mistress. Would you like me to close the window?' A young man sitting in the opposite corner was smiling politely at Nia. 'It will stop the soot coming in and soiling your gown.'

'Please do. It does get rather dirty.' She returned his smile, studying him as he tugged at the window. He was quite good-looking, in a clean-cut boyish way, though side-whiskers curled down his cheeks in the modern manner. His clothes were immaculate and his dark suit, with its short jacket, was in the latest style and obviously expensively tailored.

The young man turned to address Mrs Larch, who glanced up as he held his card out to her.

'May I introduce myself, Madam?'

Mrs Larch took the card, read it, then nodded with a smile, and put the card in her reticule.

'Miss Nia La Velle is my charge, Mr Goodman,' she replied. 'I am Mrs Larch, her chaperon.'

'And I am Albert Goodman. I am pleased to make your acquaintance, ladies,' He took his seat, then addressed Nia. 'Miss La Velle? I know the name. Are you by any chance related to Mr La Velle, of Beechwoods, the well esteemed horse-breeder?'

'I am indeed, Mr Goodman. He is my father.' Nia smiled, pleased with his portrayal of her father.

'Mr La Velle has exceptional ability,' Mr Goodman said with respect. 'He is renowned for his first-class horses – and their excellent training. Everyone wishes to buy one of his animals.'

Nia threw him a radiant smile, delighted to hear confirmation of her father's skill.

'He does have rather a special way with horses,' she replied.

'Actually, I am quite well acquainted with your father, Miss La

Velle. For years my father has made special journeys from Wales to purchase our horses from Mr La Velle. I try to accompany him whenever possible as I enjoy seeing those magnificent animals. My father has taken Mr La Velle's advice about horses for years, ever since my father bought his first mount from him. None of our family would ever dream of going anywhere else for a horse now.'

'It is amazing how many people know of my father,' Nia said. 'I believe he has great difficulty in fulfilling all his commitments.'

'I am not surprised. I hear he has a waiting list for his horses. But we are regular customers and my father makes sure he orders his animals well in advance of his needs. If you ask Mr La Velle, I am sure he will know both my father, Ernest Goodman and me.'

'I will speak of it to him,' Nia said, with a laugh.

'You seemed to be sad at leaving Gloucester, Miss La Velle.'

'No, I've enjoyed myself there immensely, Mr Goodman. I am sad to leave my friend, we have become very close in five years.'

'I can well understand. I felt the same emotions on coming down from Oxford and leaving my fellow-students.' His expression was curious, but politely did not extend to a further question.

'I have just completed my education at a young ladies' college. I found it most agreeable there.'

He leaned forward with interest. 'Obviously your parents agree with such education for ladies rather than with a governess.'

'They do. Though Mama is more conservative in outlook than Papa. She is much more attuned to the idea of ladies accepting their place in life.'

'And you? What is your opinion?'

'I believe we must each make our own choice, ladies included,' Nia said firmly. 'I certainly don't hold with the idea of ladies being considered lesser beings. Or having to remain anywhere ... unless they choose to.'

'A very unconventional lady.' His voice was tinged with admiration. 'So do you journey far, Miss La Velle?'

'To Wales. I am looking forward to returning.'

'I also journey to Wales. My parents have an estate near Newport. What about yours?'

'Well, I was born in Gower, near to Swansea town. . . .'

'I know Gower. We went there a few times when I was a boy; it is such a beautiful area. I was very young when we first visited. My parents are interested in science, and the British Association held a convention at the Royal Institute at Swansea.'

'I heard about that convention. Friends of mine attended a firework display at Singleton Abbey with their parents. They were small boys at the time, but I recall Madoc telling me about it.'

'Good heavens. I was there too. I was looking forward to it all the week. If I remember correctly, they fired a rocket out to a ship moored in the bay. I was very impressed.'

Nia nodded. 'Madoc said the ship was a schooner.'

'Who is this Madoc you mention?'

'A childhood friend. He is a mariner now, a Cape Horner.'

'A Cape Horner?' Mr Goodman sounded amazed. 'But you cannot possibly mean on a Swansea copper-barque?'

'That is so.' Her eyes gleamed like obsidian.

'But I was led to believe life on board one of those ships is primitive and harsh. He is obviously not a gentleman's son, then.'

'Oh but he is! He's the younger son of the Morgan family. They own the ship he sails, own a whole fleet of ships in fact. Madoc always had an ambition to sail around Cape Horn.'

'I see. Some men do have these foolhardy urges, I suppose.' Mr Goodman sounded disapproving. 'Personally I cannot see any point in risking your life unless it is necessary. Apart from which, it must be devilishly unpleasant. . . .' He broke off as Nia stiffened at the swear-word. 'I do beg your pardon, Miss La Velle, the word slipped out.' He reddened, looking uncomfortable, running a finger inside his elaborately folded wide tie, which was held in place with a diamond-studded tie-pin.

'I understand.' Nia's nod was gracious. 'Madoc never considered personal discomfort or danger,' she continued. 'He thrived on it, even as a boy he was very intrepid. He has an exceptionally strong character.' She smiled as she said it, her eyes shining.

'Do you see him often?'

'I have not seen him for years.' She sighed. 'In fact, but three times since we moved from Gower. I missed him dreadfully, especially before I went to college. We were always such close friends.'

'So you never kept up the friendship? I mean, as you have not often seen him since?'

'We wrote for a few years, but when he went to sea we lost touch,' she said wistfully.

'When you moved to Beechwood Hall, you mean?'

'Yes. The Beechwood estates belong to the same Morgan family I mentioned. Madoc is their son.'

'Good heavens. Then why on earth can a man from such a family endanger his life in a notoriously hazardous occupation?'

'I told you . . . that's Madoc.'

'Then Beechwood is not your father's property?'

'No. My parents and his are friends. The Morgans sometimes spend a week or so at Beechwood Hall, that's how Madoc and I have met since we moved away. But then I went to college and he went to sea. . . .' Her voice trailed off.

'Morgan is a well known name in Swansea, I believe?'

'Quite true. I told you the family owns a shipping company. I believe Emily Morgan inherited Beechwood from her father. The property came to her years ago, but they prefer to live overlooking the sea, in Gower. David Morgan was a seafaring man too, a captain with the East India Company.'

'I see. So does your father run Beechwood in his absence?'

'No. The Morgans have an excellent estate manager. My father is far too busy with his own business. David Morgan suggested we should use Beechwood when my father was looking to extend his business. They decided it would be good for the property to be occupied.' Nia sighed. 'I am so longing to be home again, and to see my horse, Surf.'

'You are fond of riding?'

She nodded, looking into the distance, seeing her beloved Surf tossing his head and snorting. 'Very.'

'You share your father's love of horses, I see.'

'Very much so. Mama is terrified of them but Papa taught me to ride as a little girl.' She laughed. 'I used to love to sneak off and ride without a saddle.'

'Not barebacked! You don't mean astride!' His mouth dropped, his face shocked. 'Surely. . . .' He broke off.

'I was but a child.' She passed it off. 'And my mother never agreed with it. She would always scold me when she found out.'

'Of course. But you would never dream of such unladylike behaviour now.' He smiled, leaning back in his seat.

Nia's lips twitched with amusement. If he only knew. But she only fluttered her fan. Some men loved the helpless lady act, she had long since discovered, and very occasionally she exploited that.

'But you are not travelling home now?'

'Oh yes, I am. My parents have come to live again in Gower. I'm delighted; I missed the sea so much living in Oxfordshire. I haven't even seen our new home yet.'

'So what will you find to do when you are settled at home? You will no longer have your studies to entertain you.'

'True. But apart from riding, there are plenty of books to read . . . and in any case, I shall have much to occupy me. I am looking forward to assisting my father with the horses.'

'You are? Do you mean train them?'

'I do. And you mentioned that your parents were interested in the sciences; well I am concerned with wildlife.'

'Are you? In which way?'

'I adore animals. When I was at home I used to rescue injured and orphaned ones, to tend and care for them. I am really looking forward to setting up my own sanctuary once more.'

'Really? That is most laudable. You are to be commended, Miss La Velle.' He seemed pleasantly impressed, Nia thought. 'How long have you had these leanings?'

'Since I was a small child. I maintained my own little refuge to treat sick animals. Everyone used to bring me orphan fledglings and other injured creatures.' She laughed. 'One time Madoc even brought me two foxcubs he had rescued from under the noses of the hunt. . . .'

'Foxcubs?' Mr Goodman was horrified. 'But didn't he get into trouble with the hunt-master? He would not approve of such subversiveness.'

Nia's expression was haughty.

'Madoc was always careless of his own safety, he never cared if he got caught. And, as I told you earlier, I do what I think best, Mr Goodman. I don't agree with hunting foxes and I'm not to be dictated to by the hunt-master.' She turned away, flapping her fan in front of her face.

'But I thought you liked riding, Miss La Velle?' He leaned forward, his hands on the knees of his well-creased trousers. Her eyes flashed back to him.

'I do, but not chasing helpless animals with nowhere to hide.' She smiled, fluttering her fan more provocatively, her coal-dark eyes demure, feathery eyebrows arched. He was immediately captivated again. He nodded.

'I understand what you say, Miss La Velle.' His forehead puckered. 'I am not certain that I agree, but I can understand. I see you really do hold unconventional views.'

The train drew into a station with a grinding of brakes, again accompanied by the metallic squealing. A vendor with a wooden tray suspended around his neck came rushing up, waving to draw their attention.

'A pork-pie, sir?' he yelled. 'Juicy and hot. One for your lady, I'm sure, sir?'

Albert raised his brows enquiringly at Nia.

'Would you like one, Miss La Velle? They do look appetizing.'

'Not for me, Mr Goodman, thank you. But please do have one yourself.'

'How about you, madam?' he asked, addressing Mrs Larch, who declined politely. As the vendor was about to pass his pie over to Albert, a flower-seller waved a small posy of heather in front of Albert's face.

'Flowers for your lady, sir?' she screamed above the noise of the busy platform. She looked at Nia. 'I'm sure you like lucky heather, miss?'

'I'll take one,' Albert said. He winked at the pie-seller, who waited good-naturedly as Albert gave the woman a coin, then paid generously for his pie. Back inside the compartment Albert presented the posy to Nia with a slight flourish and she laughed, taking it and holding it to her nose.

'They remind me of my mother. She loves flowers. My father always used to pick flowers for Mama, whatever the season, as soon as wild flowers appeared. Snowdrops, primroses ... whatever. Then once I became old enough I did the same.'

'How unusual. I've never met a man who picked flowers for his wife.'

'My father is an unusual man. Those are the special things I love about him.'

'Most unusual,' Albert said, shaking his head. They were drawing near to Newport when he addressed Nia again.

'Miss La Velle, would you object if I ask your father's permission to call on you? Mrs Larch already has my card to give to Mr La Velle and I am certain my father will have your new address.'

'I have no objection, Mr Goodman.'

'Thank you.'

He took down both his hat, and his hip-length paletot, from the rack, then pulled the overcoat over his shoulders, putting his arms through the slits. As the train pulled to a halt he called to a porter to reach down his luggage and carry it to his carriage.

'I am very pleased to have made your acquaintance. I look forward to meeting you again with impatience.'

From her seat, Nia watched him saunter along the platform, a porter trailing behind with his luggage. It was very satisfactory to be paid attention by such an attractive, obviously well-to-do, young man.

'He seems a pleasant young gentleman,' Mrs Larch offered, nodding her approval. 'I will pass the card on to your father, who is obviously well acquainted with Mr Goodman.'

Nia had learned to play the lady well in five years. Before going to college she had already had the advantage of being educated by a tutor. When her parents had lived in a cottage near to Craig y Mor, home of the Morgan family, Emily Morgan had invited Nia and her brother to attend lessons with her own sons' tutor until the boys went away to school. Then, after moving to Oxfordshire, Tom went away to a minor public school and Nia had attended a private day-school until going to college.

Having spent so much time throughout childhood in the company of the Morgan sons, Nia and Tom were naturally well-spoken and at ease mixing with the gentry. Many girls at Nia's college were daughters of merchants who, with the growing wealth and expectations of the times, wanted similar advantages for their children.

Nia leaned her head back against the cushion. Telling Albert about Madoc had stirred a deep longing to see him again. *We understood one another perfectly. I said I missed Madoc. When we left Wales I thought my heart was breaking*, she recalled. A familiar pain, which still returned, to burn and torment. *I'll always love him – but he's forgotten me.*

He never even wrote to me when I was at college. I can't believe he cut me out of his life like that – the thought was as wounding as ever.

But home again, in Gower, I'll make him remember the good times we spent together, she vowed silently, recollecting their childhood, the seemingly endless days they had roamed Gower together on their ponies. She half-smiled. *I remember he told Lucy off for being rude to me,* she reflected. And Robert was so furious.

She stared out of the window. Madoc had never hidden his admiration for Lucy's beauty. Was Lucy Madoc's young lady now – not Robert's? His wife even? Her determined chin rose. Unless they were married Lucy would not win him easily!

CHAPTER TWO

MADOC lounged against the corner of Russel Sutton's high desk, chatting to the clerk, who was an old friend of his. He glanced across as Robert emerged into the bustle of the main office of Morgan Shipping, and walked towards them.

'Are you coming with me, Madoc?' Robert stopped alongside them and put his top-hat on the desk in order to pull on his capelike topcoat. 'I did mention I was going to meet Tom La Velle in the Mackworth. You said last week you'd like to come.'

'I will come right away.' Madoc uncurled his six-foot-two frame from the desk. 'Are you going straight from here?'

'Yes. We've been meeting on a Tuesday after work, if we can manage it, and we usually have a few tankards together. He'll be surprised to see you.'

'Did you say he has a law practice?' Madoc asked as they walked up Green Dragon Passage from the Strand into Wind Street.

'No. At the moment he is still an articled clerk with Pritchard and Tudor. They seem to regard him highly. He hopes to become a lawyer eventually.'

'He was always quick.' Madoc was recalling earlier days, as children, before the Morgan boys went away to school, when they had all been taught by the same tutor. 'He and Nia could give us plenty of competition. Is he still as quiet as he used to be?'

'Not really. He is still reticent, but I think going to public school pulled him through that. It has given him tremendous confidence. He is as even-tempered and good-natured as ever, though.'

'He follows his father in that way then. That's how I recall Liam.'

'True. Though he doesn't resemble him in looks. Tom's colouring is still remarkably like his mother's. His appearance gives no hint of his gypsy heritage.'

Madoc nodded pensively, his mind drifting back to Nia; they had been so close when they were young.

'Never in a million years would you take Tom and Nia for siblings,' he said. 'They're so completely different in looks and temperament. Nia was so fiery.'

Robert cocked an eyebrow.

'Like us, you mean? Could any two people be less alike?'

Madoc smiled. 'Perhaps not.' He stepped off the pavement on to the cobblestoned road, allowing two elderly ladies room to pass with their wide skirts.

'Even your mind works completely at a tangent to mine. As a child you were so unbelievably reckless. And you can still be impulsive ... I'm often amazed at some of the things you do even now.'

'Oh well!' Madoc gave a relaxed shrug. 'I don't suppose I'll ever succeed in becoming a polished gentleman. Like you,' he mocked, elbowing Robert as he added the last remark.

Robert's expression was equally mocking.

'As if you ever wanted to.'

Madoc grinned. 'I was an unruly little beggar and I can't say it ever appealed to me ... other than wanting to attract the girls in the way that you did. What I did resent like hell was your being so much taller.' He cast an eye at Robert, their eyes now level, and they both laughed.

Two young women walked past, their lowered eyes sliding towards the tall, good-looking young men, so contrasting in appearance. Blond Robert was elegant and well-turned-out, with smooth, classically handsome features. Madoc's athletic build was intensely masculine, a distinct seaman's swagger was evident in his stride, unruly dark hair tumbled about his face, tanned skin emphasized incredibly green eyes which now, as often, held a suggestion of laughter. Noticing the women's glance, Madoc gave them an almost imperceptible wink, causing them both to gasp and lift amazed eyebrows before looking at one another and giggling behind their hands. Robert flashed a suspicious glance at Madoc, who grinned, shrugging innocent shoulders.

'So what about Nia?' Madoc asked, his thoughts returning to the past again. He was suddenly filled with longing to see her. They had been inseparable. 'Is she home with her family in Gower.'

'I'm not sure. Tom was talking about her returning, but I haven't actually asked him about her since.'

Smoke and the smell of beer hung heavily in the crowded bar as the two men ducked their heads to enter the doorway, the sawdust scattered over the floor sticking to their boots as they walked through to the back.

'I can't see Tom here yet, can you?' Robert was peering through the smoky haze, his height enabling him to see over most people's heads. He grabbed a potboy's arm as he scuttled past. 'I'll order for him as well. What are you having Madoc?'

As they sat down Tom came threading his way towards them; Madoc studied him as he approached. His colouring was his mother's, fair-skinned with honey-gold hair, revealing no hint of his gypsy blood. A slight man, wiry and light on his feet, he took after his father in build. His face was thin, but his chin was square and firm and he wore a good-humoured smile as he eased his way through the throng. His clear blue eyes met Madoc's, his expression warm as he held out his hand.

'Madoc. I wondered when we were going to meet again. Welcome home.' His voice was educated, and lacked the Welsh lilt now more noticeable in Madoc's voice since his years at sea with Welsh mariners. Tom had lived away from Wales for years before his recent return.

'Good to see you too, Tom. It's been a long time.' He noticed Tom assessing him, but whatever his thoughts were he politely passed no comment. 'Have you recently returned to Swansea?'

'No. I knew my parents were intending to move back so I decided to forestall them. I have lodgings in town.'

'But they are back now, I heard. Are they settled into their new home?'

'Very much so. They're quite comfortable now, though they are still making alterations.' He smiled, shaking his head.

'Didn't Rob say they purchased Meadow Farm?'

'That's right. They have already made a good many changes. Renovations and extensions to the house, as well as to the outbuildings and suchlike. Father's had more stables erected to house the stock.' Tom pulled out a tortoiseshell cigar-case and handed it around to the others.

'So when will Nia be home? I'm looking forward to seeing her again.' Madoc leaned forward to light Tom's cigar. 'On my last home-leave I had planned a trip to Beechwood, hoping to see her, but Mother said she was still away at college. When is she coming back?'

Tom puffed at his cigar and blew out a cloud of smoke.

'She's home.'

Madoc's face lit up. 'Here? In Swansea you mean?'

'That's right. Arrived a week ago.'

'Why didn't anyone tell me?' Madoc complained. 'I'd have paid her a visit. I wish I had known sooner, I've only a few days left now and I'd love to see her.'

Tom was amused. 'You won't recognize her. Quite the lady.'

'I will believe that when I see it,' Madoc declared, grinning. 'It must be years. . . ? How old was I? Around fourteen when you moved away. I've only seen her about three times since – when we came to Beechwood. I did come on my own a few times after that, but Nia was never there.'

'I don't think she has forgiven you for that.'

'Forgiven me? For what?' Madoc was puzzled.

'For not coming to see her. She thought you had abandoned her.' Tom tapped the ash off his cigar into the sawdust on the floor.

'Abandoned her? I like that! You were the ones who moved away. After she left I missed her like hell.'

'He was like a bear with a sore head,' Robert confirmed. 'He grumped at everyone for months.'

'And as I was at sea from the time I was sixteen, I could hardly arrange my trips to suit her holidays. I wrote to her several times when she went to college, but she never replied.'

'You must have got the wrong address. You will have to try explaining that to Nia. No excuse now, anyway, she's finished college for good.'

'I'll ride over and see her in the morning.'

'Better not make it tomorrow. I believe she has already made arrangements to go out.'

'Has she?' Madoc's heart sank. 'I'll make it the following day. If only I had known before. Not much time before I sail now.'

An hour later Tom stood up.

'I will have to be on my way. Are we on for our card-game tomorrow?' he asked Robert. He looked at Madoc. 'Can you manage to join us?'

'I'd like that. Thank you.'

★

For the rest of the evening Nia continually invaded Madoc's thoughts. Later, sprawled out comfortably in his long bed – at least, long in comparison to his bunk on board ship – he gave rein to his memories. It would be good to be with her again; the idea of it filled him with eager anticipation. He was surprised at the intensity of his reaction after all this time. Tom had indicated that she was disappointed because he hadn't visited her, which made him feel vaguely guilty – though it was hardly his fault if she had not been at home. But she had always been such a staunch and loyal friend, it seemed that the least he could have done was to make more effort to visit her. *Never mind, I'll see her soon*, he thought with satisfaction.

Nia had arrived back in Swansea the previous weekend; her parents had been waiting to meet her as the train pulled into the station at High Street. They returned Nia's wave as the train drew to a halt, her mother's face flushed a rosy pink, her father's black eyes dancing, as a porter opened the door of the carriage. Her mother Martha, with her wide skirt, was forced to wait on the platform, but Liam leapt up the steps and grabbed Nia in his arms, hugging her.

'My own sweet girl. It's wonderful to see you again.' He held his head back from her to examine her face. 'And aren't you more beautiful than ever.'

'Mrs Larch, this is my papa. . . .' Nia began, carrying out the introductions.

'May we offer you a lift, Mrs Larch?' Liam asked.

'No thank you, Mr La Velle. It has all been arranged. It was lovely to meet you, my dear.' She touched her cheek to Nia's. 'I hope you see that nice young man again.'

'Come on! Your mother's waiting.' Taking Nia's hand, her father helped to ease her dress back through the carriage door and down the steps as her mother pressed her hands against her cheeks, half-laughing and half-crying.

'Mama. You are not supposed to cry,' Nia teased. Both mother's and daughter's skirts billowed out behind them on their wire hoops as they hugged one another. 'You're supposed to be pleased.' Nia laughed.

'Oh, Nia. It's wonderful to have you home again. I have been waiting so long for this day to come. I've missed you so much, my lovely. I thought the time would never pass.'

'Where is Tom?' Nia looked around for her brother. 'I thought he would be here.'

'He had every intention of coming, but he was held up in court.' Martha's face revealed her delight.

'And is he going to be a lawyer? I'm so proud of him, he's worked very hard.'

'He has that. He deserves to get on. You'll see him later, Nia.'

A carriage and pair were waiting outside the station, the harnesses and brasses gleaming. A young man stood alongside, holding the reins and talking to one of the horses.

'Hello, Mathew,' Nia greeted him warmly. 'I didn't know you were moving to Wales as well.'

'Yes, miss. I didn't want to stay behind and leave all these beautiful creatures.' He was stroking the animal's muzzle as it tossed its head. 'Welcome home, Miss Nia.'

'Thank you, Mathew.' She sank on to the well-sprung seats inside the coach, leaned back and surveyed everything with pleasure. How many times as a child had she sat in the Morgans' carriage and wished her mother and father could own one?

As their carriage bowled along the coastal road she gazed out at the full tide lapping the golden length of Swansea beach on their left, then at the oyster-boats approaching their moorings, their sails lit up against the low, autumn sun.

'Just look at that wonderful water. I cannot really believe it yet. I am home again at last.'

Her gaze travelled over her parents, the tender expressions on both their faces as they regarded her. She was so lucky to have them. She was delighted to see how beautifully turned out they were, a real lady and gentleman. Martha's dress followed the latest fashion, and her father was wearing a sombre dark suit. Darting a glance at his ear, she saw that he spurned the gold earring which once he'd always worn. Considering him with a stranger's eye, Nia realized why so many people took him for a Spaniard; his swarthy features could easily suggest Spanish blood.

'Where are Mead Rise Stables?' she asked. This was something she had been wondering about ever since she had heard them mentioned.

'It was once called Meadow Farm.' Liam's dark eyes glowed. 'It has a fair-sized house. And the renovations and expansions are almost completed.' His tone was studiously nonchalant, but he could not prevent the grin from creeping back across his face.

Nia looked from one face to another, seeing the delight written there at their becoming landowners. It was something that ordinary people only dreamed about. She hid her own slight disappointment on hearing that it had once been a farm; secretly she had been hoping for something more imposing.

'That's wonderful.' She squeezed her mother's hand. 'And there is plenty of room for the horses?'

'Quite a few large outbuildings,' he replied. 'Sturdily built. David came with me to look over it a few times before we purchased it. He agreed it showed a lot of promise.' Nia noticed his use of Captain Morgan's first name. Then he added: 'The bank is lending us the capital . . . the cap'n offered to be our guarantor.'

Nia nodded. She knew the Morgans were eternally grateful to her father for saving their sons' lives all those years ago. Long before they moved to Beechwood, Captain Morgan had originally started her father off in business. He had offered Liam the free use of an old barn at Craig y Mor, to turn in to stables to house and treat the horses he was training.

'The cap'n wanted to lend us the money himself, but your father wouldn't have that,' Martha explained. She smiled at Liam, adding: 'You know what he's like.'

'We wouldn't have him any other way.' Nia leaned over to kiss his cheek.

'We intend building more stables as our turnover increases,' her father said with another grin, his eyes on her face. 'Do you remember asking me once if we could ever be rich? Those were the words which spurred me to try, Nia.'

She nodded. 'I remember,' she whispered, swallowing the lump which rose in the back of her throat. 'But do you remember why I asked you that?'

His smile faded, clearly knowing what she meant.

'I wanted to know if it would make it possible for me to marry Madoc.'

'Don't be silly,' her mother broke in, obviously not liking the way this conversation was leading. 'That was just childish talk.'

Nia took the hint. 'So where are we going now? Home?'

'Of course. Work on the house is not quite complete, but it is very comfortable. And I think you'll find it meets your expectations . . . as a lady.' Martha smiled at Nia, who laughed.

'If you didn't want me to change you should not have sent me to college. But I must say I couldn't have gone to a better one.'

Martha nodded. 'Miss Emily advised us to send you there. She said it would suit your temperament.'

'Miss Emily? Do you still call Mrs Morgan that?'

'Yes, I do. I was her maid for too long for Emily to come easily to my tongue, Nia. In any case it is entirely up to me.'

'I know that, Mama. I only thought—'

'That's enough,' Liam broke in. 'It is whatever your mother feels happy with, Nia.'

'I'm sorry. Of course it is,' Nia said, though she did not agree. She noticed that her mother seemed to be breathing rapidly. 'Are you having trouble getting your breath, Mama?' she asked with quick concern.

'It's nothing. I think these tight corsets don't help me at all, I wasn't built to wear the latest fashion.' She laughed ruefully.

Nia frowned, her eyes flying to her father, but he was studying Martha a little anxiously.

'I thought you hadn't had those attacks lately,' he said.

Martha shook her head impatiently.

'I haven't. I told you I think it's the corset. I'll let it out further and I will be all right.'

He nodded but did not look reassured.

Crouched low over her mount's neck, Nia galloped her horse across the beach, the deep-red skirt of her riding-habit billowing behind her as she rode side-saddle. The breeze whipped her veil free from its anchorage on her shoulder, and it too also fluttered wildly behind her.

At the same time Madoc was cantering easily across the common land, where patches of heather stained the ground purple and mauve as he guided his mount between the sheep grazing there. Out on the cliffs, gorse bushes had shed their golden blossom, and ferns were already curling and brown as he made for the path leading down to Pobbles Bay. There, on the wide expanse of sandy beach at low tide, he would allow the horse his head on the freedom of the hard sand.

A few clouds were tumbling past, and in the distance the opposite coast of Devon was clearly visible today as a dark line between the blue of the sky and the green sea. To either side of him tentacles of land reached out into the water from the many bays, receding into the distance in fading shades of green and brown. The surface of the sea was restless, broken into small white horses by the wind, which was pushing a few large sailing vessels along at a good pace towards the port of Swansea. A movement above caught his eye and, looking up, he saw a hawk drop down on to its prey to secure it with a flurry of feathers.

Looking down on to the beach he noticed a rider in the distance, galloping flat out, crouched over the horse. He could see it was a woman by her riding-habit and the veil that trailed behind her in the wind. She's a good rider, he thought, I wonder if it's someone I know? It cannot be Mother, as she is visiting the sick. A while later, the woman dismounted and appeared to be lifting the horse's foot.

Nia heard hoofs thudding against the sand and looked up in time to see a horse galloping towards her. The man sat easily in the saddle and, although the wind was chilly today, she could see he was informally dressed, hatless and in his shirtsleeves. She watched as he drew nearer, something in the bearing familiar. Shading her eyes with one hand, she studied the figure.

Madoc! She sucked in her breath, her hand flying to her mouth. *No. It can't be. He is too tall for Madoc.*

The hatless rider was dark-haired. Her gaze remained glued to him as he came into viewing-distance; she could see he was a young man. It *was* Madoc! A flare of excitement quickened her heart-beat and she dropped her head, staring blindly down at the horse's foot, where a sharp pebble was embedded in the frog of his hoof. She sucked in another breath, determined to take command of this situation.

Tense with expectation she raised her head as he arrived, leaping down from the saddle with his usual athletic grace. She painted a surprised, haughty expression on her face.

'Mistress. May I be of assistance to you?' His voice was deep and resonant. 'I could see you examining your mount's foot. Is there a stone under his shoe?'

She raised aloof brows, forcing her face to remain neutral, not allowing her eyes show interest even as they hungrily explored his

features. Her heart thumped. He was so tall, as well as broad-shoul-
dered, and radiated an aura of intense vitality. His mouth was
intriguingly sensual, contrasting with the determined angle of his
jaw, where dark side-whiskers curled down. He was strikingly handsome now, would definitely surpass his brother as she remembered
him, she decided.

A puzzled expression crept over his face.

'Are we. . . ? I feel we are acquainted, mistress.'

'Are we?' She allowed herself a disdainful smile and her eyes raked
his informal attire. 'How can I tell when you have not introduced
yourself . . . sir?' The last word held a question.

His dark hair blew over his forehead and he brushed it back, his
slanted eyes sea-green today, reflecting back the colour of the water
alongside them. He nodded his head.

'My apologies, mistress.' Looking down at his open-necked shirt,
with its pushed up sleeves, his wind-burned arms exposed, he added:
'I did not expect to meet a lady on the beach, I am Madoc Morgan.'
He paused, his glance roaming over her face. 'But I do know you, I am
certain of it. We have met somewhere before . . . I could never forget
such a beautiful woman.'

Nia laughed and hunched expressive shoulders, dropping her
haughty expression.

'That is a new turn for you, Madoc Morgan.'

His mouth dropped, recognition dawning.

'Nia? Is it Nia?' His voice was hesitant, still not quite sure.

'You don't know. You *have* forgotten me.' Her voice was cool again.

'Nia. It *is* you.' His face split in a smile, teeth gleaming against his
tanned skin, and suddenly he grabbed her in strong arms, lifting her
from the ground as though she were weightless. As he hugged her
against his chest she felt the hardness of his body beneath his thin
shirt, the fresh tang of his cologne wafting to her nose.

'Stop! I can't breathe. Put me down.'

He lowered her down gently, grinning, still holding her in his
arms, gazing down at her with delight.

'I cannot believe it . . . meeting you here. I've been longing to see
you. But it was only yesterday that Tom told me you had returned,
then he said you wouldn't be at home today. Aren't I going to get a
kiss?'

'Certainly not! What sort of woman do you think I am?' She pulled back, rigid in his arms, not willing to capitulate as he obviously expected her to do. *No mistakes, you're going to do this properly,* she thought. 'Please. Let me go, Madoc. People might see you ... embracing me.'

He dropped his arms, still smiling.

'I'm sorry. Of course, you are right. I suppose I still saw us as children together and just reacted.'

She saw his eyes studying her features before travelling on over her fashionable velvet riding-habit. She knew the rich ruby colour suited the warm honey of her skin well. The short jacket, nipped in to display her small waist, also did justice to her well-developed figure. Her black hair was gathered into a large knot, with the latest gentlemen's-style topper perched above. She grabbed the recalcitrant veil attached to it, and redraped it under her chin to the opposite shoulder.

'You have matured into an exceptionally lovely woman, Nia.'

Not wanting him to see her pleasure at his words she dropped her head and brushed sand from her skirt. Then she squinted back up against the light, to where he towered over her. She measured him with her eyes.

'You've grown a bit since I last saw you.' She knew he had always worried that he would never grow as tall as his brother, his great rival. 'I imagined you were going to be the runt of the litter.'

He burst out laughing. 'And who would know more than you that I thought so too?' His admiring eyes returned to wander over her body. 'And you were such a skinny thing. Whoever would have expected you to. . . .' He broke off, obviously reconsidering his words.

Nia put her haughty expression back.

'I will thank you, sir, not to scrutinize me in such an ungentlemanly manner.'

'Was I?' His voice was innocent, though a smile lurked at one corner of his mouth. 'Please forgive me.' He looked down at her gelding's leg. 'I was going to offer to remove the stone from his foot, but I suppose you will not need any help.'

She pretended surprise.

'Why not? I would be pleased not to mark my skirt with the wet sand. I'll accept your offer, Mr Morgan.'

His forehead wrinkled; he seemed slightly nonplussed.

'Am I Mr Morgan now, Nia?'

'All right, Madoc, if you prefer. Though you must realize that after all this time we are almost strangers.'

'Strangers?' His laughter faded. 'We can never be strangers, Nia. We can never forget our shared childhood years. What about. . . .'

'But I wish to forget them. I want to forget how I followed you around.' She allowed herself an incredulous laugh and scrutinized his pushed-up shirt-sleeves again, his tumbled hair. 'I cannot imagine now what I ever found so attractive about you. Evidently, by the way you choose to dress and act you have still not developed into a gentleman.'

She saw his mouth tighten. Her barb had found its mark and she wanted to take back her words, tell him she didn't mean it. To tell him she loved him! But she held her counsel. She must make him see and think of her in a different way first.

'Allow me . . . Miss Lovell.'

He reached down and took her mount's foot in his strong hands. As he turned it up on to his palm she noticed how calloused it was by his years of handling ropes and canvas at sea. His pushed-up sleeves revealed a scar snaking up his forearm, ugly and puckered, and she wondered how he had acquired it; the thought of his being hurt was unbearable. It looked as if the wound had been inexpertly pulled together and roughly stitched, leaving it ragged and knotted. I could have sewn it up neatly for you, she thought tenderly.

She looked down at the back of his head as he worked on her mount's foot, his unruly hair, rather longer than was fashionable, blowing about his face in the wind. She longed to ruffle it further in her hands, to lift up his head and stare into those fascinating up-tilted cat's eyes she remembered so well, eyes that always stared out of her dreams. She knew all their vagaries, aware they changed colour with his mood and his surroundings, from the clear green of rock-pools, right through to an aquamarine when he was happy, to a swirling mossy amber when emotional or disturbed.

Madoc put down the horse's foot.

'There we are. I'll leave you to continue your ride . . . Miss Lovell.'

'Nia, please,' she broke in. 'And we are known as La Velle now. Everyone seemed to address us as such in Oxfordshire; they assumed we are of some Mediterranean descent.'

'A natural mistake, I suppose.' Madoc's glance was on her face again. 'Your appearance certainly bears a Spanish quality.'

'As you will understand, my father was ill-pleased at first. But then he could see that the assumption was of benefit to his business and he allowed it to mature. People are more inclined to accept a Spaniard's advice than a Romany's.' Her voice was bitter.

'Unfortunately. Though my father never held that view.' He cupped his hands to assist her to mount and, as she gripped his arm, she felt the muscles taut and hard. She ached to throw her arms around his neck and hold him close. Never to let him go.

'Do you wish to accompany me, Madoc?' She affected indifference as she took her seat. 'I was about to return home.'

'I'm afraid my horse is impatient for his exercise. And perhaps I am not suitably attired?' His face was deadpan, but there was a wicked gleam in his eye. 'After all, you do not want to be seen out riding with a common seaman. Good afternoon, Miss La Velle.' He gave a formal nod of his head, but she saw one corner of his mouth curling up as he smothered a grin. She pursed her lips and raised her chin.

'Good afternoon, sir.'

She touched her gelding with her crop and trotted off, aware that he was staring after her. She swallowed hard, blinking rapidly. *I still love him*, she thought. *But what does he think of me? What did he say when he recognized me? He'd been longing to see me – but he never once visited after he left school. At least now he can see I am a lady, surely he must regard me in a new light? Not just as the maid's daughter, his tomboy friend.* Unshed tears broke the reflection from the sea into a million brilliant shards before she brushed them away impatiently.

Madoc watched her ride away, grinning at her grand-lady act. She always had liked to boss him about, he mused. Pity, but Storm was not ready to return to his stable yet. He remounted, and continued his ride, taking the opposite direction from Nia, his mind overwhelmed with her. It had been so long since he'd seen her. Far too long. It was marvellous to talk to her again, just to be with her.

There was no one else like her. And all this time he'd been besotted with Lucy. He was amazed it hadn't hit him before how much Nia had always meant. How much he'd missed her. She was the same Nia beneath all that grandeur. He frowned slightly – wasn't she? That she seemed to find the idea of their friendship amusing was disquieting. He should have understood that she'd have matured, would no longer be his tomboy pal, he mused. He should have treated her differently.

But she was absolutely glorious, he reflected, his eyes gleaming as he deliberated about her delightful figure. Who ever would have thought plain, skinny Nia would metamorphose so astonishingly? As a child, tough, wiry and agile, Nia's slight frame had seemed to be taking after her father's. But now she had developed that coveted hour-glass shape. A small waist, which surely he could have encircled with his hands. Not forgetting those titillating, swelling mounds – though those had begun developing early, even as a skinny girl, he remembered. Her breasts were the first he'd ever noticed and wanted to touch, he recalled. Did touch, he remembered with a jolt of disquiet. And he certainly had the same feelings about them now, he decided with a grin.

Her high cheekbones had appeared gaunt in a child, but now they sculpted her face into aristocratic lines. And what about those full sensuous lips, deep claret in shade? Begging to be kissed. Her mouth might be too wide for fashion, but it suited her face. Yes. She was impressive, not pretty but vivid and exotic, with the air of a Spanish grandee's lady. He grinned again, nodding his appreciation. She is beautiful . . . exciting!

He couldn't wait to meet her again.

'Mama.' Nia left her horse with a stable-boy and rushed through the house. 'You'll never guess who I met on the beach?'

Martha, sitting sewing in a rocking-chair near the window, smiled at her daughter's animated expression, her flushed face.

'Someone special, that's sure. Let me guess. . . .'

'Madoc. Madoc Morgan. He's as tall as Robert now, Mama, and very handsome.' She hugged her mother. 'It was wonderful to see him after all this time. He said he's been longing to see me again.'

'Don't go getting ideas above your station, Nia,' Martha broke in, a worried expression creeping over her face. She dropped her sewing on to her lap; her hands were trembling slightly.

'Don't be so old-fashioned, Mama. Anything can happen. I can make things happen.' She picked up a biscuit from the plate on the lacquered table alongside her mother. 'At one time, you never thought you'd have a servant bringing you tea and biscuits either.' She nibbled the biscuit with sharp little teeth. 'That you would be sitting here being idle, as you used to call it.'

'That may be true enough, but . . .' Martha stopped mid-sentence.

'Don't get carried away with Madoc, Nia.'

'What do you mean? We have always been friends.' Nia sank into a chair near her mother and took her hand. 'What is it?'

'He's a gentleman's son . . . my employer's son.'

Nia laughed. 'But that was years ago – not now.'

'Still, nothing can ever come of anything between you.'

'You were told that too, weren't you, Mama? Before you and Papa got married.' Her voice had dropped its laughing tone.

'Yes. But that was my choice,' Martha pointed out.

'And wouldn't it be my choice, too?'

'That is just it! It wouldn't. You have forgotten the Romany blood running through your veins. You are . . .' Her voice trailed away.

'Half-gypsy,' Nia spat. She flung the half-eaten biscuit back on the tray. 'I have never forgotten that, Mama. I have been proud of it. People are interested by it, attracted . . .'

'But it might prove unattractive in a wife.'

Nia gasped, her face going stiff, and snatched her hand from her mother's.

'I never believed I would hear you say words like that to me, Mama. Not my own mother!'

Martha looked stricken and reached out for Nia's hand again, but Nia backed away, clenching her fists, pressing them against her rigid body.

'I am only trying to warn you, Nia. You have never experienced prejudice as I have, and I don't think you realize that you can come up against it. Sometimes where you least expect it.'

Nia closed her eyes in disbelief and shook her head.

'You can't mean Madoc,' she whispered. 'You cannot possibly think that about Madoc?' Her eyes flashed open again, dark as midnight as she stared at her mother. Her voice rose: 'Do you?'

Martha's face sagged, her eyes flooded with tears.

'Of course I don't mean Madoc. I love him almost as a son,' she choked, dabbing at her eyes with her sewing. 'I am just concerned that you should be aware. That you will not be hurt. I cherish you so, my . . . Oh!' she broke off, gasping, and pressed a hand to her chest.

Nia flung herself on her knees alongside her mother, fiercely hugging the solid form, now thickening with middle age.

'Mama? What's wrong? Have you got a pain?' She leaned back to study her mother's face, which had suddenly lost its colour. 'You're still having that breathing problem, aren't you. Don't tell me that's the corset now. Is there a pain in your chest?'

Her mother managed a weak nod, and slumped back in the chair. Her breathing became laboured, her hand still pressed against her chest. Her face was waxen, and slight beads of perspiration began appearing on her upper lip which had acquired a slightly blue tinge. Frightened, Nia leapt to her feet.

'I'm going to call Papa.'

'Not here,' gasped her mother. 'Gone ... to ... treat ... sick ... horse.'

'Don't try to talk! I'll send the stable-boy for a physician.' She dashed over and pulled the bell-cord.

'No!' Martha put her head back against the chair, closing her eyes. 'Please.' Nia just caught the whispered words.

'Papa will want me to. You look terrible, Mama. I'm frightened. I'm afraid it's your heart.' She turned as the maid entered. 'Bethan. Call Mathew for me please, and will you bring a glass of water for my mother.'

'Yes, miss.' The maid cast a concerned look at Martha. 'Is Mrs La Velle unwell, Miss Nia?'

'Yes. Please hurry, I'm very worried about her.'

She returned to her mother and knelt alongside her again, taking her ice-cold hand and chafing it gently. Relieved, Nia thought she was beginning to recover. Colour was returning to her cheeks, though her breathing was still laboured.

Bethan hurried in, carefully carrying the water, watching anxiously as Nia held it to her mother's lips. Thank God the blue look around her mouth had gone.

'Mathew is coming now, miss. Is Mrs La Velle going to be all right, miss?'

'I think so. But I'm sending for a doctor in any case, I don't want to take any chances.'

Martha's strained face was beginning to relax.

'Pain's ... going. Don't ... need him.'

'Papa will say I've done the right thing. You are Papa's life, Mama. He would be heartbroken should anything happened to you.'

'Please, Nia.' Martha gripped Nia's hand weakly as her breathing became easier. 'Don't send for a doctor. I'll tell Liam, I promise.'

Nia's face puckered anxiously. Her instincts urged her to send for help, but Martha's pleading expression warned that it would further distress her mother. Worry was the last thing she needed if her heart was at risk. Indecisive, Nia chewed her lip. Martha seemed to have more or less recovered now, perhaps it would be wiser to capitulate in the circumstances.

'Very well, I won't send for him. Will you tell Mathew I don't need him please, Bethan,' she said to the maid.

Martha took the glass from Nia's hand and sipped at the water.

'I don't want him worried, Nia. He has enough with the business. Can't you give me some herbal medicine?'

'Of course. If I can find them. Where does Papa keep his herbs these days?

'Mathew will know. Somewhere in a loft above the stables I believe.'

'Has he ever given you anything for this?'

'No.'

'Never? Why not?'

Martha's expression became slightly defensive.

'I try not to show him, Nia. I told you I don't want him to worry unnecessarily.'

'Mama!' Nia heaved an exasperated sigh. 'Very well. Let me see what herbs I can find. Papa must surely have some foxglove leaves. That's what you need.'

She found her father's herbal store and she rummaged through the boxes for some dried foxglove leaves. Her father had taught her this gypsy remedy many years ago, and in the past she had administered it to village patients. Nia was fairly certain that it was her mother's heart that was causing her breathlessness, and this was the remedy of choice. After carefully making up an infusion of the leaves and boiling water she took the medicine back to her mother, who sipped it obediently.

'Thank you, my lovely,' said Martha.

Still upset about her mother's condition, Nia was studying her, wondering how ill she really was.

'Nia. About what we were talking about. . . .'

'I'm sorry, Mama, but I will have to tell Papa when he gets back,' Nia insisted.

'No. I mean before this happened.'

'I see. Yes, I know what you mean, Mama. So let me say that I understand what you were saying about my Romany blood, and I shall remember it. I promise.' She managed a smile. 'And just to set your mind at rest, I can tell you I have no wish to be married. Not yet, anyway. Not for years and years. I want to enjoy myself, to do something, be someone, not just be a wife . . . a man's property, his chattel.'

Martha looked at her mutely and Nia had no way of reading her thoughts: *Unless the man is Madoc Morgan!*

CHAPTER THREE

T HE following morning, intending to ride over to Mead Rise to see Nia, Madoc carefully pulled on his jacket, folded his wide necktie with meticulous attention and secured it with a gold pin. Nia will not fault me this time, he thought with a grin – though I could do with some new clothes with shorter jackets, like Robert's. His brother had been making fun of his tailed coat, saying he was old-fashioned.

The air was cool again today, the sky grey and cloudy, though the sun was trying to break through. On the horizon a few silver rays had escaped, slanting down to the water to form a shimmering path across the sea. He stopped his mount at the lane leading to the one-time farm and studied the new notice-board that hung to one side. Burnt expertly into the wooden board were the words:

Mead Rise Stables
Top Class Mounts
Breeding and Training

Smiling, he approached what had once been the farmhouse. It had been refurbished and renovated, with sizeable extensions added, making it an attractive residence. Impressed, Madoc rang the bell, looking around at the well-tended lawns and paths. A young housemaid opened the door; she bobbed a curtsy, smiling at him.

'Good afternoon, sir.'

'Good afternoon. Is either Mrs La Velle or Miss Nia at home?' he asked, holding out his calling card.

'Please come in, sir.' She took the card. 'I'll go and see.'

Waiting in the hall, Madoc noticed the good-quality rugs on the flagged floor, the huge vase of greenery standing beside the newel post at the foot of the stairs.

'Madoc!'

He turned towards the inner regions of the house to see Martha coming towards him, smiling. As she reached him, she gave his hand a squeeze.

'I was wondering when you would call on us.' She stood back, looking up at him. 'My goodness. You're so big. You were only a boy last time I saw you.' She stretched up to kiss his cheek and he returned her kiss, beaming down at her.

'Lovely to see you, Martha.'

'Come in. I've asked Bethan to bring us some tea.' She led the way into a light and airy drawing room, twin glazed doors in the French style replacing the ordinary windows, bringing the attractive garden right into the room.

'This is a lovely room, Martha. And I like your windows,' Madoc said, looking out through them.

'It was your mother's idea. She said they are very popular. We need to get as much light in as possible because of Liam.' She undid the latch throwing the windows wide open. 'See. It is like sitting in the garden.'

'Indeed. Just the thing on a fine day.'

She gave a mock shiver. 'It's too cold for that today, as far as I am concerned,' she said, closing them again. 'But Liam leaves them open most of the time when he's here. Even now he would still prefer to live outdoors.'

'Hmm. I can quite appreciate that viewpoint.' Madoc was thinking of the *Gower Girl* and the hated cramped quarters below deck. 'Nia isn't here then?' He waited for Martha to sit down, before taking his own seat near her at the window. An occasional table alongside Martha held a crystal vase filled with sprigs of hawthorn, the red berries bright against the greenery.

'I am afraid not. She is in town with a young gentleman. Liam knows him well, his family are very good customers of ours. He visited a few days ago, to ask our permission.'

'I see?' Madoc was disappointed. 'I must have mistaken what Tom said the other day. Did she tell you I met her yesterday, on the beach?'

'Yes. I think she did mention it. She and Albert travelled to Wales in the same carriage; he was very taken with Nia. He seems a nice young man.'

'Is he from Swansea? I might know him.'

'He's from Newport. He studied at Oxford University. His family are in the wine-importing business. He has business in the Swansea area for a few days, and decided to call on us.'

'I see. I had no idea Nia had returned home or I would have called sooner. I've been looking forward to being with her again. Does she wish to see me?'

'I am sure she does . . . both you and Robert. After all, you were all children together.' Her tone was neutral.

Madoc had the impression that her reply sounded negative, as though Nia had no particular wish to see him.

'I thought Nia seemed to have changed a great deal.'

Martha smiled. 'In some ways, not in others.'

'I was hoping she'd be here, I want a chance to get to know her again.'

Martha nodded without replying and he sensed her withdrawal, wondering what caused it. He thought Martha appeared paler than he remembered, her face was lacking the rosy, apple-cheeked, healthy look he'd always associated with her.

'Is Liam around?' Madoc glanced out of the window.

'No. I'm afraid you've missed him also, Madoc. He's gone to Pembrokeshire to purchase a new horse. He wants it for breeding.'

'He's worked hard, Martha. I am so pleased for you both.'

Many people had wondered how pretty Martha, lady's maid to Mrs Morgan, had chosen to marry a gypsy. But Madoc had spent much time in their cottage with Nia, knew how happy they were together.

'Thank you, Madoc.' Her expression softened. 'He is a good man. Would you like me to show you around the stables?'

'Thank you, Martha, but no. I'll wait until Liam is here. I remember your feelings about horses.' He smiled at the memory.

'You're right. I still don't like the smelly creatures . . . though they have provided us with a good living. I like them well enough when I can ride in a carriage.'

Madoc's mind wandered back to Nia once more, flooding with childhood memories.

'Did Nia get my letters at college?'

'I didn't know you wrote any.' Her brow puckered slightly.

'I did. She received a few when I was in school, because she wrote back to me. But since I've written to her address in college I've heard nothing.'

'I don't know. She didn't speak of any. So for how long are you home, Madoc? Have you had enough of the Horn to get it out of your system? It was always your ambition, as I remember.'

Madoc shook his head.

'Not yet. I want to skipper my own ship around the Horn before quitting.'

'You want to be a captain? Like your father?'

'Not quite. Copper-ore barques are much smaller than the East Indiamen he sailed.'

'I expect your mother is hoping you will stay home. I know she hates you sailing on the copper-barques.'

Madoc laughed. 'Does she, now? You're giving away secrets, Martha. She has never admitted as much to me.'

'Oh dear!' Martha put her hand to her face. 'I didn't mean to . . .'

'Don't worry.' He grinned at her. 'I won't give you away.' He finished his tea and stood up. 'I'll be going now. I'll call again to see Nia and Liam'

Taking his leave, he felt ill at ease and dissatisfied and, which was completely out of character for Madoc, plagued by a slight feeling of inadequacy. He would never make a fortune in his work, he thought, and as the younger son he'd have no inheritance. Nia's brother was already settled into a lucrative profession, and this young man who was calling on Nia seemed to be financially well-off. Had he done right to leave school early? Might it have been more sensible to have continued his education or joined the Royal Navy? He dismissed the idea, but was left feeling vaguely unsettled.

The following day Nia's maid came upstairs to her bedroom and tapped on the door.

'Miss Nia. There's a gentleman to see you. He gave his card. He's very handsome, miss.'

Nia sucked in an unsteady breath when she read the card.

'Thank you, Bethan. Tell him I will be down presently.'

She rushed over to the mirror to smooth down her hair and pinch her cheeks to make them glow. She picked up a glass bottle of toilet water, touching a little of it lightly behind her ears. Her heart was thudding erratically and she took several steadying breaths. I must not show him how much I care, she told herself firmly. Be aloof, keep him guessing. After all, he did refuse to ride with me the other day.

Though I know he was teasing – and it was my own fault, she conceded.

She ran along the corridor, then, near the top of the stairs, she slowed to a sedate pace. Descending regally, she arranged her face into a ladylike smile before she reached him.

'Madoc. How lovely to see you.' Her voice was pitched low and melodious and she held out a hand to him.

'Well, that's a relief.' He took it, kept holding it, looking deep into her eyes for a few moments as she struggled to hold her neutral expression. He released her hand and he spread both his own, palms up, saying: 'See. I'm dressed in my best rig today. I hope it meets with your approval.'

She thought he looked wonderful but chose to ignore his remark.

'Do come into the drawing room.' She led the way, adding: 'I'm afraid Mama is not here, she would have loved to see you. . . .'

She broke off as Madoc, after a quick glance around to make sure the room was vacant, pushed the door shut with his foot and twirled her into his arms, crushing her against him and kissing her passionately. His lips were tender and sensual, his smell sharp and spicy. For one endless moment she managed to remain passive in his embrace, then, as if of their own intention, her arms stole tightly around his neck and she kissed him back with equal fervour. Her lips clung to his as he began to pull away, but he pressed his mouth back to hers for a second lingering kiss, his tongue gently caressing her lips. As he lifted his head, still holding her, she saw the look in his eyes, a smoky amber, smoulder across her face. Her own eyes, wide, dark and uncertain, hung on his.

'I've missed you, Nia.' He hugged her close, his voice gruff. She dropped her head, but not before he had noticed the tears flooding her eyes. 'Nia? What is it?'

He put his hand gently under her chin, tried to lift her head, but she jerked it away, pulled out of his arms and ran from the room.

Dismayed, Madoc stared after her.

'Now what have I done?' He rubbed reflectively at his chin, screwing up his face. God! I shouldn't have kissed her. I shouldn't have taken her response for granted – but there was no denying she had responded with equal measure. And her perfume wafting around him, flowery but heady, had enhanced his ardour. Robert was right; I do jump right into things, he decided, shaking his head. Now what?

He went out into the hall but there was no sign of Nia. He was standing there looking around when the young maid came back.

'Can I help you, sir?'

'Er . . . did you see where Miss Nia went?'

'I believe she went upstairs, sir. Shall I tell her you are looking for her?'

'No . . . thank you. Is Mr La Velle in the stables?'

'I think so, sir. Do you wish me to send someone for him?'

'No, that's all right. I'll walk around to see him. If Miss Nia comes back will you tell her where I am, please?'

'Of course, Mr Morgan.' Her expression was curious. 'Do you want your hat, sir?'

'I'll collect it later, thank you.'

Nia had raced up the stairs and into her bedroom, slamming the door behind her. She leaned against it, trembling slightly.

'Oh God! Now what should I do?' She touched her lips with her hand, running her finger gently across them, reliving the thought of his mouth on hers, the feel of his arms around her, his hard body pressed against hers. *I love him – but does he love me?*

Or is he playing with me? Unbidden the thought leapt into her mind. *He is so attractive, he could have any woman he chooses – why should he pick me?* Surely that was not the kiss of a novice? He was obviously well-practised in the art.

I must remain aloof, like Lucy did, she decided. *Not be eager*. He always wanted Lucy and she never paid him any attention. *I'll make him think I am not interested in him. But can I do that?* She poured water from the china jug into its matching flowered bowl, dipped a cloth into it and pressed it to her face, trying to calm her shattered equilibrium.

She sank on to the bed. This could be one of the most important things she would ever do in her life; she must do it properly. She could not afford to make a mistake.

Madoc went out through the front door and made his way around the house towards the outbuildings that extended beyond. He could see a few mares in a large fenced paddock, where the grass was lush and green. A stable boy was brushing one of them. On noticing Madoc he began walking over but before he could reach him Liam emerged from one of the stables with another young man.

'Madoc!' Walking over, Liam held out his hand, pumping Madoc's arm warmly once he held it. 'Good to see you after all this time. Martha told me you had called. Nia is around somewhere. I'm sure she'll be pleased to see you again.'

'Yes. I have seen her. She's gone upstairs ... I believe.' He felt uncomfortable, wondering whether Nia might come storming back. What would Liam's reaction be if she told him what happened? 'A wonderful place you have here, Liam.'

'Your father has been very good to us, he started it all off. We are more than lucky; Martha is well pleased.' There was quiet satisfaction in his voice. 'That was always my wish in life, to make my own sweet woman happy. Both my women.'

One of the horses in the paddock had seen Liam and snickered a greeting to him.

'It's not luck, Liam, you've more than deserved all you've had.' Madoc was recalling Liam risking his life all those years ago. Could he ever forget it when Robert had been left disabled? 'You can be justly proud of your achievements.' He smiled as the horse came cantering over to Liam.

'Thank you, Madoc. And you? Are you content with your life at sea?' Liam reached his hand between the rails to the animal.

'It suits me well enough for now. Maybe sometime I'll try a different ship, but not yet. And I cannot see where I would fit in at home with the firm at the moment.'

Liam lifted the latch on the paddock gate, and as the men entered the other horses trotted over, crowding around them.

'These are ready to be sold on,' Liam explained.

Madoc noticed he looked downcast as he smoothed an animal's glossy flank.

'You don't want them to go?'

Liam gave a wry smile. 'I'd like to keep them all. But then I'd have no business.'

'Do you still train them all yourself?' Madoc reached to smooth another velvet nose.

'In the early stages. But Mathew ...' he nodded towards the young man he had been with, '... is coming on very well. He's got a feel for the animals. I've started letting him take a hand once I get the horse under control. I have two other young assistants as well, and of course

I have Nia back to help me now.' He smiled at Madoc, who returned his smile.

'When we were children she always wanted to help you. Does she actually do anything with the horses now?'

'She was becoming very useful before she went to college. In these last years she has been away so much she's had no opportunity. She is anxious to try her hand again, though.'

Madoc noticed that Liam's Irish accent was hardly noticeable and wondered whether he was deliberately trying to bolster the Spanish heritage idea. Why not, if it helped with his business?

As they were talking Nia came round the corner of the yard. Madoc watched her approach, her steel hooped skirt swaying as she walked. It was nipped in at the waist by a belt above which she wore a blouse with little pin-tucks decorating the bodice. A demure rounded collar finished off the neckline where an exquisite cameo brooch nestled. She looked perfect. He gave a slight nod, smiling as she reached them, wondering what she was going to say. She returned his nod and came up to lean on the fence.

'Are you showing Madoc the animals, Papa?'

'I am.' Liam's glance flashed between them, and his brow puckered; obviously he sensed an atmosphere. 'I thought maybe you were coming to help me.'

'Not today.' She glanced down at her clothes. 'I am hardly dressed for it. But I could always change, I suppose.'

'Would you like to come riding with me, Nia?' Madoc asked.

'I might.' Her reply lacked enthusiasm and Madoc saw Liam's frown deepen.

'Don't feel obliged because I've asked. Maybe you'd prefer another time.'

'Why would I feel obliged?'

'If you will excuse me, Madoc, I'll be getting on.' Liam began moving away. 'I hope I'll see you another time.'

'Yes, of course. I'll call.' Madoc looked back at Nia, who was now facing the other way. Her black hair was naturally wavy, but today it was drawn back on to the nape of her neck, where intricate coils and plaits held it in a sleek, wide knot. It must have taken ages, Madoc thought with amazement. She turned back to face him and he threw her a wry smile, but held her gaze.

'Nia. Will you accept my apology? I realize I was precipitate. It was inexcusable of me to be so unthinking. You looked so lovely I got carried away. . . .' His voice trailed off. She wasn't responding, her expression was remote, and she was silent for a few moments.

'You really expect me to give in, don't you? To say it's all right,' she said eventually. She gave a little snort. 'Am I so lightly to be trifled with?' Her voice was cold. 'Like a scullery maid, to be grabbed and kissed in the corner.'

Madoc stared at her, appalled.

'Nia! Of course not! You know that's not how I think of you. That's not what I meant . . . thought! You know me better than that.'

'Do I really, Madoc? I knew you as a boy. I haven't seen you for years . . . you couldn't even bother to visit—'

'I did,' he broke in. 'I came—'

'When your mother brought you with her—'

'No. I also came on my own. Several times. The first time I came home after rounding the Horn, for one. I was dying to tell you all about it, but you were away at college.'

Her eyes narrowed. 'Are you telling me the truth?'

'Did you ever know me to lie to you?'

'No.' She fed a handful of grass to one of the horses. 'But it is strange no one told me you had called.'

'By the time you got home they had probably forgotten. And I wrote to you at college too.' He reached forward to where her hand rested on the fence, covering it with his own, but she snatched hers away. Madoc stiffened, pulling himself erect, his face harsh. 'And another thing,' he barked. 'I have never grabbed a kitchen maid and kissed her. Or any other maid for that matter. I would never force myself on any woman.'

Her head jerked up, her eyes meeting his blazing ones and she flushed.

'What makes you think you didn't force yourself on me?'

His mouth tightened; his eyes were glittering and he stared at her, saying nothing. Tension crackled in the air between them.

'It is time I left.' He gave her a formal nod. 'Good afternoon, Miss La Velle.' Turning on his heel, he stalked away from her, his face bleak, his heart in his boots.

She watched him walk away, and swallowed hard, forcing herself not to run after him or call him back. Her face was unutterably sad as she recalled a similar despair many years before.

★

She had been around fourteen years old, Madoc fifteen, when he came home from school and she told him her family was leaving Gower. They had wandered along paths winding through the gorse bushes, thorns catching their clothes as they passed.

Downcast, they sat on the cliff grass, gazing out to sea. The air had been crystal clear that day. On either side, the cliffs bordering the Gower bays vanished into the distance, fading from shades of green to pewter. Not a ripple disturbed the sea, flat as glass, other than where two cormorants were diving under the water in their search for food. A few seagulls floated on the surface, their inverted reflections floating with them.

'So when do you leave?' Madoc chewed a stem of grass.

'On Monday.' Overcome with misery, Nia's voice wobbled, unable to bear the thought of never seeing Madoc again. 'I don't want to leave, Mad.'

She leaned her head against his shoulder. After a moment's hesitation, he put an arm around her and held her against him.

'Never mind, Nia. You can always come back to see us . . . and I'll come and visit you.' His voice was gruff.

'Will you really?' She turned her face up to his. 'Promise?'

'I promise,' he murmured, drowning in those pleading eyes, empathizing with her, completely understanding her misery. It was pleasant to be holding Nia like this. Her hair smelt of fresh herbs, and she was softer than he ever remembered; not skinny and bony. He swallowed, aware of a tightening and tingling in his loins and, surprising himself, he leaned his head down and kissed her.

His firm lips met her soft ones questioningly, hers clinging to his for a brief moment before he lifted his head from their first kiss, studying her as though he had never seen her before. Her face was luminous, her black eyes brilliant with gold flecks as she reached up both hands and slid them around his neck. He turned more to face her, leaning his head down to repeat that kiss.

As their lips met, the hand resting around her shoulder slid down, as if of its own accord, and his fingers inched towards her breast. She didn't stop him and, his fingers reaching their goal, he found it yielded beneath his hand, sending shivers crinkling down his spine to his groin. She gave a little whimper and turned to him, pressing against him, his hand trapped between their bodies. Panting slightly, he crushed her to him, his lips and hand more demanding as she responded, kissing him back. Suddenly, feeling himself harden alarmingly, he pulled away from her, flooded with acute embarrassment. He leapt to his feet.

This was Nia, his greatest friend! He shouldn't be treating her this way. This was the way some boys at school gloated about, getting lucky with the maids, the gloating accompanied by lecherous laughter.

'I'm sorry, Nia.' Ashamed to look at her he turned away, brushing a distracted hand through his hair. He fought to control the wild emotions coursing through his body. His pulse pounded in his throat and he was panting, as if he had been running. Nia was quiet and he half turned back to her, risking a glance down, expecting her to be scowling up at him. But she was still sitting with her knees drawn up, both arms resting on them, her head buried in her arms.

'Nia. Are you all right?' She never moved and he took a deep breath. 'Nia, I'm sorry,' he repeated, wondering what to do.

She still didn't answer and he dropped to the ground beside her again, keeping a space between them, afraid to risk touching her. To his relief, she lifted her head and smiled at him.

'I'm all right, Madoc,' she whispered.

'I'm sorry. I don't know what I . . .' His voice trailed off and he looked down, blushing hotly.

'I forgive you.' She didn't sound angry. Her eyes wandered over his face, hanging on his eyes as if searching for something. 'Madoc. I . . .' She bit off the words and her face crumpled.

'Nia? You're not going to cry are you? I didn't mean to upset you.'

'No. I'm not going to cry, Madoc.' But she sounded sad. 'I'm not upset.'

The following Monday a cacophony of noise had filled the station; traders promoting their wares, trolley wheels squeaking past, clacking over the cobblestones. Nia glanced at Madoc whose hands were thrust into his pockets, his mouth turned down, his eyes brooding. Struggling to hold back tears, she brushed her hand across her eyes, aware of her mother's concerned gaze. She's not happy about it either, Nia knew.

'I don't want to go. Mama, please can I stay at Craig y Mor?'

'What would we do without you, my lovely?' Martha took her arm.

'Who would your father talk to about his precious horses?'

Nia sighed. Her mother knew just the right words to get her on to the train. Leaning precariously out of the window, her arm pumping, black mane fluttering around her face, she watched Madoc grow smaller, then disappear, in the trail of the clouds of steam from the engine's funnel. She sank down on to her seat, her shoulders shaking as she sobbed softly into her hands.

Now, her harsh words had forced him away a second time. Would he come back?

CHAPTER FOUR

FROM inside the stables Liam was observing Nia and Madoc through a window. As Madoc turned on his heel and stalked away, his glance returned to his daughter. She was standing motionless, holding her head high. Then her shoulders slumped, and turning listlessly, head down, she walked across the yard to the house, her distress plain.

Liam's love for his daughter overwhelmed him sometimes; he still found it difficult to accept that affection for a daughter could be so powerful. He loved her mother with a passion undiminished since the day they met, but was astonished at the strength of his feelings for his daughter. Before having children, he had assumed it would be a son who would give him most pleasure. And he did love his son dearly, knew he had all the qualities of an admirable man, but it was Nia who filled him with joy. He was so proud of her abilities, her strength of character, her intelligence.

Once again Liam wondered what was amiss between the couple. Nia had appeared abrupt with Madoc, who seemed to be trying to coax her into a better temper. Although they had been apart for years, Liam had fully expected them take up their friendship where it had broken off, had been hoping for this. He wondered if Nia could be simply heeding her mother's advice?

Martha had always discouraged Nia's interest in Madoc, not believing a romance between them to be possible; but Liam realized this was because of Martha's past position as Emily Morgan's personal maid. Martha was not normally interfering, but he knew she was anxious about Nia's marriage prospects, wanted her to find a good husband.

In Liam's opinion, Nia and Madoc were made for one another, two free spirits with minds in harmony. Well, they could only sort it out

49

for themselves – as long as Martha did not try to disrupt things and prevent their romance from developing.

He sighed. He was extremely anxious about Martha's heart condition. Her breathless attacks were getting more severe and more frequent, and the slightest emotional episode did seem to trigger one off. He had been upset to hear she had had a severe attack the other day, in front of Nia, who had been frightened and distressed. Martha's increasing incapacity was becoming a huge worry. Liam kept urging Martha to rest, which she found hard to do, and he had been dosing her with foxglove tea. At first she seemed to be responding well, restoring his faith in the old and tried remedies, but Nia, since she had come home, had been urging him to send for a physician. Having little faith in doctors himself, Liam had bowed to Martha's insistence not to call one. Still, he did wonder if he should ignore her protests, just in case. These days they could easily afford treatment and he would never forgive himself if . . . No! He was not going to follow that line of thought.

He reached up to lift some tackle from the stable wall, when the twelve-year-old Nia's words came echoing back to him from the past. She had been asking him details about being ostracized by his tribe for marrying a non-gypsy, wanting to know exactly what it involved.

'Papa, have you ever regretted marrying Mama?'

He regarded her with surprise.

'Never. Don't be foolish, Nia. You know your mother is the most important thing in my life.'

'But you do miss your people, I know you do. You talk about them all the time.'

Liam said nothing. She spoke the truth. It *had* been hard, very hard, making up his mind to leave the tribe for Martha. He had agonized through long nights about making the break – but she had been worth any sacrifice.

'You love Mama very much, don't you? I want to marry someone who will love me like that. Do you think Madoc could ever love me as much?'

Aghast, Liam sucked in a breath.

'Nia. Don't speak foolish words. You are both so young. Just children and good friends.'

'But I love him, Papa.' Her voice was quite certain. 'You told me you knew you loved Mama the first time you met her.'

'I was older than you. . . .'

'What has age to do with it?' Her expression was earnest.

Liam didn't reply for a moment, trying to gather his thoughts. He pulled off his felt hat, scratching his head. Quite apart from her gypsy blood, how could he explain to her the huge gap existing between master and servant? The Morgans were unconventional in their outlook – hadn't they educated his children with their own? But the daunting chasm still yawned between them.

'Papa?' She was waiting for an answer.

'Nia . . . Madoc has gone away to school now. He'll change, he might forget about you. . . .'

'He'd never! I know he won't.'

'But your mother and I are their . . . servants, Nia. We are not . . .' he groped for words, 'not on an equal footing. His parents will be expecting him to marry another from his class. Do you understand what I'm saying?'

She nodded, and brushed a hand across her pony's head as he flicked his ears, trying to get rid of a fly.

'I don't think Madoc thinks about things like money.'

' 'Tis right you are about that.'

'And he is the second son. Doesn't that mean that Rob will inherit everything?'

'I can't give you an answer because I don't know much about it,' Liam admitted. 'But how do you know about such things?'

'I heard the servants talking, I think.'

'But that still doesn't alter the facts. Madoc is from the gentry . . . and we are not.'

'Can we ever change it?' She looked hopeful. 'If we made a lot of money, could we change it then?'

He was daunted by her words. How could they ever change the situation?

'I don't see how we can, my little Nia.' He hated the shadow clouding her face. 'You'll find a man to make you happy, I know you will.'

He saw her mouth tighten, the defiant tilt of her chin.

'Madoc,' she mouthed silently.

But later he had deliberated about her words. *How can I change it? What can I do to make money? Something with horses, perhaps?* The idea set his mind racing.

For some time, as well as treating sick horses, Liam had been breaking them in and training them for the local gentry. Captain Morgan, ever helpful, had suggested that Liam might turn an unused barn into a stable for his own use, to house the animals. It had been a huge success and he earned a very acceptable extra income from it, which he was sure he could expand a great deal further.

Was there anything else I could do in this line? he pondered. All the Morgans' friends and neighbours sought his opinion on buying their horses. Was there a way he could really make money with horses?

And when he asked David Morgan's advice, it was he who once more proposed a solution, by offering him the use of his wife's inherited property, Beechwood Hall, to breed horses.

Liam's smile was self-mocking as he led a horse out of the stable. *And here I am today, a respected businessman, a landowner – not just a gypsy. And my daughter is a 'lady'.*

But would it bring her one day her heart's desire? he wondered.

CHAPTER FIVE

NIA waited all the following day, hoping Madoc would return. She kept going over the previous day's events.

She should never have said those awful things to him, she reproached herself, recalling her unforgettable words. She stared sightlessly out through her bedroom window, both arms wound across her chest.

I implied he'd forced himself on me ... still, it had been his own fault! No gentleman would kiss someone he regarded as a lady in such a way. Not in such an intimate way! The tip of her tongue slid across her lips and she closed her eyes, reliving that kiss. *Is Mama right after all? Does he see me as the maid's daughter?*

But that would not be like Madoc; even as a boy he'd been courteous to the servants. And he did apologize. She should have accepted his apology and forgiven him. Reluctantly perhaps, showing a little reserve and coolness towards him to let him know she was displeased. But why should she forgive him? He did not behave as a gentleman would ... to a lady. That was the thing that hurt. But she *had* returned his kisses, he must have realized that.

Unable to settle to anything, she went riding, eyes hopefully scanning the cliffs and the beach. There was no sign of him, but he still filled her thoughts. She saw his huge, strong hand reaching out to cover her own, remembered snatching hers away. *I never gave him a chance*, she reflected.

He had looked appalled when she had virtually accused him of forcing himself on her ... why had she said it? She hadn't struggled ... in fact she'd responded. He'd been positively shocked that she'd thought he could do such a thing. It was not in Madoc's nature to hurt any woman. He had been justly offended. No wonder he hadn't come back.

Tom would have news of him, she decided. He and Robert often met and Madoc would have gone with them.

But Tom did not turn up for their evening meal.

'Mama, is Tom not coming for dinner this evening? He's very late.' Nia shook her napkin out on to her lap.

'I'm not expecting him, my lovely. He often plays cards with Robert on Wednesday and Friday evenings.' Martha beamed. She enjoyed the idea of Robert and Tom being friends on equal terms. 'Did you want him for anything in particular, then?'

'Nothing special.' She kept her voice neutral, not wanting to admit the truth to her mother. She caught her father's quizzical glance on her, but he said nothing.

It was almost bedtime when she eventually heard Tom's voice in the hall. She hurried out, pretending she was going through to the kitchen.

'Hello, Tom. You're back then. Have you been playing cards with Robert and Madoc?'

'With Rob, not Madoc. He sailed on the evening tide.'

'He's sailed! Oh! How long will . . . are his trips at sea?' She tried to sound nonchalant, but Tom cocked a teasing eye at her.

'I thought you were no longer interested in Madoc? What about this Albert fellow, then?'

'I am *not* interested in Madoc.' She gave a dismissive nod. 'I was merely asking if he'd been playing cards with you, that is all.'

'Ahh. That is all.' His expression was mocking. 'I see.'

'Shut up!' Her face was venomous.

'Very ladylike, I'm sure. Did you learn that at your ladies' college, Nia?' He laughed when she poked the merest tip of her tongue out and flounced away. He called after her. 'Several months, I believe.'

Slowly she walked up the stairs. *I won't see him for months!*

Bethan had already lit the lamp in her room, which emitted a faint oily smell as Nia turned up the wick. It cast a pool of warm light around her as she sank, dispirited, on to her bed.

'Madoc. I'm sorry,' she whispered. 'I didn't mean it. Please come back safely.'

In bed, she tried to read for a while before turning out her lamp. At last she fell back, closing her eyes, but sleep refused to come. She kept worrying about her mother as well, and time and again, just as she was drifting off to sleep a huge wave came crashing into her drowsy state, jerking her back to full awareness, leaving her shivering and troubled.

Madoc! I love you. Maybe she could send her thoughts to him wherever he was in that pitiless ocean. *Madoc please don't drown.*

Eventually she fell into an uneasy sleep. She woke late the following morning.

Regarding her face in the mirror, she found it drawn, with dark shadows under her eyes. After washing, pulling on an unhooped skirt and a plain dark blouse, she laced her hair into a thick plait down her back and tugged on a pair of riding-boots before going downstairs. The family had already eaten and Nia drank only a cup of tea, unable to face eating.

Outside, she went to lean on the paddock rail, watching her father who was shepherding a young untrained filly into a smallish ringed area he had dedicated to his charges' initial training. Catching sight of her he turned, pleasure on his face.

'Nia. Have you come to help me, then?'

'I thought I might, Papa. If you will have me? I feel I must do something useful.' She laughed. 'Not embroidery.'

He joined in her laughter, knowing she hated such feminine activities. But as he noticed her drawn face, his smile faded.

'Are you feeling all right, girl? You look a bit off colour.'

'I'm tired. I didn't sleep too well. I kept waking.'

His dark eyes were searching.

'And would Madoc have anything to do with that?'

Her mouth turned down, trembling, and she nodded wordlessly. Immediately he leapt up and over the fence and put his arms around her, holding her tightly. She curled up against him, thankful for the comfort of his arms.

'I thought he left in a hurry yesterday. Was that your doing?'

'Yes. And now he's gone back to sea, and all night I kept thinking about him.' She gazed up at him. 'Papa, what if he drowns?'

'Nia, girl. He's been doing these trips for years. He'll be back safely.'

'I know that. But I still can't help worrying.'

'That's natural enough.' He stood, holding her shoulders to study her pale face. 'Look. Would it be wiser if you gave the horses a miss today? You'll not want to get exhausted. And most likely they will pick up your distress.'

'I never thought of that. I'll watch you a while, anyhow. I'll enjoy that.'

He supported her arm as she hitched up her skirt and climbed up to sit on top of the fence.

Liam never used conventional methods of breaking in horses, which Nia knew he considered cruel.

'There is no need to break an animal's spirit,' he would quote, ever since she'd been old enough to understand. 'You must listen to the horse, communicate with it in its own way.' And this was what he acted upon in his methods. Nia loved watching him. His understanding of animals, and of horses in particular, still seemed like magic to most people.

Expectant, unwittingly she leaned forward as her father entered the ring which now housed the unbroken filly. The filly's eyes immediately flared wide, showing the whites, revealing her fright. She began prancing skittishly, tossing her head and kicking her back legs up behind her, keeping as far away from Liam as possible. He appeared not to look at her, to ignore her almost and, without touching or drawing near to the young animal, he walked around with her, circling as she circled, weaving and turning as she did, sometimes even turning his back to her. The filly gradually slowed, and once she stopped racing around the arena and calmed a little, Liam picked up a long rope. Still not approaching her, he flicked the rope out near the animal's rump, not touching her but causing her to bolt forward in a rush of renewed panic. After he repeated this a number of times, she seemed to realize that there was nothing to fear and her terror subsided; lowering her head she reached her neck forward. Liam discarded the rope and once again began walking around with the filly, his eyes not meeting hers, turning as she did, mirroring her movements, walking up to her then retreating, talking softly all the while, reassuring her. Eventually her eyes were calm.

Liam approached cautiously, coming right up to her this time. The filly raised her head, slight alarm evident again until he was near to her head. Nia held her breath – this was the best bit. Liam put his face close to the filly's, found eye-contact, seemed almost to breathe into the animal's nostrils. The fear left the filly's eyes and she dropped her head, snorting. Liam stroked her soft nose, murmuring to her, then he walked away, leaving her standing calm and quiet on her own.

The first part, the hardest part, was over, the rest was relatively easy. Liam approached the filly again, but there was no fear this time as she snickered softly, reaching her head forward to nuzzle the sugar-lump he held out on his palm.

Nia felt a lump in her throat, wonder in her heart. She was emotional every time she saw the miracle her father accomplished and beamed at him as he returned to sit on the fence with her. Even though the late October day was chilly, she saw slight globules of perspiration beading his upper lip; he pulled a coloured handkerchief from his pocket and wiped his face. The breaking-in looked easy, but Nia knew it took immense concentration on his part. One false action could mean hours more work to train a horse, and some animals were more easily reassured than others.

She and Madoc had spent hours watching her father, forever enthralled by the whole scene. Many were still convinced it was some sort of trick, but Madoc's family had always acknowledged and respected Liam's skill. Tomorrow she would begin to learn this magic, Nia resolved.

Trying to put Madoc to the back of her mind and set it firmly on training the horses, Nia slept better that night, awaking fresh and rested the following morning. A cool wind was gusting the few remaining red and gold leaves across the cobblestones, their feet crunched through them as they were blown into the corners.

'Before you can begin to understand what the horse is saying, you have to listen to it. And to do that you must be relaxed,' her father told her. 'You have to reassure the creature, otherwise your tension will communicate itself to him. You realize what I'm saying?'

Nia nodded. 'Yes. You taught me that when I was a girl. You said it applied to handling any animals, especially wild ones. They have to trust you.'

'That's right. Horse and man must understand each other, otherwise there will be no trust, only fear. And that is not good. We have to imitate the body movements they use to communicate with one another. That is how the horse talks to us in the ring.'

Nia and her father discussed it for a long while and, eventually trying out these theories with a fairly placid filly, Nia began to gain some success.

'She did it, Papa. She listened to me.' Nia's excited voice rose, her cheeks flushed with triumph as she came out of the ring.

'Of course she did. You've always had an understanding of wild creatures, Nia. I knew you would be good at it.' His face mirrored her exhilaration. 'Try again with a slightly friskier foal.' He turned enquiringly to the young housemaid, hovering alongside.

'Please, sir. Mrs La Velle asked me to tell Miss Nia that Mr Albert Goodman is at the house.'

'Thank you, Bethan,' Nia replied. I'll come right away.' She began walking towards the house, and saw Albert approaching.

'Good morning, Nia. Mr La Velle. I was in Swansea and I took the opportunity of calling. I hope you don't mind?'

'I am pleased to see you, Albert. Though I am hardly dressed for company.' She looked down ruefully at her working-skirt and blouse, the old jacket she wore, her muddied hands.

'You look as lovely as ever.' His eyes assured her that he meant it. 'Your mother said you were working with the horses. When I said I'd come out to see, she said she thought you'd rather change first.'

Nia laughed. 'She is not impressed with my unladylike behaviour. I will be scolded when you leave.'

'Oh dear! I'm afraid that is my fault.'

Nia started to thread her hand through his arm but stopped with a little laugh.

'I can't take your arm with these filthy hands.' In the short time she had known him, already she realized Albert was fastidious about his clothes. Impeccably groomed at all times, he always wore the latest fashion.

'How long are you in Swansea?'

He hesitated slightly. 'I could stay a few days.'

'That's good.' Nia wondered about offering him accommodation at Mead Rise, but decided it could complicate matters. 'Do you like riding? I can show you something of Gower?'

'I do like riding. I can book a room at the Cambrian Hotel . . . our family always stays there.'

'We can send a stable boy with a letter, if you wish. To secure your room.'

So Nia spent the next few days in Albert's pleasant company, trying to forget her worries about Madoc. Chaperoned by Nia's mother, one evening they went to a play at the theatre in Swansea, on another they attended a concert in the Assembly Rooms. The temperature dropped sharply and, both wrapped up warmly against the biting wind blowing in from the sea, and a stable boy trailing them discreetly in the distance, Nia took him riding in Gower, taking delight in his admiration of the scenery. But Madoc dominated her mind; she kept comparing him with Albert.

Albert was kind, gentle, attentive. Polite and even-tempered, he was pleasant company. Whereas Madoc...? He was impulsive, his temper flared quickly, but died just as easily. He was kind and thoughtful too, though he had often hidden it beneath a tough exterior. She recalled his care for wild creatures as a boy, freeing them from traps, with much risk to himself. Several times he had tackled the local village bully, a sadistic boy far bigger than Madoc, in order to rescue animal victims from his evil clutches. Madoc never cared how he looked ... and he was just the same now she realized, remembering his casual dress that first day. She smiled at the thought. Albert could never be accused of not behaving like a gentleman. Albert was ... nice. And Madoc? Was virile and strong and ... stirring! I always felt safe with him, she remembered, a trifle sadly.

They were making their way back to Mead Rise one afternoon when Nia noticed a bundle of muddied fur slumped alongside the road. Her mount snorted out a cloudy breath in the cold air as she drew to a halt.

'Look! I think that's a dog.' Nia held her arms out to Albert. 'Help me down please, Albert.' She was dressed in a riding-habit and it was difficult to alight from a side-saddle without a mounting-block.

He regarded her with astonishment. 'You don't intend touching it, do you Nia? It looks—'

'Of course I do. Please lift me down.' She held her arms out to him again.

Sucking in a breath, he dismounted, his face disapproving.

'Shall I take a look and see if it is alive?' he asked, his lip curling slightly with disgust as he looked down at it.

The bundle must have heard their voices and, giving a little whimper, moved slightly, and two glazed eyes looked up at them in appeal.

'It is a dog. Poor thing. Please, Albert. If you won't help me down I'll have to manage on my own.' Nia began gathering up the folds of rich material draped from her waist.

'No, wait! I'll help you.' He reached his hands around her waist and lifted her down, his face concerned. 'I think you should be most careful, Nia. It could be rabid.'

'I'll take a look.' She shrugged out of her heavy jacket and draped it over her saddle. 'Will you hold back my skirt please, Albert.' Once again she gathered the material together, but this time drew it behind her out of her way, waiting for Albert to hold it. Dumbfounded, his mouth a thin line of disapproval, he held her skirt back as she crouched alongside the dog. She murmured softly to it, and it gave another little whimper as she moved it gently with her gloved hands.

'I think it has been run over by a wagon and left for dead. How could they? People are so cruel.' She looked back at Albert whose mouth was turned down more than ever. 'Will you call Bertie, the stable boy, for me please, Albert. He can fetch my father.'

'You mean to say you intend staying here with the creature?'

'Of course I do.' Her voice was sharp and angry. 'Did you expect me to just leave it here to die? Will you try and secure my skirt back out of my way, somehow? Perhaps you can use my veil. I don't want to handle it with these gloves now.'

Silently, stiff with censure, Albert unhitched her veil from her hat and tied her skirt back as best he could, and went for the stable boy.

'Explain to Papa, please Bertie. He'll bring a cart to carry it home.' She flashed Albert a grateful smile and his face softened slightly. 'You have no need to worry. I will be perfectly all right, I assure you.'

Nia was sitting on the ground alongside the dog when her father arrived. Liam, wearing an old jacket, examined the dog with Nia and agreed with her assessment. Murmuring soothingly to the dog, he wrapped a sack around it and gathered it up tenderly in his arms. As if it understood, the dog's tongue reached out to lick his hand and Liam smiled.

'You'll be all right, my friend. We'll soon get you mended.' He laid it in the back of the cart. 'I'll see you back at Mead Rise.'

Nia peeled off her suede gloves and threw them in the cart with the dog before undoing the veil that held back her skirt.

'This habit will have to be laundered.' She shook her skirt, brushing ineffectively at the mud with which it was liberally covered. She allowed Albert to help her into her jacket, then gripped his arm to remount. She was reminded of that day on the beach, the day she had held Madoc's iron-hard arm, and was once more aware of another difference in the two men.

Albert's manner was more amiable to the dog once it was installed in a warm corner of a stable, its wounded leg bathed and splinted, its muddied coat cleaned up a little with a damp cloth.

'He's going to be fine. Aren't you pleased we rescued him now?' Nia's face was glowing with pleasure.

'Certainly. I was merely concerned about you.' He heaved a big sigh, his eyes hanging on her face. 'You really are the most unusual woman, Nia. I cannot imagine another disregarding her own welfare as you did. I don't think I will ever get used to your ways.'

'Would you change me then, Albert?' Her voice was playful.

He smiled, looking perplexed. 'I cannot imagine you any other way. I believe I am growing to love you, Nia.'

She dropped her eyes. She liked Albert, enjoyed his company, but had no wish for their friendship to be spoiled by his getting serious. How could she explain this to him?

'I should not speak this way. It is too soon. You hardly know me yet,' he said. She looked back at his face, expectant, hopeful. 'Have you. . . .' He broke off mid sentence.

'I regard you as a very good friend, Albert,' she whispered. 'But you know little of me. I will always be interested in rescuing and tending animals. That is how I am, and I would not change.'

'I do understand. But I would like to get to know you more, Nia.' He took her hand, held it. 'You are willing for me to do that?' When she made no reply he took it for her acceptance. 'Thank you.'

'Your Albert is a true gentleman,' her mother said as they watched his hired gig drive away. 'I like him a great deal.'

'My Albert, Mama? I hardly think he is mine.'

Martha threw her a speculative smile.

'I think he is. He's smitten with you, Nia. He would make you an excellent husband.'

Nia bit back the retort which rose to the surface: Why Albert and not Madoc? What about my gypsy blood now? But she was trying hard to keep life as placid as possible for her mother, remembering that a confrontation had set off an attack once before. Instead, Nia brushed her mother's remark off with a laugh.

'He is very likeable, I agree, but I hardly know the man, Mama.'

'Then get to know him. Next time he comes to Swansea you must offer him accommodation here.'

Nia frowned. 'I don't know if that is a good idea. I find it easier as it is. Please do not ask him to stay, Mama. I can suit myself this way.'

'Just as you say, but you may issue an invitation if you wish.'

'Thank you, Mama.'

CHAPTER SIX

THE day after Albert left, Nia set about starting up her animal infirmary, like the one she had kept as a girl. That one had been a small lean-to shed attached to their cottage, but her father, who thoroughly approved of the plan, suggested she might use part of the building where the dog was already settled.

'You can have that end entirely for your use,' Liam told her. 'We'll set it all up for you. We can make the loft up as a workshop, and you can also use it for the storage of the herbs and plants for your healing medications.'

'That would be wonderful, Papa.' Delighted, she kissed his cheek. 'Can I start clearing it out now?' She made towards the ladder leading up to the loft.

'I'll send Bertie over to give you a hand. Perhaps you should be thinking of wearing gloves if you want to keep your hands ladylike?' he added, a twinkle in his eye.

Nia pulled a face, looking at her hands.

'You are right. If I get them rough Mama will be annoyed. I'd better find some gloves.'

Nia's skill in training the horses began to improve rapidly, much to her father's delight. And although this work, along with her developing infirmary, occupied much of her time, her thoughts kept returning to Madoc as she counted the weeks to his expected return. Albert's visits became more frequent; often he stayed in Swansea over the weekends. He seemed amused with her infirmary and its assorted occupants, and if he disapproved he hid it carefully, obviously not wanting to earn Nia's censure as he had the day they found the dog.

Laddy, now Nia's dog, had recovered well from his ordeal, his coat was glossy and sleek, his eyes bright with intelligence, though he would always bear a slight limp. A sheepdog, he would have been only too eager to round up the horses, had he had been allowed. His first attempt earned Nia's disapproval, so he never did it again, but at times he gazed longingly at them, crouched low on his belly, a sly look on his face. He followed Nia everywhere, his nose just touching her skirt, sitting to gaze up with adoration whenever she stopped.

'Aren't you glad we rescued Laddy now?' Nia asked Albert.

'Of course. He has turned out a jolly good dog,' he agreed.

Albert turned up one day when Nia was out. He went straight out to the stables to Liam. There he formally asked Liam's permission to court Nia.

'You have my permission, Albert,' Liam responded thoughtfully. 'But my daughter has a mind of her own, as you well realize. Nia will marry the man she chooses. Nothing I say would alter that.'

'But you and Mrs La Velle have nothing against me?' Albert stretched his neck, running an anxious finger inside his collar.

'We both like you, Albert. I am sure you would make Nia an admirable husband.' Seeing his expression lighten at those words, Liam continued hastily: 'But don't hold any false hopes. I am not convinced that Nia sees you in . . . in that way.'

Albert nodded, crestfallen.

'Do you believe she is in love with someone else?'

Liam remained silent, his eyes on Albert's face.

'This . . . Madoc, perhaps?'

Liam rubbed a hand over his face, looking away, wanting Albert to realize that this was exactly what he thought.

'You think she loves Madoc?' Albert's voice rose. 'But she has hardly seen him for years.'

'I cannot speak for my daughter, I am just trying to warn you, Albert. I know what it is to be in love. I know the despair a man can face at the idea of not winning her.'

Albert's brow wrinkled. 'You are very frank, sir. Not many men admit to such emotion.'

Liam gave a twisted smile, but said nothing. He was hoping Albert would not see Martha and express this idea about marriage to her, but that hope was in vain. She knew Albert had arrived and sent Bethan out to ask the men in for refreshment.

'Nia is out riding, I'm afraid, Albert, but she should not be too long. Will you wait for her?' Martha asked.

'Thank you Mrs La Velle, but I am afraid I unable to stay. I am actually on my way to a firm in Carmarthen.' He glanced at Liam, as if expecting him to say something, then he continued: 'I have been asking your husband's permission to court Nia with a view to marriage, Mrs La Velle.'

Martha's eyes widened, her face lighting up with delight.

'I am more than pleased to hear that, Albert.'

Albert's face mirrored Martha's joy.

'You would accept me as a son-in-law, Mrs La Velle?'

'I would welcome you, Albert.'

'Thank you. Thank you so much, Mrs La Velle. Do you believe Nia will?' he blurted.

Martha hesitated, then pressed her lips together in a determined line.

'I think so.'

'Martha,' Liam broke in. 'You can't tell Albert that! You have no idea of Nia's thoughts.'

Martha opened her mouth as though to speak, then changed her mind, looking away.

'If you will excuse me, please, I have to be on my way.' Dejected, Albert rose to his feet and was seen out by the maid.

'Martha. You should never have said that to the man,' Liam said as the hall door closed.

Martha's expression was defiant.

'She must be sensible, Liam. This man is so perfect for her.'

'I know it is what you want ... but it may not be what Nia wants, my love.' He put an arm around his wife's shoulders, aware that her breathing was becoming shallow. 'Why don't you lie down for a while, my dear. Just let things take their own course.'

'Albert. I am greatly honoured but. . . .'

'But you don't want to marry me,' Albert broke in hoarsely.

'I was about to tell you that I don't want a commitment.' Nia's expression was haunted. 'I don't know what else to say. . . .'

He took her hand, touched it to his lips.

'I love you very much, Nia. I am content to wait ... and hope. You may feel differently in the future.'

'I don't think so, Albert. I am very unsure of my own mind.'

'Is there someone else?' he blurted.

Her eyes widened, dark as coal, then she spun away from him, her chest heaving.

'Nia. Please? Is it Madoc?' He caught her arm, but she shrugged his hand away.

'I don't wish to discuss it further.' Her voice was cold.

'But I may still visit you? You don't mind my coming?'

She turned back, contrite.

'Albert. Of course you may come. I truly am sorry, I never wanted to hurt you.' She put a gentle hand to his face. 'I like you very much, and I value your friendship. But I cannot be more positive.'

'I am prepared to wait.'

Nia swallowed hard and shook her head.

'No. I don't think you should, Albert. I don't want you to hold false hope.'

'I am prepared to wait,' he repeated.

Nia said nothing to her parents about Albert's proposal. But her father had already warned her that Albert had mentioned marriage to her mother, and Nia was aware of her mother's eager expectancy each time he called.

After Christmas Albert's parents had sent an invitation for Nia to come and stay with them at the end of February, but Nia had been unwilling to go.

'You must accept, Nia. It seems most impolite not to, and Madoc will be back long before the end of February,' Martha had advised. 'It's something to look forward to. It will take your mind off worrying.'

So Nia had been coerced into accepting the invitation, and was already regretting it.

February was ushered in by further icy winds and heavy snow; the fairylike scenery was at odds with Nia's mood as the expected time for Madoc's arrival came and went and she became increasingly anxious about her mother's health.

Martha's health was deteriorating, the number of attacks increasing; at last, her father, gaunt and drawn with worry, sent for a physician.

'Breathing problems, you say? Pains in the chest? Will you undo your mother's garment for me please.' Taking a listening tube from his bag, he pressed it against the linen shift covering Martha's chest.

'Mmm, yes.' He put the tube back into his bag. 'I will get the apothecary to make up a prescription for you. You must take that when you feel an attack is imminent.'

Nia followed him out to join her father, in time to hear him pronounce her mother's heart was failing, which both she and her father already knew.

'Is there anything you can do, Dr Martin?' Liam asked without much hope.

'Nothing. Mrs La Velle must get plenty of bed rest and not get upset or excited. I will send my servant with some medication for her and I will call again next week.'

The air around Madoc seemed to smoke, filled with ocean spume churned up by the wind's frenzy as they ran before it. His clothes sodden, icy water trickling down his neck, he brushed an impatient hand through his ice crusted curls, flicking the hair off his face to have it immediately whipped back across his forehead by the wind. To prevent being washed away by the angry water, he was secured to his station by rope, where he swayed instinctively to counter the angle of the ship, a practice born of years at sea. He peered out once again at the ocean on the starboard side, where a sailor had earlier reported seeing icebergs. None were evident now, though the visibility was dreadful.

Eyes narrowed against the driving sleet, which clung to his dark beard, he risked darting a glance behind him at the gigantic wave pursuing the ship. The prevailing winds at Cape Horn blew continuously from the west to east and, unobstructed for a thousand miles, the waves rolling before them built up to tremendous heights. Their awesome violence was notorious amongst mariners and the one towering behind the *Gower Girl* was a 'greybeard', a nickname given to particularly mountainous waves. Taller than the others, it reached near a hundred and thirty foot high, its head turning an ominous translucent green and Madoc knew that if it overwhelmed the ship it would likely capsize her. The two seamen alongside him, their hands also secured to the ship's wheel, struggled together to keep the boat on course and Madoc prayed his ship could outrun the wave and none of her gear would rupture under the strain.

The wind sang through the rigging, the sails taut, as the *Gower Girl* hurtled along before it, her bow appearing to tilt down towards the boiling ocean. Gradually the 'greybeard' began to lose some of its height and Madoc was later to be thankful that it was a great deal lower by the time it eventually crashed down on them like a solid force, shuddering the ship from end to end. As the freezing water engulfed them, fighting for his life Madoc struggled to add his weight to that of the men holding the ship on course, his hands stiff and cold. Then, above the noise of the storm he heard a crack like an explosion and knew one of the masts or spars had fractured.

CHAPTER SEVEN

STILL they waited. Fear held Nia's stomach in a tight knot, leaving her agitated and frantic, unable to sleep. Madoc was still not home and the time for her visit to Albert's home drew nearer.

'Have you heard anything?' Nia leapt up, running towards her brother as he entered the drawing room. 'Is his ship back yet?'

'No.'

'What about the others? Are any of them home?'

He nodded reluctantly. 'Yes.'

'How many?'

'The rest of the fleet are home.'

'Did they say anything about Madoc?' He avoided eye contact, turning away. 'Tom? Please tell me.'

'They don't know,' he admitted, glancing at her face.

'What do you mean, don't know?' She gripped his coat in both hands, shaking it. 'Tell me! You must tell me!'

'One captain reported seeing Madoc's ship in trouble near Cape Horn. The weather was too rough for anyone to. . . .' His voice faded as he saw the anguish on Nia's face.

'Oh my God!' She buried her face in her hands, surrendering to her fear, sobbing softly. 'I'll never see him again. I know it.'

'Shorten top sails aloft,' Madoc yelled to the sailors on the yards above who, anticipating his order, were already beginning to gather in the canvas. A Swansea pilot barque drew near, and Madoc flashed an assessing glance up at the *Gower Girl*'s sails as she spilled the wind from her canvas, going into irons to allow a line to be cast. Along with the tugs, the pilot barque had been waiting for business near the Mumbles lighthouse in Swansea Bay, and a line was thrown to it, a rope ladder dropped down for the pilot to clamber aboard.

'Hello there, Madoc,' the pilot called above the noise of the waves. 'They'll be glad to see you.' Casting a swift look around at the devastation evident, he pulled his mouth down. 'I heard from another barque master that you'd had a rough trip.'

'Aye.'

'Are you taking the tugs?'

'Aye. My crew can do with a break.' Madoc indicated acceptance to the tug captains and they drew alongside.

'Where's Captain Davies?' Looking around for him, the pilot hung on to one of the stays as the ship lurched to port.

'Indisposed,' Madoc growled, watching the bosun deal with the tugs as they washed around in the waves.

As they reached the lock gates at Swansea's North dock a relief crew was standing by to come aboard to take the *Gower Girl* into the busy docks and up the river Tawe, a service often performed for fatigued Cape Horn crews on their return. With Madoc's assent they raced on board to take up their positions as the *Gower Girl*'s exhausted crew thankfully made their way ashore, leaving just Madoc and his acting first mate. They would pay the relief crew the following day when they returned to sign off officially. Pulled through the lock by the tugs, the *Gower Girl* continued on her way into the North Dock. Workers on the quay waved as they recognized the ship, and a young lad raced off to tell Morgan Shipping that the *Gower Girl* was approaching her moorings. Ropes were secured to bollards as the anchor chain dropped, rattling and grating against the hull. Madoc's father and brother stood waiting for the ship to berth.

'You made it, then,' Robert said, half-serious, half in jest, when a gangplank had been lowered and they joined Madoc on board. 'Didn't have time to shave, I take it.' He was eyeing the untidy black growth on Madoc's face.

'Shave! Bloody hell! Been too busy nursing the ship.'

'The rest of the fleet was home over a fortnight ago,' David said. 'We were told you were having difficulty making headway.'

'Difficulty.' Madoc managed a twisted grin. 'Is that what you call it?' He gave a mirthless chuckle.

His father's scrutiny turned on the ship, his expression solemn as he took in the repairs that would be needed to the damaged spars and masts, even the hull itself, the ragged, patched sails. Eyes narrowed, he studied Madoc's exhausted face, the dark shadows beneath red-rimmed, weary eyes.

'You've had a rough sail.'

Madoc shrugged. 'You could put it that way. We lost two men overboard.'

'You didn't get either of them back?' David asked tensely.

Madoc's expression was bleak.

'No! I regret to say. We spent quite some time searching, but conditions were too bad. I'll see their families tomorrow. Captain Davies was injured; I thought we were going to lose him as well. Look, I'll tell you about it later. Why don't you go down and see the skipper?'

Madoc rejoined the crew, leaving the other two, to wend a way through the activity on deck, dodging sailors bustling about. David left Robert lounging against the rail watching proceedings, brows drawn down, his expression morose. When he caught Madoc's eye, he threw him a smile. Madoc's answering smile was forced as his eyes alighted on Robert's useless right arm.

Upon entering the captain's cramped cabin at his bidding David was disconcerted to find him lying on his bunk, deep lines of pain etched into his grey face. He had aged ten years since David had last seen him, looked an old man.

'Captain Davies. Welcome home.' He walked over, extending his hand which was taken by the captain's horny one.

'Thank you, sir. It took us longer than we'd expected but it's good to be home ... though you'll know that feeling well enough, Cap'n Morgan.'

David nodded. 'I hear you met with an accident.'

'Ay.' Captain Davies heaved a heavy sigh. 'One that will finish my Cape Horn days. Not that I haven't been toying with the idea of retiring, but this has decided it for me, I'm afraid.'

'What happened?'

'Everything. On our outward trip we caught a big squall; it couldn't have happened at a worse time. We were approaching the Horn on a starboard tack, beating straight towards the rocks. It came from nowhere and hit us so suddenly we nearly went over. It washed a man overboard.' He shook his head sadly. 'We never saw sight of him again. And one of the big water-casks broke free and crashed into me.' His voice was matter of fact. 'I was out cold for a few days.'

'My God! We need to get you straight to a physician—'

'A few hours will not make much difference. I did see a couple of them in Valparaiso. A fat lot of good they were.' He pointed with the stem of his pipe at a deep drawer below his bunk. 'I'd be obliged if you would pour us both a tot of rum, sir. I am not a believer in liquor aboard my ship, but I am so relieved to be home I think I could appreciate one now.'

He pulled his pipe from his mouth again and poked the glowing tobacco with a hard thumb, then put it back, sucking it experimentally to ascertain its merit. Satisfied, he pointed at a chair, its leather seat cracked and worn.

'Take a seat, Cap'n.'

As David put the two glasses of rum on a little table he added: 'You won't have to find yourself a new captain. Your son managed the whole trip very well without me.'

'That's good to hear, apart from the circumstances. I'm glad he lived up to your expectations.'

'Lived up to them be damned! That's an understatement, Cap'n Morgan. He may be young, but he's a very able man, is Madoc. He's a first-rate Cape Horner and, what's more, the crew like and respect him. They'll do anything for him. I can't say more.'

Hobbling with the aid of crutches made by the ship's carpenter, Captain Davies accompanied Madoc to Morgan Shipping. The staff crowded around, pumping Madoc's arm and thumping their backs as someone brought a chair for the captain.

'This calls for a tot of brandy.' David walked over to an oriental lacquered cabinet and poured a few fingers of the golden liquid for everyone present and handed them around.

'Here's to *Gower Girl*'s return, Captain Davies.' He raised his glass.

'It's Madoc you should be toasting, not me.' Captain Davies shook his head. 'He acted as master for practically the whole voyage . . . and with two . . . no . . . including me . . . three men short. He's a good man to have around in a crisis.' He held up his glass: 'To Madoc.' As everyone raised the toast he extended his other hand towards Madoc, who gripped it firmly.

'Thank you, sir.' Madoc glanced at his father, whose blue eyes were glowing with pride, though his face was impassive.

David tapped his glass with a paperknife.

'May I have your attention, please. I think it is a good time for another ceremony.'

With a formal little nod, he handed Captain Davies a flat cardboard box.

'Please accept this plate as a gift on behalf of Morgan Shipping. In appreciation of your years of service to the company.'

Captain Davies' smile was bitter as he accepted the gift, knowing he would never sail again in the *Gower Girl*. He took out a presentation plate decorated in blue, bearing an engraving of the *Gower Girl*, scrolled with both ship's and captain's, names. Cambrian Pottery had now closed but David had had this specially commissioned from Landore Pottery.

'Thank you very much, Cap'n Morgan. I'll treasure this, as I know will my good lady.' He ran his hand gently over the plate. 'Very acceptable indeed, Cap'n. I thank you.'

David raised his glass. 'My pleasure.'

'Are you sincere in this talk of retiring?' David asked quietly.

'Ay. At least from the Horn trips.'

'But you might change your mind once you are recovered?'

'I'm not going to recover,' Davies said frankly. 'It wasn't just that my legs were crushed. Some of my internal organs are affected.'

'I see.' David nodded gravely. 'But a good physician could put you right.'

'Maybe enough to manage a steam-packet in the channel . . . but not the Horn. This last voyage was a nightmare.' He raised eloquent brows at Madoc. 'Everything that possibly could go wrong did. On our outward journey, just as we were changing over to the heavy sails in readiness to round the Horn, we had a fire in the hold. I think the merchant must have put dry coal over the top of wet because, as you know, we always make sure it's dry before we let them load.'

David frowned. 'You weren't the only barque with fire in the hold. You think wet coal was deliberately covered?' Damp coal in a hold was notoriously highly combustible.

'Well. . . ?' Captain Davies raised his shoulders. 'I won't say it was intentional . . . and I don't like to point a finger. But the merchant knows we won't take it if it's wet. If it hadn't been for your son's quick reactions in pulling a man out we'd have lost another mariner in the fire too. As it is Cliff and Madoc were both burned . . . not a convenient place to have two men injured as you can imagine.'

'I was hardly affected,' Madoc reassured his father, in answer to his anxious glance. 'Cliff Rowlands was not so lucky.'

'Lucky enough to escape with his life,' Captain Davies put in drily. 'As were you.'

'It was nothing,' Madoc protested.

'I don't expect Cliff Rowlands would agree with you.' He turned back to David. 'The squall that I've already mentioned came a few days later. That was when I was injured. Madoc had to take full command then, even though he'd been burned. So with Rowlands burnt, the one lost overboard and myself, we were three men short on the outward trip. Then to cap it all, on the way home we broke a spar when a greybeard caught us, lost another man overboard . . . then got tangled with a bloody iceberg. Before we could continue our journey, Madoc was forced to make for port at the Falklands to get emergency repairs.' He shook his head. 'No. I think I am getting too old for this lark. You can have her, Madoc.'

'But I have another year to serve as first mate.'

'In theory, maybe. But you acted as first mate for the whole voyage eighteen months ago, when Howard fell from the yards. I can testify to that. I am sure you will be a very able new skipper.'

'With the damage she's sustained, it's going to be quite some time before we even think about sending the *Gower Girl* back to Valparaiso,' David said.

'Her copper-plating has been ruined too,' Madoc put in. 'So she'll need inspecting for terdo worm.'

'Then there's no need for a decision at this time, Captain Davies. You might have recovered by then.'

'Maybe.'

Someone had hailed a cab for Captain Davies and Madoc gave him a hand as he painfully climbed the steps to get inside.

'I'll call around to see you,' Madoc promised, then the driver cracked his whip in the air above the horse and the cab bowled away. Feeling an empathy with the ruined man, Madoc watched them go away, his face gloomy.

'Before going home I'll get a bath, shave and haircut in the public bathhouse.' Madoc rubbed a hand over his shaggy beard. 'And I'm starving.'

'I think you'd better take a change of clothing with you.' David was examining Madoc's salt-encrusted jersey and ragged trousers, the unkempt growth on his face, the dark hair tangled down on his shoulders. 'I always keep some in the office and I'd hate your mother to see you in those rags.'

Madoc laughed. 'I'm glad you thought of it.' He turned to Robert with the question he had been longing to ask. 'Have you seen anything of Nia while I've been away?'

Ever since he'd known that they were safely nearing home and he could relax his concentration he'd had time to think about Nia. Now he was impatient to see her again.

'I've met her once or twice. Mother asked them all over one evening; she brought that fellow Albert with her. But you haven't heard the other news ... Lucy is home.' His face was alive with underlying excitement.

'Home?' Madoc said, surprised.

'I forgot. You don't know. She's been widowed. Randolf was killed in action.'

'Killed?' About to take a mouthful of his brandy, Madoc paused, hand in mid-air, his face shocked. 'My God! Poor girl! She's young to be a widow.'

'Yes, she's back from India, living in Oxfordshire. Apparently her husband was quite rich.'

'Was his home in Oxfordshire, then?'

'Yes. Lucy's mother stayed with her for a while. Lucy was prostrated with grief.'

'Have you seen her?'

Robert nodded. 'We travelled over from Beechwood to pay our respects. She was pleased to see us. She's talking about coming to Swansea for a holiday.'

'I'll pay my respects then.' Madoc said, thinking how little the prospect of Lucy's return affected him now ... other than sorrow for her grief.

Robert grinned sourly.

'Still keen on her, Madoc?'

Madoc shrugged, laughing.

'I gave up on her years ago. I thought she was going to marry you.'

Robert's smile slipped slightly and he dropped his glance, swirling his brandy in the goblet. Madoc could have kicked himself.

'It seems she had other ideas.' But Robert's expression showed that he had been more hurt than he had revealed at the time.

'How long will she be in mourning?'

'I'm not sure. About a year, isn't it? Seeing her in black makes her look even more fragile.' Robert's voice was wistful.

Maybe he'll get another chance now, Madoc thought. But he should make sure he doesn't leave it too late this time.

Madoc, his toilet completed and too tired even to hire a gig, took a horse-cab and sank back inside. He felt as if lead weights were tied to his drooping eyelids, and dozed all the way home in cosy comfort. It was completely dark when he arrived home, and he savoured the light and warmth enveloping him as he entered the door. It contrasted sharply with the gloomy, damp quarters he occupied on board, without heat in the freezing cold, the only light provided by an improvised lamp, with a canvas-thread wick.

Jenkins, their manservant, came through into the hall, his stiff manner deserting him slightly as he saw Madoc.

'Mr Madoc. Good to have you home, sir.' He allowed himself a smile as Madoc took his hand.

'It's good to be home, Jenkins.'

Some of the other servants heard and came crowding through from the kitchen, their faces lighting up with delight.

'It's Mr Madoc. Thank God.' Mair, the cook, began, waddling over to him.

'Shh!' He put his finger to his lips. 'I want to surprise my mother.'

'There's lovely to see you safe home,' the cook continued in a whisper as she gave him a hug. Madoc returned the old lady's embrace. She'd always had a soft spot for him as a boy. 'There's pleased your mother'll be. Worried sick, she's been, even if she pretends she's not. I'll put a meal up for you, Mr Madoc. There's some *cawl* on the hob, do you fancy that?'

'Fancy it? It would be wonderful. I've been thinking about your soup for weeks.' This was perfectly true. The small copper-barques had little room for storage other than the cargo, even for necessities. Fresh food was always short by the time they reached port either way. Being so weary he'd made up his mind to go straight to bed, but the thought of Mair's soup changed his mind.

She was pleased at his words.

'Poor man. You must be starving. I'll leave you greet your mother before I send it in.'

'And fresh bread, please. Great big chunks of it.'

As Mair bustled off, Mary, a housemaid, came forward, her head dropped shyly, her limp hair hanging around her face.

'Welcome home, Mr Madoc.' She took his hat, blushing as he threw her a grin and squeezed her arm.

'Thank you, Mary. It's good to be home.'

A very pretty maid whom he had never seen before was staring at him over Mary's shoulder, eyes wide.

'This is Sîan, Mr Madoc, the new housemaid,' Mary offered, explaining to the girl: 'This is Mr Madoc Morgan, the seafaring son. You've heard us talking about him.'

'Pleased to meet you, sir.' The girl bobbed a quick curtsy, her eyes roaming boldly across his face, continuing on admiringly across his broad shoulders and chest before returning to meet his quizzical gaze. She seems very forward, he thought with surprise. As he mounted the stairs to his mother's sitting room he heard her perky voice drifting from the passage leading to the servants' quarters:

'My goodness. There's handsome he is.'

'Enough of that, my girl,' Jenkins corrected swiftly as the door was closing. 'You show respect for a son of. . . .'

Madoc opened his mother's door quietly and crept towards her, but before he could reach her she looked up from her book.

'Madoc!' Her face was a picture of joy as she flew towards him. She reached both arms tightly around him but kept her head buried against his chest. He frowned, lifting her head gently, a hand under her chin. Her eyes were brimming with tears and she released a hand to brush them away impatiently.

'Mother?' he said, surprised.

She blinked her lashes rapidly, laughing at herself.

'Don't take any notice. I must be getting old or something.'

'Old? That will be the day.'

'Thank God you're back,' she whispered as he kissed her cheek. She hugged him again. 'I was uncommonly frightened this time. I was convinced you were at the bottom of some dreadful southern ocean. One of the other captains told us you had broken a spar near the Cape. He was very concerned but said they could do nothing to help because of the terrible weather conditions.'

'They couldn't have. I'm glad they didn't attempt it. We could easily have got entangled, then both ships would have foundered.'

Her eyes were travelling eagerly over his wind-burned face and she reached up to touch his cheek, still staring up at him, her slanted cat's eyes wide.

'Madoc. Every time you return I can't believe how much you resemble your father now. It's uncanny.'

He grinned at her, not displeased. In the past he had heard more than one young lady sigh about his handsome father.

She smiled, nodding. 'Except for your eyes, of course . . . at least you've followed me in one aspect. . . .'

'More than one, I'd say,' he laughed. 'What about the impulsiveness and fiery temper? I never got those traits from my father.'

She gave a little smile. 'Maybe. Why are you wearing his clothes?' She was looking at the outfit he wore.

'Er . . . mine were a bit . . . disreputable.'

She frowned suspiciously, but didn't query his answer.

Sîan brought in a tray; along with the tea things was a bowl of rosy apples, their waxy skins reflecting a glow from the lamplight. Mair knew that on coming home from a voyage Madoc was always eager for fresh fruit and vegetables. His face lit up, his mouth watering as he saw them, and he reached for an apple without being asked, crunching it with relish, savouring the juice, licking his lips before taking another bite.

'Wonderful.' Madoc closed his eyes, gulping it down in big mouthfuls, then reached for another.

Emily laughed, but her expression was unhappy. She was always disturbed at the idea of his doing without fresh food.

'So Rob tells me Lucy is a widow,' he murmured, as his mother poured his tea.

'Yes. We were all so distressed when we heard.' She added milk and sugar to his cup and handed it to him.

'Did they have any children?' He took the dainty bone china cup and saucer, which always felt ridiculously fragile when he returned from a voyage.

'No. Though I am uncertain whether that is a good thing or not. She would have his children to remind her of him, but then, it is sad for children to be brought up without a father.'

'I shouldn't think they would be without one for long.' Madoc stirred his tea with the tiny silver spoon. Emily paused, her eyes questioning. 'I mean, she should soon marry again.'

Emily carried on pouring. 'That depends on whether she wants to marry again. I wouldn't. But your father is rather special.'

Madoc smiled at her unconsciously complacent tone. He knew his parents still had eyes for no others.

'She would have to be out of mourning before remarrying anyway.' She went on to tell him about their visit to Lucy.

'Did I tell you I paid a visit to the La Velles last time I was home?' Madoc asked. 'Martha and Liam have done very well for themselves, haven't they?'

'Indeed. Their business has expanded unbelievably since they first moved away. They have become quite prosperous, though I think Martha finds it difficult to accept her new status in life – not like Liam. He has adapted so well; he's very much a businessman now. Most people seem to believe he is Spanish.'

'So Nia told me last time I was home. I was surprised that he could accept that. I'd have thought he'd object to not being acknowledged as a Romany.'

'He is a shrewd man, and realizes that he gets more business that way. After all, the Spanish are renowned for their horses.'

'That's true. Wasn't Liam involved in helping the original agent with the estates at Beechwood?'

'Yes. Particularly after Drummond became incapacitated with the rheumatics. It was fortunate that he seemed to take to Liam completely. He was able to offer him much valuable advice with his business accounts in the early years.'

'So what is happening now at Beechwood?'

'We have a new agent, he is very able.' She took a breath, her eyes flying to his face. 'But . . . Robert is keen to take it on.' She was studying him, obviously seeking his reaction.

'Now?' he asked with surprise, though Robert had always loved Beechwood. 'I see. The elder son taking up his inheritance,' he said slowly. He had never given consideration to this before, but it was the accepted law of succession. *And I am the younger son*, he thought, with a sudden awareness of the inevitability of it all.

She didn't answer for a moment, then said reluctantly:

'That's true, I suppose. Madoc.' He looked at her, his face detached. 'You will not be left a penniless younger son – neither I nor your father want that, I assure you.'

He forced a smile. 'That's how it is, Mother. We cannot fight the system. Anyway I have a career at sea. I can always earn a living there. Captain Davies spoke of retiring ... he suggested I take over as captain.'

'Surely you are too young to be captain on a Cape Horner?'

He was amused at his mother's appalled expression.

'Not too young, but I haven't officially served two years as first mate, which is a condition.' He did not repeat what Captain Davies had said. 'I already have my master's certificate.'

'And you've enough experience?'

Madoc gave a barking laugh.

'After this voyage? I certainly have.' He was grateful when Sîan tapped on the door and halted the conversation.

'Cook said to say your food is ready, sir. Do you want to have it put on the table in the dining room?'

'Yes please, Sîan. I will be straight down.'

'And I'll have another tea tray in the dining room at the same time, please,' Emily said.

Emily sat near Madoc at the table as Mary placed a silver tray in front of her, then another in front of Madoc, spooning a ladleful of the rich stew into his dish.

'Shall I leave the tureen, sir?'

'Please.' He swallowed the saliva rising in his mouth as he smelt the appetizing food and immediately began wolfing down his meal. Realizing that his mother was watching him he forced himself to slow down and eat in a more gentlemanly manner.

'You seem particularly hungry tonight.'

'This is delicious, I'm starving. We've had nothing hot for ...' He snapped off the rest of the thoughtless remark, knowing he should never have mentioned it. He was so tired he was not thinking rationally.

She pounced on it. 'Why didn't you have hot food?'

Madoc shrugged with a laugh.

'Madoc?'

'The cook-house got washed away.' He injected a light-hearted tone, trying to make it a joke.

'Washed away? Are you jesting? How did that happen?'

He made a show of swallowing the food, then put another spoonful in his mouth, hoping she would not repeat the question. He had said too much already. She allowed him to eat in peace, but as soon as he put down his cutlery she asked again, forcing him to answer.

'A wave swept it overboard. Anyway the fire had gone out as the cook couldn't get it to stay alight.' He would have replenished his dish but instead rose to his feet to evade further questions. 'If you will excuse me now, Mother?'

'Of course. I expect you are ready for your bath.'

He made for the door, not telling her he had already bathed.

'Madoc! How did you manage? Without hot food?'

Madoc grinned at her from the doorway.

'We managed very well with water, ship's biscuits and salt pork. It's a good job I've got strong teeth.' He clicked his teeth together, then pulled a face as he added: 'Not forgetting the lime juice, of course.'

Now that he had eaten he couldn't wait to sleep: to be able to sleep for longer than just the half-hour he had been snatching for much of the voyage. As he pulled off his borrowed shirt and trousers he thought about Robert going to Beechwood, coming into part of his inheritance earlier than expected – then a bleak realization swept through him. One day Morgan Shipping will be Robert's as well, he thought bitterly. Even the ship I sail in will be his – not mine!

CHAPTER EIGHT

Madoc lounged in the bath the next morning. Leaning his head against the upswept back, eyes closed, he revelled in the luxury of soaking in hot water, had been imagining it for weeks.

His mind lingered on Nia again. Not the elegant woman she had now become, but as he recalled her, a skinny, coltish child, all arms and legs, sallow-skinned with a plain face and a wide mouth. Her only claim to beauty had been her huge, almond-shaped eyes, surrounded with sweeping black lashes. When she was happy golden glints shone in them, lifting her whole face as they sparkled with life. Her black hair, thick and wavy, had always tumbled in an untamed mane around her shoulders. With a rush of unexpected emotion Madoc smiled, picturing the child Nia so clearly.

How I love her, he thought tenderly, still unable to understand why he hadn't recognized this before. No wonder the girl in my dreams often had dark hair! It was never really Lucy at all!

Much to her mother's despair, Nia had hated wearing frocks, being much more at home in her brother's outgrown breeches.

'I can't ride as well in a skirt,' he remembered her grumbling when Martha insisted she wore one.

'Well you will just have to learn. Miss Emily manages very ably. I don't see why you can't do the same. If you want to grow up into a lady.'

'I don't!' Nia howled. 'Why can't I do the same as Madoc?'

'He is a boy. You are a girl.'

'It's not fair!'

'That's how it is, my lovely. Life isn't fair.'

So when Nia had been forced to wear the hated skirts she hitched them up to sit astride her pony, white petticoats billowing up around her thighs, making Madoc laugh.

Nia, my love. You will never believe how much I am longing to see you. To see your impish grin, your dancing black eyes taunting me. We'll soon sort out all the nonsense then nothing will ever part us again. I promise.

'There you are.' His mother looked up from her newspaper, smiling as he dropped a kiss on her cheek. 'I've been lingering here hoping you would emerge before I finished my breakfast.'

Madoc lifted the lid on one of the chafing-dishes, sniffing at the delicious aroma of cooked bacon and scrambled eggs being kept hot, pilling his plate to carry over to the table. His mother gave an amused smile.

'You haven't lost your appetite I see,' she said, as he returned with a second helping.

'I wonder what makes you think that?' His green eyes danced at her as he stirred milk and a huge spoonful of sugar into his tea, both items luxuries aboard the *Gower Girl*.

'Have you any plans for today?'

Madoc's face grew solemn. 'Yes. I have to visit the families of the men we lost. . . .'

'Lost? Men were drowned this trip? More than one?'

Madoc pursed his lips.

'Two,' he answered unwillingly.

'Two! My God! How awful.' Emily was aghast. 'Do I know them?'

'Mat Stephens was one. I don't believe you knew the other.'

'Poor Sarah! With all those children. I must visit her too.'

'I'm sure she would appreciate that.' He looked around for more bread.

'It could as easily have been you.'

'Would you pass me the bread-basket please, Mother,' he asked, not replying. He knew it was true. When the greybeard struck the ship they were fortunate not have lost the whole crew.

Although his mother was used to his occupation she had never really accepted it. Something like this reawakened all her original fears for his safety.

'I was thinking about Nia. I decided to leave visiting Sarah until this afternoon and I'll ride over to Mead Rise this morning to see if Nia is at home.'

His mother raised her brows.

'You are aware that Nia has a suitor?'

'A suitor? You don't mean that fellow she met from Newport?' His voice was dismissive.

'Yes, Albert,' she said slowly. 'She has been seeing quite a lot of him. Albert came with the La Velles when they had dinner with us. Martha told me Albert's intentions are serious. He asked Liam's permission to court Nia, but she doesn't know whether he has proposed yet. When he does, Martha is keen for her to accept.' Correctly reading his expression she added tentatively: 'You mind?'

He clenched his jaw, feeling as though he had been punched hard in the stomach, and stared at his plate, his appetite vanished along with his peace of mind.

Do I mind? The bottom has dropped out of my world and she asks if I mind, he thought savagely.

'Madoc?'

He looked up without expression, but his eyes gave him away.

'She probably has more prospects there than with a seaman.' His voice was expressionless.

'Don't talk like that, Madoc. You don't mean it. I didn't realize you still ... cared ... about her. Anyway, as far as I know, she has not agreed to anything yet.'

His eyes narrowed and he was aware of his heart thudding.

'Why not? Do you know?'

She shook her head. 'Martha seems cross with her.'

He gave a tight smile.

'Nia will do what she wishes, she always did. She will not be coerced by her mother.'

'I am not so sure. Martha's health is not good, it's her heart. Liam and Nia are very worried about her. They don't want her upset.'

'I see. You mean you think Nia could marry him for this reason?'

Emily's eyes were troubled.

'I don't know about that but I think it could influence her.'

Madoc said nothing, suddenly not as certain as he had been about winning the woman he loved.

Madoc reined in Storm outside the house at Mead Rise. As he dismounted Nia came around the corner with a young man. She was smiling up at him, holding on to his arm and he was looking down at her, his feelings for her written on his face for all to read. Madoc's throat constricted, jealousy flooding through him like a hot wave.

Noticing the horse and rider in the courtyard, the couple looked over at him.

'Madoc!' realizing who it was, Nia shrieked out his name and raced across, her shawl dropping to the ground as she clutched at her skirt, stumbling over it in her haste. A dog was running excitedly alongside her. She flung herself against his chest as she reached him, her arms wound tightly around his waist. But when he put his own arms around her and hugged her against him, she became rigid, and pulled back stiffly, dropping her hands to her sides, fists clenched. She looked up at him wide-eyed, slightly breathless.

He gave her a lopsided smile. She still doesn't want my arms around her, he thought.

'Madoc. Thank God you're back.'

It is my welfare as a friend she cares for, he thought. Not me, the man. She is relieved that I am home safely and not lying at the bottom of the ocean. His horse tossed his head, spooked by the dog near his legs, and Madoc bent down to fondle its ears.

'Hello there. Who are you then?' he asked the dog. As Laddy's rough tongue lapped eagerly over his face, he looked back up to see Nia scrutinizing him, her eyes agitated.

'We've all been worried sick. When did you get back?'

'Late yesterday.' His glance strayed to the man who had arrived alongside them, his cold eyes studying his rival as he tried to fight down the surge of hostility which rushed through him. He managed a tight smile, reaching out a hand as Nia introduced them.

Albert's hand felt soft and feminine, compared with those of the men Madoc usually associated with, though his grip was firm enough. A nice-looking young man, he and Madoc were probably near in age but, to Madoc, Albert appeared almost boyish, his rosy-cheeked face smooth and rounded. Albert was not considered a short man, but Madoc reached a good four inches above him, lean, hard and solid muscle. Madoc was gratified to realize that Albert's eyes were assessing and wary, his expression disconcerted.

So he is not certain of her, Madoc thought with satisfaction. And she must have told him of me if he is regarding me as a challenger. Storm caught Madoc's attention again as he tossed his head impatiently, his harness rattling as he snorted out a cloud of breath in the cold air. Madoc rubbed his nose affectionately, as a young groom came up to take the reins.

'What happened to make you so late?' Nia asked.

'Ran into bad weather.' His reply was laconic but his eyes drank in her exotic beauty, and he longed to kiss those dewy lips.

'But isn't the weather around the Horn always bad?'

His expression was impassive. 'Mostly. This time it was just worse than usual.' His attention slid back to Albert, who was listening intently to this conversation.

'Tom told me a captain from another ship was terribly anxious,' said Nia. 'He was concerned that you might have foundered and would not make it home.'

Madoc grinned. 'That was him . . . not me.' A glint of amusement shone in his eyes as he dared her to comment on that deliberately boastful observation.

'Madoc! You conceited. . . .' She rolled her eyes skywards. 'Trust you to come out with a remark like that.' She scowled with good humour at his wicked grin. 'I heard you were acting skipper. Your captain was injured, wasn't he? Is he all right now?'

Madoc's smile dropped away.

'No. He's in a pretty bad state, I'm afraid.' A movement in the fields beyond flashed across Madoc's vision as a few horses cantered past in a little group, manes flying as they kicked up their heels.

'What happened to the captain?' It was the first time Albert had spoken. 'I mean, how did he receive his injury?'

Madoc sucked in a breath.

'He was unlucky. We caught a bad squall and a water-cask broke free and crashed into him. He could have been killed or swept overboard. One man was.'

'He will recover, though?' Nia asked with concern.

'I don't think he will. He suffered internal injuries as well as two shattered legs.'

'The poor man. Perhaps once he gets medical attention. . . ?'

'He saw two physicians in Valparaiso. Their prognosis was not good.'

'Valparaiso? You mean the accident occurred before you got there? Were you near the Horn?'

'Too near for comfort, we nearly ended up on the rocks.'

Madoc, usually reticent about the harsh conditions and adversities of his life at sea, realized that he had said that to impress Albert and was amused at his own foolishness. I must be in a bad way, he thought, trying to overawe the opposition. And Albert's expression clearly revealed that he was appalled at the whole idea of these voyages.

'Why do you go on those ships? I mean ... as the owner's son surely you have no need to sail on them yourself?' Albert asked.

Madoc stared wordlessly at him for a moment, as Albert's face coloured uncomfortably, as if he wished he could take back his words.

Madoc felt an unexpected rush of empathy towards the other man. After all, he thought, this poor sod is in love with Nia as well ... and I'll be the one who gets her, Madoc vowed.

'In one way, I have no need. I could easily work for the firm on dry land. It is a personal thing, I suppose.'

'I see.' Albert nodded without understanding, then added: 'So you feel you continually need to prove yourself?'

'Prove myself? I'm not trying to prove anything!' Madoc exploded, his goodwill vanishing. 'One trip—' He snapped off the words, realizing that he was rising to the bait, and regarded Albert with new respect. He was not going to be such an easy adversary as he'd first believed.

'Then why don't you sail on a less hazardous ship? It—'

'Come on!' Nia took Albert's arm and threaded her other arm though Madoc's. 'Mama will be delighted to see you. We tried to hide it from her, that you were overdue, but she found out, somehow. She has been very distressed.'

Madoc swallowed his fury and allowed her to lead him to the house to be made a fuss of by Martha. He managed to make polite conversation with her mother, but his glance kept straying to Nia, drinking in every detail. He saw that Albert had noticed his distraction. He was sitting next to Nia on the settee, looking far too cosy and content for Madoc's peace of mind. He was even holding her hand! What if she's already accepted his proposal? The concept speared through him like a physical pain.

'Madoc?'

He started, his eyes flashing back to Martha, who was waiting for an answer to an unheard question.

'Er ... sorry?' He gave a roguish smile, which usually managed to win over most ladies, but she was not taken in.

'You were not listening.' Her voice was accusing, and she left him feeling ill-mannered and uncomfortable.

'Would you like a biscuit, Madoc?' Nia broke in, holding a plate towards him. Her face was serious, but the mischief dancing in her eyes revealed that she was aware of his discomfort. It reminded him of when they were young, of how they had both tried to rescue each other from awkward situations.

'Thank you.' He threw her a grin, accepting one, and flicked a glance towards Albert who was frowning, obviously realizing that he was missing something between them. He might as well get it first as last, Madoc thought, Nia and I belong together!

'Well, there's nothing to prevent you going now, Nia,' Martha said, looking at Albert. 'When did you think of leaving, Albert?'

'Whenever Nia wishes.' Albert appeared pleased at her interruption.

'Nia is accompanying Albert to his home today,' Martha said to Madoc. 'He wishes her to meet his parents.'

Madoc's complacency vanished and he tensed. Carefully he placed his cup and saucer on the occasional table beside him.

'Then I must not keep you,' he said. 'Are you taking the steam-packet?'

'No. The train.' Albert pulled his pocket-watch from his waistcoat, flipped up the lid. 'We could make the next one if we leave fairly soon, Nia, my dear.'

Nia nodded, looking at Madoc as if waiting for his reaction, but he turned to stare out of the window, not wanting her to see that he was disturbed and unsettled.

He doesn't care, Nia thought, a lump rising in her throat. For a few moments it had seemed like old times, each grinning secretively at the other . . . and he did seem rather hostile towards Albert. Could he be jealous? Trust Mama to remind her that she was free to leave now; Nia had already warned Albert that she couldn't go until she knew Madoc was safe.

She had been badly shaken to hear about a man being drowned, and the captain seriously injured. The ache returned to her stomach: an ache that had been captive there for months, like a live thing gnawing at her entrails. With Madoc's precarious occupation death and danger were ever present; but either of those men could have been Madoc. Imagine him not able to walk again? Madoc! Who was so physical, so alive. Like a huge predatory tiger, each movement smooth and co-ordinated, with no wasted effort. Madoc's being an invalid did not bear thinking about.

She didn't want to leave yet. She was enjoying sitting in the same room with Madoc, where she could admire him as much as she wished. *I always thought he was wonderful as a boy, but now!* She studied his features, the lean, strong planes of his face, his glowing cat's eyes, the firm angle of his jaw beneath that sensual mouth. *Who could have believed that Madoc would turn out to be so stunningly attractive?*

Her mother rose from her chair and Madoc immediately stood up, his eyes meeting Nia's again. For a single instant he gave a surprising impression of being vulnerable, as if something troubled him, then it was gone, replaced by his normal relaxed expression and manner.

He smiled, extending his hand, first to her mother, then to Nia, lastly to Albert.

'Good to have met you, Albert.' In the hall he turned to Nia. 'May I call again when you return?'

'Of course. You'll still be here?' Her voice sounded eager, even to her own ears. 'When are you returning to sea?'

'Not for some months, after my ship has been overhauled.'

Flooded with relief Nia beamed at him and caught her mother's disapproving glare. Glancing at Albert she saw his crestfallen expression. *What am I going to do about Albert?* she wondered, not for the first time.

Before they left Martha called her to one side.

'Nia. Can I ask you a question? Has Albert proposed to you yet?'

Nia caught her breath. 'Why do you ask that, Mama?'

'Because he told your father and me that this was his intention.'

'I see.' Wary, Nia was unwilling to upset her mother. 'Would you wish me to marry a man I do not love, Mama?'

'You cannot know that at your age, Nia. You can learn to love a man after marriage. Most women do.'

'As you did Papa?' she asked, knowing this was something her mother had not experienced.

'Well . . . no. I admit I knew I loved him before. . . .'

'Then please leave me the same choice, Mama.'

Martha nodded, began turning away, then said: 'It would make me very happy, Nia. Content to know you are settled in a good marriage . . . before I die.'

Nia caught her breath. 'Please don't say that, Mama! You are not going to die!'

'I hope you are right, my lovely. I cannot imagine how your father would be, should that happen.'

Stricken, Nia regarded her mutely. *Neither can I!*

The tide was out so, on his way into town Madoc rode Storm on a short cut across Swansea Bay. He always took every opportunity to ride – something he missed a great deal while at sea. He intended going to Carmarthen the following day to see the family of the other drowned sailor, but he was on his way to visit Mat Stephens's widow today; their cottage was in the Strand. He left his mount at the livery stables on his way to Morgan Shipping.

Eli, the senior clerk, came up to him as he entered the office.

'I am told you will be here with us for a while, Mr Madoc.'

'If you can put up with me, Eli. It will give me time to get my land-legs back, if nothing else.'

'And a chance to learn the business, sir.'

'Madoc.' He heard his name and saw Russel beckoning. 'Come by here!' As Madoc reached the group, Russel indicated two new young office boys. 'These lads are dying to hear all about Cape Horn. They want to know what it's really like.'

'Is it as bad as they say?' The smaller boy's eyes were round with wonder. 'Are the waves truly that high?'

The two boys were regarding him with awe. Madoc frowned; he had no intention of making heroics out of his experiences. He'd had plenty of opportunity for this but always avoided it.

'Why don't you find out for yourselves?' Madoc teased. 'I've got room for an apprentice next trip.'

'Oh come on!' Russel sounded disappointed. 'Well, what about this fire on board? We were told you were a hero—'

'Don't talk rubbish! That's nonsense.'

'But he said you were burned pulling someone out. . . .'

'Just talk.' Madoc lightened his remark with a grin.

Robert came into the general office. 'I was just about to go to lunch,' he said. 'Do you wish to join me?'

'Not me, thanks. I feel as if I've just finished breakfast.' Madoc patted his stomach. 'I ate too much. I'll walk along with you, though, I'm going that way. Are you coming too?' he asked his father, who had been observing the exchanges with Russel and the young boys.

'No, I have a business appointment. I'll see you later on.'

The two men walked along the dock, a bustling hive of activity. Copper ore was being unloaded from ships on to barges for its journey upriver to the smelting-works, dockers passed with laden baskets, sailors were busy with heavy ropes or making their way to and from berthed ships. Raucous voices called to each other, dogs barked and children shrieked as they darted between crates. The air reverberated with the noise of hammering and sawing, and a resinous smell of pine emanated from one ship. Men touched their caps, some called friendly greetings, or shook Madoc's hand, glad to see him safely returned.

'Mother was telling me about Lucy. How did she seem when you called?' Madoc asked his brother.

'Very sad and downcast, but as beautiful as ever. She looks wonderful in black, it emphasizes her delicate beauty.'

'How long has she been widowed?'

'It must be around seven months. Of course we didn't know about it then, we didn't hear until after you had sailed.'

'I expect she will remarry. She must have plenty of suitors,' Madoc said, acknowledging a greeting from one of his crew.

'That thought occurred to me.'

'Well, don't leave it too long this time. Someone might steal her from under your nose.'

Robert's eyes narrowed.

'You for instance,' he said curtly. He was smiling, but his eyes were suddenly assessing.

Madoc regarded him with surprise.

'Come on Rob. You know I didn't mean me.'

'Well you can't say you haven't always wanted her,' he challenged.

'So? She never even glanced at me when you were around.' Madoc laughed, trying to lighten the conversation.

'That's the only reason you'd hesitate?'

Realizing that Robert was still in earnest, Madoc caught his arm.

'Rob. I assure you I have no interest whatsoever in Lucy.'

Robert nodded rather morosely. As Madoc left he was aware of his brother staring moodily after him.

CHAPTER NINE

Some days later Madoc pushed his way through the crowded tavern, and fought his way to the counter. Holding his tankard of ale he weaved his way to the rear of the room where he was to meet Rob and Tom. He managed to find a table between leaded-light glass screens which sectioned off parts of the bar. There was room for two on the bench seat along the wall and he looked around for a third seat. He saw a spare stool at the next table.

'This anyone's?' he asked the two men seated at the table.

He pulled it over with his foot, and sat on it, taking an appreciative sip of his beer. He was wiping the froth from his mouth when he heard a familiar name mentioned in conversation in the next booth. He pricked up his ears.

'Yes, he is! That bloke who did the deeds of sale for your uncle. What's his name? La Velle . . . he's a gypsy.'

'Gerroff! 'E's no bloody gypsy. 'E's fair. He don't look like no gypsy I ever seen,' a second voice objected.

'I don't care about that, I knows what I'm talking about. His old man used to be a groom with the Morgan family and he married the Morgan's maid or something.'

Madoc leaned back slightly to take a quick peep around the screen at the speakers. There were three men, two of whom he recognized as villagers from Whitesands. The informant was unknown to him: a whey-faced man, wearing a red cravat. The second speaker was an ugly, lumbering man, over-developed muscles across his shoulders almost bursting out of his jacket, which pulled at all the seams, huge hands on the end of enormous wrists thrust out of the too-short sleeves. He had been a hateful bully as a child, bigger than everyone else even then, and given to ill-treating animals. Madoc had had more than one fight with him in the past, often coming off second best – though not always. This man was now well-known in the town as the 'Bull', a professional bare-knuckle fighter. The third man, Dick Maddis, wore the garb of a farm labourer.

'Never. You got it wrong somewhere, Bert. This bloke is a toff, 'e's quality o'right. Have you heard 'im talking?' Bull scoffed.

'I don't care about that, I'm telling you. . . .'

'But where would 'e learn to talk like that?' Bull was incredulous. 'A gypsy's son, for Chrissake?'

'Does it matter?' Dick broke in.

'Well, if Bert's right it does. It means my uncle just sold 'is farm to a bloody gypsy. This La Velle bloke was doing the business of the sale for his father, he was.'

'But gypsies don't live in houses.' Dick sniggered and they all joined in. 'And what's more, I never heard of a gypsy having a fancy foreign name like that.'

'But if 'e *is* a gypsy, this lawyer bloke, I reckon 'e's too big for 'is boots. What do you think, Bert?' Bull growled in his gravelly voice.

'Yeah! Maybe we could take him down a peg. You're good at things like that aren't you, Bull?' Dick gave another snigger.

'You want to make sure of your facts before you go starting anything,' Maddis warned. 'You could end up in bad trouble.'

'Don' frighten me like that mun, Dick,' Bull chuckled. 'Anyway if Bert's right, it could be fun.' He gave a sickening laugh, which turned Madoc's stomach over. 'I'll get 'old of a couple more of my boys. Right?'

Madoc banged down his pint, stood up and walked around the screen, standing over the men sitting at the table.

'Good afternoon, gentlemen. An interesting conversation you were having.'

Their heads jerked up in surprise, guilt flashing across Dick and Bert's faces but Bull just leered at him. Rising slowly from his seat Bull towered to his full height of six foot six inches. From inside folds of unwashed skin his piggy eyes looked down at Madoc and he sneered.

'Well, well. If it is not Madoc Morgan. Still not as big as me, are you, boy?'

'I don't need to be, Bull . . . or wasn't it Bullock's Balls we used to call you?' Madoc jeered, grinning.

The smirk dropped from Bull's face and he pulled his mouth down.

'I've given you more than one hidin', Morgan. I can do it again, easy.'

'Not so easily now, I've grown some. As I remember it, you preferred picking on things smaller and weaker than yourself, didn't you? Like animals that couldn't fight back.'

Bull grabbed hold of Madoc's jacket-front, jutting his head forward menacingly. Madoc's smile vanished, his eyes hard slits of jade as they fixed firmly on Bull's face.

'Get your hands off me,' Madoc asserted through his teeth, his voice cold. 'Right now!' As he said the last words, in one swift movement he brought both hands up through Bull's arms, knocking them out sideways, then he dodged nimbly as Bull swung a punch at him. Bull's fist went straight through the glass panel of the screen, which cut his hand.

'Missed!' Madoc laughed as Bull uttered a string of choice profanities. The place was so crowded that only people sitting nearby noticed, but a few men hurriedly sidled away.

'Leave off, Bull.' Bert, in the red cravat was looking around furtively. 'You'll get us all put on the mill.'

'What? Let 'im get away with saying that—'

'Come on, man,' Dick said. 'His family got influence in the town. He's not a kid no more.'

Bull held Madoc's eyes for a while, screwing up his face into an intimidating expression as Madoc, mouth pursed aggressively, faced up to him. Then Bull turned away.

'Come on,' he grunted. 'Let's get outa this place. There's an awful stink.'

'Couldn't agree more. The air will be much fresher once you've gone.' Madoc watched them going to the door, making sure they left before sitting down again at his table.

He was about to go to order another tankard when he saw Robert and Tom looking around for him. He waved to them and they joined him at the table.

'I met Albert the other day.' Madoc brought the subject into their conversation. 'Has Nia returned from her visit yet?'

'Not yet.' Tom laughed. 'I think my mother is hoping she will return with a ring on her finger.'

Madoc gulped at his drink, trying to swallow down his alarm with it.

'Really? Do you think she will?'

'I don't know. It's my mother; she's been ill and is very unlike her usual, cheerful self. She is being most persistent.'

'Is she?' Despondent, Madoc let the matter drop and told them about Bull.

'God. I thought I'd left all that nonsense behind.' Tom groaned. 'How on earth did they get on to that?'

'They're not certain . . . in fact Bull was quite incredulous.' Madoc frowned. 'But I'd watch your back, if I were you. It's years since I've seen him but he looks a pretty nasty piece of work. He was always a sadistic bastard as a child.'

Tom grimaced. 'Yes. I remember. I used to avoid him like the plague. I recall something about him hurting Nia's dog. . . .'

'That's right,' Rob said. 'Wasn't that when he beat you up, Madoc?'

'One of the times.'

'Maybe you should be the one keeping out of his way. Not me,' Tom said.

'He was always itching to get Madoc.' Robert shook his head. 'I don't know why you never told the old man about him and got him off your back.'

'I liked to settle my own fights, that's why. Nobody could ever say I was hiding behind my father's coat-tails.'

'No point in having family influence if you can't use it,' Tom observed.

'My sentiments exactly. Have they gone now?' Robert wanted to know.

'Yes, but not before I showed myself. I wanted to make quite sure they knew I'd heard what they said. I thought they'd be more wary of carrying out any—'

'The devil you did! Are you mad?' Robert exploded. 'What if that monster had started on you?'

Madoc banged down his tankard.

'I'm not an innocent, Rob. Nor the idiot you imagine. And I'm not forever looking for a fight, whatever you may think.' To soften his words he added with a grin: 'Anyway, I didn't know you cared.'

Rob raised his eyes skyward.

'I am quite aware you can look after yourself.'

'So I'll repeat my warning. Just watch your back for a while, Tom. Keep out of Bull's way.'

CHAPTER TEN

As the Gower Girl went for her much-needed repairs and refurbishment Madoc was glad of a respite from battling his way around the Horn. He began working in the office of Morgan Shipping, luxuriating in the slower pace of life with its regular hours and unbroken restful nights. He easily settled into the routine; by comparison most things seemed less important, less urgent than the immediacy of imperative decisions aboard a sailing-ship. Pleased to find that he and Rob got on well together, they shared an office, enjoying an easy companionship, one they had not experienced since early childhood years.

'I intend to take this opportunity of going to Beechwood Hall next week,' Robert told him. 'I'm getting to grips with the economies of an agricultural business . . . it makes a change from ships and shipping.'

Madoc looked up from the ledger he was working on.

'Do you ever have regrets about not going to sea, Rob?'

Robert pursed his lips.

'I'll concede I sometimes feel I would like to have tried a trip or two.' Seeing Madoc's grim face he added: 'But, even with two good arms, I don't think I'd have had the stomach for what you do. I'd never want to sail around Cape Horn on a copper-barque.' Laughter rippled through him.

Madoc rubbed a hand through his dark curls, not enjoying his brother's amusement.

'God, Robert. If you knew how I've—'

'We were children . . . and I think that that was one time I deserved your wrath. I thought it was such a good lark to go behind your back and give Lucy a kitten.'

'I never understood why Nia let you have that kitten.'

'You don't understand?' Amazed, he realized that Madoc really did not know. 'Because Nia was as jealous as hell of Lucy.'

'Nia jealous? Don't be silly. I always stuck up for Nia against Lucy.'

'Lucy was a rival.'

'Never! She knew Lucy couldn't stand me. All Nia ever wanted was to compete with me. She hated being a girl.'

'Well, she changed, take my word for it. She grew up and was crazy about you.'

In the act of dipping his pen into an inkwell, Madoc paused, remembering the first time he'd noticed her skinny figure beginning to blossom. Rubbing a hand over the back of his neck he threw Robert a rueful grin.

'She certainly grew up.'

They both laughed.

Madoc dipped his pen again, swearing as he dropped a blot of ink on to the page. Robert threw him a disapproving frown.

'You should curb your language now you are home, old man. Not the done thing.'

Madoc pulled a face, giving a non-committal grunt, and began scratching away with his pen again.

With the tide out, Madoc and Robert drove the gig home across the hard sand of Swansea Bay. A flock of gulls flew up into the air as they drew near to them, screaming their objection, before landing again further along the beach.

'So whilst you are at Beechwood, I take it you intend paying Lucy a visit?'

'Of course I shall.'

'Has she changed at all?' Madoc asked.

'She is still serene and beautiful. Her figure has matured slightly . . . but I believe it suits her. She is quite wonderful.'

'So what are going to do about Lucy? Will you ask for her hand?'

Robert looked outraged.

'Of course not. What sort of man would do a thing like that when she's so recently been widowed? Really, Madoc. You sound just as impetuous as ever you were.'

Madoc was stung. His eyes flashed green fire.

'I thought you might miss the tide again. You should at least make your intentions understood. Some other man might be just as eager to—'

'You said that before.' Rob's face was accusing.

Madoc groaned. 'Look, Rob. I'll repeat what I said previously. Not me! If you must know I am far more interested in Nia.'

'Nia? Good lord.' Robert's forehead puckered. 'I . . . I thought she was going to marry Albert.'

Madoc pursed his mouth.

'Not if I can help it,' he growled. 'In any case, Rob. I would never play such an underhand trick on my own brother. I fully understand that Lucy is your . . .' He paused, at a loss for a suitable word.

Rob looked uncomfortable.

'Point taken, old man. You are probably right anyway. Perhaps I should ask her to give it consideration . . . for the future, of course.'

Madoc sucked in a breath, thinking that he had more positive ideas about approaching a woman. He gave a little frown, his glance straying to Robert's face, for the first time seeing his brother as just another man. Maybe he could teach him a few tricks after all. He half-smiled, and Robert caught it.

'What are you laughing at? What's funny about it?'

'I'm not laughing. Just thinking.' Madoc raised eloquent eyebrows and grinned. 'I was just deciding that another, more impulsive way of expressing your passion might be more effective.'

Robert's jaw dropped slightly for a moment.

'Just what are you suggesting, Madoc?'

'I'll leave that to your imagination, Rob.'

'I think you've been mixing with uncouth men for too long. I dread to think what you have been up to on your travels.'

Madoc gave a lopsided grin. 'Yes.'

Rob regarded him uncertainly, but changed the subject.

'Anyway about Beechwood. As you know, I've been reading a lot about managing estates and I am confident I can make it even more prosperous than it is now. It's been out of family hands for so long that it is bound to improve with some loving care.'

'But I understood the new manager is excellent.'

'He is, don't get me wrong. I'm just anxious to be permanently installed at Beechwood. I need to think about moving soon.' His eyes lit up. 'Being in such close proximity to Lucy's home, I'll be able to see her quite often. It is an excellent property to offer to her, don't you think?'

Madoc snorted. 'Definitely. She could play the lady for the rest of her life.'

'What do you mean?'

'Just that Lucy would not consider marriage to a man without property.'

'Why on earth should she? Any woman would be unwise to do so. But a woman of Lucy's outstanding beauty could choose whom she wishes.'

'Definitely. I never held any false illusions about her. In any case, I believe she always thought I was an idiot.'

Rob laughed. 'You certainly gave that impression at times. You were a wild little renegade, did things just for the hell of it.'

'Or maybe I behaved like that because I could never live up to you?'

Madoc turned the gig towards Oystermouth, and both men got out before they reached the soft sand. Madoc led the horse to the road.

'Am I right? Did I hear that Lucy's husband was a colonel?' Madoc asked, once they were on their way to Gower.

'Yes. Quite a bit older than she was but an attractive devil. Bewitched all the ladies. He was due for promotion any day, so I heard.'

'Sad. But at least she's home from India now. The climate must be hard on a delicate woman like Lucy.'

'It must be. I gather she was none too keen on the heat. It is devilish hot out there from what Father says.'

'It certainly is hot.' Madoc's first voyage as an apprentice had been to India, before he joined the Cape Horn vessels.

'I will think on your advice, brother. To approach Lucy about marriage.' His expression was contemplative. 'She may even be waiting for me to mention it.'

'She probably is. I'll admit I could not believe it when she married someone else. She always favoured you, I used to be as jealous as hell.'

Robert sucked in a deep breath, shrugging his shoulders. Madoc tapped his brother's knee.

'You get your oar in there before anyone else does, Rob. Some of her husband's friends might be interested in her. Get there first this time.'

Robert mulled over Madoc's words, still considering it too soon to approach Lucy about marriage. He would hate her to get the idea that he was crass and unfeeling. But on the other hand, as he intended paying her a visit, if the time seemed right he might ask her. If not, he'd leave it for another time. He smiled, anticipating his imminent trip.

The sooner he was living there permanently the better, he decided. With Madoc home he'd have more time. He could engage more staff to run the place properly. Then he would invite Lucy and her parents for a weekend; they were bound to be impressed with the property.

He wondered what she would think of Madoc? His eyes narrowed thoughtfully; he realized that Madoc certainly attracted much female admiration these days. Robert had perceived that ladies noticed as his brother entered a room, had seen their fascinated eyes hang on him, had watched them whispering behind their fluttering fans and nudging one another. And Madoc was well aware of it, too, Robert decided. Because when he had laughingly joked about it to Madoc, he'd just grinned without surprise, his eyes dancing wickedly. Even that new maid, Sîan, ogled him every time he came in.

He had a relaxed authority he had never had as a youngster; obviously the result of commanding men at sea. Though how going to sea on a copper-barque and mixing with a crew of largely unrefined men could have improved him, heaven only knew. What appeal could Madoc have found in enduring all that deprivation? But Madoc had always been a daredevil on the look-out for danger. Robert would have opted for a commission in the Royal Navy. His mouth twisted wryly; his useless arm had put paid to any ideas in that direction. Even though he had never intended to harm his brother, Madoc had got his own back with interest, Robert thought, slightly bitter in spite of himself. Had his arm been the reason Lucy had chosen to marry Randolf?

Randolf Chilcott had been another dashing, adventurous character with appeal to the ladies. It might be prudent to get Lucy's promise before she met Madoc again, just to forestall any difficulties. He'd see about arranging to go to Beechwood as soon as he could, he decided.

'Madoc. May I have a word with you please?'

Madoc was just about to leave the house when his mother called from the top of the stairs.

'I'm sure they can manage the office without me for a short while.' He put his hat back on the hall table and bounded up the stairs and into her sitting room.

'You're spending quite a lot of time at the office these days. I have something to discuss with you.' She sank on to the brocaded *chaise-longue*. 'Do sit here with me, Madoc.' She noticed him pulling back the tails of his coat as he sat alongside her. 'You badly need some modern clothes. Those tails are very out of fashion for young men.'

He pulled a face.

'I've already realized that. I thought I might go along to a tailor today . . . but that isn't what you wanted to say?'

'No. Before your father left this morning he asked me to tell you something. We had a long talk yesterday evening.' She paused.

He studied her animated face with amusement.

'And?'

His heart missed a beat when she continued: 'And we have decided we want you to inherit Morgan Shipping.'

'What?' He sucked in a breath, hardly daring to breathe. 'But what about. . . ? You can't. . . .' He stuttered, trying to mask his excitement.

'We can . . . though we have spoken about this to no one.'

'Not Robert?' He glanced sharply at her.

'To Robert, of course. Your father broached the subject with him before he went to Beechwood. He is in complete agreement. Your father asked his opinion before speaking to me.'

'I see.' Madoc tore his gaze away, still unwilling to reveal his exhilaration. 'What if Robert changes his mind?'

'We wouldn't have told you if we believed he would do that.'

'That doesn't mean he won't.'

'He wants to be a country gentleman. He has been eager to move permanently to Beechwood Hall for some time.'

'Yes. He told me.' Madoc's eyes were reflective as he rubbed his hand across his chin. 'But what if he regrets this decision? He is within his rights to object to my receiving part of his inheritance.'

Emily sucked in an exasperated breath.

'Have you really such a low opinion of your brother?'

'No, Mother. I'm trying to see it from his viewpoint.'

'So? Would you begrudge him if the position were reversed?' she asked softly.

'Good Lord, no!'

'So that's all right then. The matter is settled. You are pleased?'

'I'm lost for words.' He ran his tongue over his lips. 'I can't take it in properly yet . . . you can never appreciate how much it means to me, Mother.'

'I think we can. You have always loved the sea and ships, just like your father. They have never held any appeal for Robert. Your father will be glad to have you in the business, especially once Rob moves away.' She reached down to pick up her journal which had slid on to the floor.

'Wait a minute!' he said with sudden suspicion. 'Was this *your* idea, by any chance? To keep me from going to sea?'

'How on earth did that idea cross your mind?' Her expression was innocent.

Madoc slapped his thigh, erupting with laughter.

'You must be the most scheming woman in the whole world.'

She widened her eyes.

'I . . . might have considered it. But as I told you before, we had no intention of leaving you penniless.'

'But what about when I go back to sea?'

She nodded. 'We recognize that possibility. But it won't make any difference to your inheritance. In any case, with Nia home again you'll be pleased that you won't have to leave.'

'She seems not over-eager to be in my company these days.'

'Don't be silly.' His mother dismissed his remark with a wave. 'She has not long come to terms with her new status as a lady. She probably wants you to see her in this light too.'

Madoc stared at her. 'Of course she does; why didn't I think of that?'

'I must say, she is a very elegant young woman these days. Until I met her again I couldn't imagine her being anything other than a hoyden. Martha used to become quite distracted . . . do you remember?'

'Yes. Martha used to blame me.'

Emily laughed. 'Not only you. She said you took after me. She used to despair of me because I liked wearing boy's clothes to go riding.'

'I'm glad to have you with us for a while.' David was about to leave for Bristol and was putting Madoc in charge.

'I am pleased I have your confidence, sir. And about the inheritance . . . it means a great deal to me.'

David gave a satisfied nod. 'We reached a definite decision last night and I was afraid I might not get the chance to talk to you before I left. That's why I asked your mother to tell you. You know Rob

intends settling in at Beechwood soon. It will leave us without him.'
He looked questioningly at Madoc. 'Though if you are set on going
off to sea again I shall understand. . . ?'

'Will you? If I don't, I think I'll always be sorry I was never officially master of a Cape Horner. It would give me immense personal
fulfilment.'

'I can understand that. I'd be the same in your shoes.'

'So you'd not be disappointed if I sailed a few more trips?'

'You've never disappointed me, Madoc.'

'But as a boy I was such an unruly little beggar.'

David laughed. 'That's part of the process.'

'Rob seemed to bypass it. I could never manage to do the right
things.'

'At least you wanted to please . . . I wanted only to annoy my foster-
father.'

Madoc's brow puckered. 'You never knew your own father, did
you?'

David pulled a sardonic face. 'Not even his name. Of course, you
know I was a bastard?'

'I had heard.' Madoc was slightly uncomfortable to be talking
about it. 'You inherited Morgan Shipping through your mother's
side, didn't you? But why didn't she tell you who your father was?'

'She died when I was two. If my foster-father knew, he never
revealed it to me.'

'Have you any idea? Any suspicions?'

'None whatsoever and I can't say it worries me.' David was uncon-
cerned. 'But never mind all that. We are to have the pleasure of your
company for the next few months anyway, until the *Gower Girl* is
seaworthy. And if you decide to take those other trips, then I am sure
we can manage a while longer without you.'

'I like that idea.' Madoc beamed. He put out his hand and his
father took it warmly. 'And I want to learn everything about the shipping business.'

'Especially as it will one day be yours.' David's blue eyes glowed
with pleasure.

Madoc was satisfied with his original decision to embark on his
chosen career, glad that his father had understood and backed him,
against his mother's protests.

CHAPTER ELEVEN

MADOC did not bother to turn his collar up against the rain. As he hurried along the Strand he realized that he was cutting it fine for his appointment. As he entered the office the damp odour of wet wool drifted over from the coats hanging on hooks, mingling with the smell of ink and musty papers. Russel Sutton got down from his high stool as Madoc walked towards him.

'Mr Madoc, Mr Edward Lewis sent word to cancel his appointment. I made a tentative one for the same time tomorrow. Is that all right?'

'Excellent. Thank you, Russel.' Madoc nodded, but as he went to walk on Russel held his arm.

'Er . . . that man was here.'

'What man?'

'The one I was telling you about. The foreigner.'

'Oh. Yes, I remember. You said someone has been hanging around outside the office.' Madoc shrugged out of his coat and shook the rain from it.

'That's right. I've seen him there several times now.'

'Didn't you say he was an Indian?'

'I think so, definitely an Eastern type. He was wearing a big turban around his head, anyway.'

Madoc laughed. 'Sounds like an Indian . . . you're sure it wasn't a bandage?'

'Get away!' Russel laughed.

'When you said he was here, did you mean inside the office?'

'Yes, that's right. He came in this time. Ever so polite he was, and asked for Lieutenant Morgan.'

'Lieutenant Morgan? God, that must go a long way back. It's ages since my old man was a lieutenant.'

'Yes. At first I thought he might have meant you, like. Got it wrong. But then he said no, of the East India Company. I told him your father had been a captain and he said that must be him.'

Madoc was curious. 'Must be someone he hasn't seen for many years. Not since he was sailing to India. I wonder who he is?'

'Well, you may have a chance to find out. I told him the captain was away in London, but that you would be here later.'

'We shall see if he returns then.'

With Robert still at Beechwood and his father in Bristol, Madoc was on his own. After the staff had all left that evening he was outside the offices, about to lock the door, when a singsong voice sounded from behind him, making him jump.

'Good evening, sahib.'

The figure had seemed to materialize from nowhere, and Madoc jerked around in surprise, dropping his keys. The man plucked them from the ground before Madoc could reach them, handed them to him gravely, then both hands pressed together in salutation. He bowed his head over them, touching his forehead.

'Thank you, sir,' Madoc said. 'And good evening to you. I didn't see you come up.'

'No, sahib.' The man inclined his head again. 'I am sorry to be startling you, Mr Morgan. . . .'

Madoc pushed the door open again. 'Do come in Mr. . . ?'

'Aseem, sahib.'

'Mr Aseem.' Madoc waved an arm for the man to enter, but he deferred to Madoc, with another little bow.

'After you, sahib.'

It was quite gloomy in the corridor, and Madoc lifted the glass shade from the wall light and put a light to the gas-mantle, then led the way through to his father's office, which he was using in his absence. He also lit the oil lamp on the desk.

'Do you wish to take off your cloak?' The man was wearing a thick cloak over his clothes and as Madoc helped him out of it, he caught the smell of sandalwood drifting in the air around them.

'Thank you, sahib.'

'How do you know who I am? Have we met before?'

'No, sahib. I am remembering your father as a young man your age.' Mr Aseem allowed himself a smile. 'You greatly resemble him.' He studied Madoc's eyes. 'Except for your eyes. They are not the colour of precious sapphires.'

Madoc smothered a grin, curious to know the Indian's business.

'Please sit down, Mr Aseem.' Madoc pulled up a chair for him but the man waited until Madoc had dropped into his own chair before taking the one he had been offered. 'Would you care for a cigar, Mr Aseem?' Madoc held out a case made from an albatross foot, popular with Cape Horn sailors.

'No thank you, sahib. Please you do so.'

Before Madoc could light up, the man whipped out a box of friction matches, struck one on a strip of sandpaper and lit Madoc's cigar. Madoc nodded his thanks and, leaning back in his chair, studied the man with interest, just as the dark eyes, deep-set in his face, seemed equally to be studying Madoc. It was disconcerting, as he did not blink and his expression was inscrutable as he looked down his hooked nose. He was definitely of the Indian race, Madoc decided, probably from the north, as he was not very dark, though his skin was lined with age and the effects of the sun, his curling moustache and beard were white. A mark tattooed on his forehead proclaimed his caste, though Madoc had no idea of its significance, but he noticed that Aseem's loose trousers and jacket were of the finest silk, braided with silver threads. On his head he wore a huge turban where, pinned into the folds, a jewel gleamed as he moved his head.

'I am afraid my father is away on business.' Madoc looked questioningly at the man. 'It was him you wished to see?'

'It is, sahib. I understand he will be returning?'

'That's right.' Madoc turned his head, blowing out a cloud of cigar smoke to one side.

'Very soon?' Aseem leaned forward in his chair, for the first time giving a sense of urgency.

'I am sorry, but I don't know precisely. Next week sometime. You wished to see him sooner?' Aseem did not reply. 'If it is business, can I be of any assistance, sir?'

'No, sahib. It is Captain Morgan I need to see.'

Madoc quirked one eyebrow.

'It must be many years since you last saw him?'

'Indeed, sahib. It is more than thirty-five years.' Madoc was amazed that he knew so exactly. 'Your father was a young lieutenant serving with the East India Company. He used to visit the home of my master, Prince Lokesh.' His head seemed to wobble slightly from side to side as he talked, as if it were mounted on a fine spring.

'A prince?' Madoc was impressed. 'I don't remember my father telling us that . . . he used to tell us stories about India.'

'You have brothers and sisters?'

'I have one brother, no sisters.'

'And your mother, she is very beautiful?'

'She is, very.' Madoc pushed his hand through his hair, wondering why on earth he was telling this stranger these facts. 'Look, Mr Aseem . . .'

Aseem smiled. 'Your father has just such a habit, sahib.'

'What?' Madoc's mouth curled up on one side. The man was talking in riddles.

'With your hair. Brushing it back. Your father does it also.'

'Does he? I hadn't noticed. Look, perhaps you should come and see my father, Mr Aseem.'

The man rose to his feet, making his obeisance again.

'I will be taking my leave, Mr Morgan. And I may call again? To your father?' His deep-set eyes were watching him again. 'You believe he will see me?'

'Of course. I am sure he will be delighted to see you again after all this time.'

'I hope so, sahib,' said Aseem enigmatically. 'But he will not be returning until next week?'

'That's right. Towards the end of the week I believe he said.'

'Then I will come to see him when he is home.' Aseem salaamed with his hands again and was gone.

Madoc laughed. If Russel hadn't told him about the Indian man earlier, he'd have thought he was dreaming, Madoc decided. Wait until he told his mother that the old man had been hobnobbing with princes. She would be fascinated. He wondered whether his father had ever told her before?

But Madoc had arranged to play a card game that evening and the Indian man slipped right out of his mind.

CHAPTER TWELVE

ROBERT'S train pulled into the station. Trailed by a porter bearing his luggage, he made his way outside.

'Shall I call you a cab, sir?' The porter put down the two leather bags and waved down a passing horse-cab. Placing the luggage inside with him, he asked. 'Where to, sir?'

'Beechwood Hall, please.'

Having given the driver his instructions the porter touched his cap as Robert gave him a generous tip.

Robert sat back smiling. Tomorrow morning he intended travelling to Lucy's home to ask for her hand in marriage. Madoc was right. If he left it until later someone else could approach her. How often had he regretted not proposing before she met Randolf Chilcott?

Robert had spent much time with Lucy as they were growing up, attending parties, balls and other social engagements. When he had mentioned the future to her, indicating that they would make a good couple, she had always seemed to be in agreement. Assuming that their future would be together, he had been taken completely by surprise when she told him she was to marry Randolf.

Robert, who had never met the man previously, had been late arriving for a ball at the assembly rooms in Swansea. He had not expected to see Lucy, who had been away for several weeks with her aunt in London. She had not sent him word that she was home. He was pleasantly surprised to see her present, dancing with an army officer who was resplendent in a scarlet uniform lavishly embellished with gold braid. A flamboyant man, he was attracting a great deal of attention from the ladies present. During a break in the dancing, holding Randolf's hand, Lucy brought him over to introduce him to Robert.

'. . . and he is serving in the Indian Army. A colonel,' she put in proudly. Then she held out her hand, revealing an extravagant diamond ring, the gems sparkling on her finger as she moved it in the lamplight. 'Do you like my ring, Robert? Randolf and I are engaged to be married.'

'Married?' It was like a bombshell exploding; then the room went quiet, the hum of voices faded. His heart began to pound erratically, and he was aware of a loud throbbing and thudding in his ears. 'I . . . I . . . congratulations,' he managed at last, reaching to take the other man's hand, hoping his own hand was not shaking.

'Thank you, Robert. I am an exceptionally lucky man, don't you think?' Randolf flashed a flirtatious smile down at Lucy, who gave him a radiant one in return.

'Yes . . . very.' Robert forced the words through his dry throat, desperately trying to conceal his crushing devastation as his world toppled around him.

'I didn't see you here, Robert, but I saved a dance for you in case you turned up. A waltz, I know you like those.'

'Thank you, I'd like that.'

His jealous eyes followed the man as they walked away. Robert had the impression that Randolf was fully aware of his own good looks as he sauntered across the floor, his rakish smile enthralling matrons and their daughters alike. Robert had managed to gain a modicum of control over his emotions by the time he danced with Lucy, keeping his voice aloof and neutral, not revealing his deep hurt at her betrayal.

'I believe you said Randolf is serving in India?' he ventured, for something to say to cover his dismay.

She nodded, her face animated, the smell of violets drifting around her as ever.

'Yes. It will be an exciting adventure for me. Don't you think?'

'I suppose. Though I have heard the climate is exceedingly hot.' Was there possibly some way he could change her mind before she left? he wondered.

'He will be going back when his leave ends in two weeks' time.'

'Two weeks?' Robert's spirits rose, upon learning that the man would be soon gone. 'And when will you leave?' he asked in a neutral tone.

'I'm going with him, of course.' Her glance drifted over to Randolf where he stood with her parents. 'You don't think I'd let him go without me, do you? I might lose him to some other woman.' She gave a possessive smirk. 'I believe they are jealous. They are all admiring him . . . don't you agree?'

Robert managed a weak smile. There was no possible way he could change her mind, in two weeks.

'I shall be hard pressed to get my trousseau prepared in time.' She sounded delighted with the prospect. 'Naturally all the garments I need will never be completed in time, but Mama said she can send them on. As long as I have sufficient until they arrive I am sure I shall manage. It is all such fun, Robert.'

He felt physically sick, wanted to rush off and vomit. Had she no inkling of the anguish she was causing him? Surely he had made his feelings clear on more than one occasion? It took all his will power to keep his expression bland and hide his pain. Not wishing to hear any more about what she was going to do with Randolf he was almost overcome by the temptation to dash away from her, to leave her on her own on the dance floor. Impatient to end it, as soon as the dance was finished, he escorted her back to her seat and went home.

Lucy looped her arm through Robert's as they walked in the grounds of her home. He looked down at her hand where it rested on his arm, so pale and frail-looking, in spite of her years in India. He felt the familiar surge of protectiveness towards her that he always had. It was a bright spring day and they were strolling along the path around a pool, where frogs croaked at one another, or dived in the water with a plop, leaving concentric rings of ripples on the surface. Daffodils swayed their heads as they brushed past them, leaving a smattering of pollen on Lucy's black skirt.

They sat down on a bench carved into the back wall of a little arbour. Lucy wore a thick cloak but still shivered slightly.

'Are you cold?' Robert asked. 'Would you rather walk?'

'No. I am all right here, thank you. But I do find it cold today. Especially since living in India. I think I'll have my shawl now, please, Robert.'

He opened out the soft cashmere shawl, woven in a soft grey-and-white paisley pattern, which he had been carrying for her. He draped it gently on top of the cloak around her shoulders.

'Thank you.' She smiled at him and once more her ethereal beauty moved him. Her pale hair peeped from beneath her black bonnet, and the black-lace-edged ruffles around the edge of the tiny parasol she was holding over her head cast fluttering shadows on her face. He loved his fragile, delicate Lucy. It still pained him to recall how destroyed he'd been when she married Randolf Chilcott; but now he had a second chance. He was not going to let her slip from his grasp this time.

'Lucy.' He reached for her hand. 'I know you are still in mourning for Randolf, but I . . . I wish to say something to you. It has been on my mind for some time and I feel I must mention it now.'

Her trusting eyes were on his face.

'What is it, Robert? What has been on your mind?'

'I fully realize it is much too soon . . . but . . . I wonder . . . I wonder if you will do me the honour of considering marriage to me?' His voice, normally so self-assured and confident, was unusually hesitant, causing him to stumble over his words. He hastened to add: 'I don't mean now, of course, but in the future. I do love you, Lucy. Very much . . .' His voice trailed off.

Lucy cast her head down for a moment and Robert was convinced she was about to refuse, but then she raised it, her violet eyes shining, a wistful smile on her mouth.

'Thank you, Robert. You have done me a great honour and I will certainly consider it. I believe I do return your love, but with my husband so recently departed . . .' She broke off with a little sob, her shoulders shaking prettily, and dabbed at her eyes with a scrap of fine linen, also edged with black lace. Robert put a protective arm around her.

'I understand, my dear. Please don't upset yourself. Perhaps I should have left it until a later date. . . .'

'No. You have done nothing amiss in asking. I will consider it.'

Robert beamed with happiness. 'I know you have inherited these beautiful estates from your late husband, but if we were to marry you would become mistress of Beechwood Hall also.'

'Beechwood Hall?' She raised her eyes again to his face. 'But surely you will have to wait a long time before you inherit that property?'

'No! I am to take over the management and occupancy almost immediately, if I so wish. My parents intend never to live there, and the whole of the estates and property will be mine.'

'Really? Immediately you say? That is exciting news.'

'I would like you and your parents to come for a few days, once I have made the necessary arrangements, of course.'

'I've heard Beechwood Hall is very grand with vast estates. You will be like the lord of the manor there.'

'And I hope that you will be its lady. Have I reason to be hopeful?'

'Yes, Robert, you have every reason to be hopeful.' She gave a quiet smile.

He took her hand, feeling as though a great weight had been lifted from his shoulders.

'Have you any idea when you will be able to give me an answer?'

'If you wish . . . you may consider us to be unofficially engaged. . . .'

'Lucy! You make me the happiest man in the world.' He was hardly able to believe she had agreed.

'But this is to be completely unofficial as yet. I am in mourning, and you must allow me a little longer to get over . . .' Her voice trailed off and her face was sad once more.

'I will tell no one until you permit me to.'

'Thank you.' She reached up and pressed her soft lips to his cheek.

'Have you other suitors?' He wanted to be certain of her commitment.

'No one else has approached me so far. But I know . . .' She let the sentence trail off unfinished.

Robert swallowed his anxiety at her words. She has given me her promise, he told himself. They got up and began strolling back along the path.

'If you are to come to live at Beechwood what will happen with the shipping business? Aren't you needed there?'

'Not now Madoc is home, he'll be in the business as well. . . .'

'Has he finished with the sea then? Didn't he sail on one of those copper-ships?'

'That's right. A Cape Horn copper-barque. . . .'

'Why did he do it? Isn't it terribly hazardous?'

'It is. Very hard and dangerous. But you know Madoc, he courts danger.'

'I see.' Lucy nodded, her violet eyes contemplative. 'And has he decided to stay home now?'

'His ship was badly damaged, it is being refurbished. He may still return to sea. But it has been decided that Madoc is to inherit Morgan Shipping.'

'Madoc inherit. . . ? But he is the younger son! It should come to you.' She was astonished. 'Don't you mind?'

'Why should I mind? Beechwood will be more than enough for me

... it is a very rich property. . . .'

'But Morgan Shipping is most successful too, is it not?'

'Indeed, it has a fine fleet of ships. My parents discussed it with me first, of course, and I was perfectly happy with the idea.'

'And naturally Madoc is too,' she said a trifle tartly.

'He is delighted. He was doubtful at first, wanted to make sure I was fully in agreement with—'

'But now you have convinced him.' Her voice was derisive. 'I think it is extremely generous of you. More than generous, I believe. Not many men would give up their inheritance so easily.'

'If you are thinking that we will be short of money, you need have no worries on that score.' Robert wondered whether she was considering that aspect.

'If you say so.' She fiddled with her parasol.

'Please do not think ill of Madoc . . .' he began.

'He was always such a ruffian. What is he like these days?'

Robert laughed. 'It is years since you've seen him, you will hardly recognize him . . . though perhaps I shouldn't say that. Everyone insists he is the image of my father. . . .'

'Your father? Never! I can't believe that.' She looked at him with surprise. 'Do you consider them alike?'

'I suppose they are.'

Lucy raised her eyebrows. 'I cannot imagine Madoc looking anything other than disreputable. Still, perhaps I shall see him soon. I am coming to my parents for an extended stay.'

'That's wonderful news.' Robert was delighted. 'I'll be able to see so much more of you. Are you willing for me to drop a hint to my parents about. . . ?' He broke off hesitantly.

'You may tell them that . . . that we are unofficially engaged.' She dimpled prettily at him. 'Very unofficially.'

'May I kiss you, Lucy?'

She looked up at him from under her lashes.

'You may, Robert.'

He took her delicate form lovingly in his arms, afraid to crush her against him, and was overwhelmed by her familiar violet perfume as she reached up soft arms to wrap around his neck. He lowered his lips to hers, finding them warm and yielding. Her mouth opened slightly under the pressure of his kiss and he was rather shocked when the merest tip of her tongue probed his lips. At last he drew his head away reluctantly, looking down at her flawless beauty as those dazzling eyes met his gaze.

'I love you deeply, Lucy. I will always take care of you, I promise.'

Her smile dimpled again, and she reached her head towards him, waiting for another kiss, which he was elated to supply.

The following week Madoc arrived at work to find Aseem waiting in the vicinity of the office. Madoc nodded politely to him and he came over.

'Good morning, Mr Morgan. Your father has not returned yet?'

'I am afraid not. Sorry.' Madoc shook his head. 'He has sent word he will be home by Saturday, so it will be Monday, now.'

'At what time please, sahib?'

'Say three o'clock. Will that suit you, Mr Aseem?'

'Very suitable, Mr Morgan. Thank you.' Aseem salaamed again and silently retreated.

'Did I see you talking to that foreign gentleman?' Russel asked, balancing three huge ledgers in his arms.

'Yes. That's the second time. After you told me about him, he suddenly appeared behind me when I was closing up last week.' Remembering it, Madoc laughed. 'It was most disconcerting. You were right, he wants to see my father and he remembered him as Lieutenant Morgan.'

'You think he would have forgotten him after all these years.'

'The same thought occurred to me, but he recalled him remarkably well. He even told me I had a similar mannerism.'

Russel screwed up his face. 'A similar mannerism? What's that?'

'Brushing the hair off my forehead.' Madoc reached a hand to grab the top ledger as it slid off the pile in Russel's arms. 'I wasn't even aware that I did it.'

Russel laughed. 'He's right. I've noticed you both do that. He must remember him very well, then.'

'Must do. This is most mystifying.'

Aseem returned to his lodgings in The Burrows, a fashionable area of Swansea where his mistress had a suite of rooms. He tapped at her door and it was quickly opened by her maidservant.

'Aseem. Was he there?' His mistress's voice came from within the room as she spoke to him in their native tongue. As the maid stepped to one side he saw that her face was alive with expectation.

He salaamed to her, answering in the same language.

'No. I am sorry, Princess Charu.' He shook his head, distressed to see disappointment shadow her face.

'Did they say when he would return? Did you see either of his sons this time?'

'Yes. I spoke to the same one as before, Mr Madoc. The one who resembles him. He said we might expect him on Monday. He has arranged a time of three o'clock.'

'So long to wait.' She sighed deeply, her expression disheartened. Aseem's glance followed her as she glided across the room, the silk of her sari swishing around her, causing the numerous anklets which she wore to tinkle together at each step. Her every movement graceful and feminine, she sank down into a chair near the fire, dropping her head into her hands, her shoulders sagging.

'Princess. Because of the urgency, do you think ... perhaps we should speak to his son?' He spoke hesitantly.

She raised her head, her luminous eyes regarded his face.

'No. I must speak to his father. You do understand, Aseem?' she said passionately. 'It is essential for me to speak only to Lieut ... Captain Morgan himself.'

'I understand, Princess.' He salaamed low over his touching palms; he would give this woman the earth if it were possible.

CHAPTER THIRTEEN

ROBERT returned to Swansea in good humour and hurried out to join Madoc and Emily in the conservatory. The moist earthy smell was heavy in the air, the plants luxuriant with fresh new growth.

'I have some wonderful news for you. Lucy and I are unofficially engaged.' His delight was evident. 'We can tell no one outside the family as yet, but she has more or less consented to be my wife.'

Emily, who was trimming a plant, put down her cutters and reached up to hug him and kiss his cheek.

'That is wonderful news, Robert. I am very happy, it is what you wanted. I suppose there can be no official engagement whilst she is still in mourning.'

'That's right. Until her mourning period is ended, she said she could give no more definite answer.' Robert, normally so calm and composed, was beaming widely as Madoc thumped him on the back.

'Congratulations. I am glad you put it to her. You'll make a fine couple.'

Robert hunched his shoulders.

'I still can't really accept it. I am longing for her to name the day ... though unfortunately that cannot be for some months. Anyway, I'll be seeing her again soon. She is travelling to Swansea next week to stay with her parents.'

'Good. I can think about arranging that soirée I mentioned now.' Emily's eyes slid thoughtfully towards Madoc. 'Is Nia back yet, Madoc?'

'I haven't heard, Mother.'

'I shall send Trevor round to find out. Do you like this new plant? It is from the Mediterranean.'

'It is very nice, Mother.' Robert looked around at the abundant greenery with good humour. 'But soon we shall have no room left to sit at this rate.'

Madoc was turning away when Robert caught his arm. 'By the way, Madoc, Lucy has invited me to her parents' home. She specifically asked me to bring you along too.' He sounded as though he was conferring a treat.

Madoc nodded, smiling. 'Good. I'll look forward to that.' His voice was polite, though he thought how strange it was that he felt such little interest in Lucy. She was no competition for Nia.

Liam took Nia's hand to help her down from the carriage.

'I'm glad my girl is home again. Did you enjoy yourself?' He studied her face as he kissed her cheek.

'Yes, thank you. How is Mama? Any better? I've been worrying about her all the time I was away. I don't think I should have gone.'

As she was talking, Martha's voice called from the doorway.

'Nia. You're back, my lovely. I'm so pleased to see you, I have missed you dreadfully, it seems so long.'

Nia hurried over to hug her mother.

'I've missed you too, Mama. How have you been?'

'Not too bad, at all. I believe that doctor's medicine is doing me good.' Nia and her father exchanged glances, but passed no comment. 'Come in and tell me all about your visit. I'm dying to know everything. What were Mr and Mrs Goodman like?'

'Very friendly, I really took to them. They both made me feel very welcome.'

'That's good to hear. Let's have some refreshment. I expect you are thirsty after your journey.'

Nia looked around the airy drawing room with pleasure. After being away for several weeks she enjoyed seeing it with fresh eyes.

'It's so good to be home. I truly love this house, Mama. You have done it out so beautifully.'

Martha was pleased. 'We are well satisfied with it. So?' Her tone was expectant. 'Have you any other news?'

'Other news?' Nia hedged, knowing exactly what her mother was alluding to. 'I met Albert's sister and her family. She is married with two delightful small children.'

'Nia,' her mother sighed, 'not that sort of news. You know what I mean, real news.' Her eyes were eager. 'What about Albert? Did he propose?'

Bethan tapped on the door and brought in a tray, allowing Nia to be distracted.

'Nia. You didn't answer me,' Martha said as the door closed. 'Did he ask you to marry him?'

'When I was away, you mean? Er . . . no.'

'Oh! I thought . . . that is. . . .' Martha's face fell.

This was more difficult than Nia had imagined. She had been practising what to say all the way home, had intended to be quite firm if her mother brought the subject up. But now she found herself at a loss for words. Martha had obviously been expecting her to announce her engagement. How could she admit that she had already turned Albert down, even before she went away? She looked hopefully at her father for help, but he half-shrugged.

'I'll get back to the horses,' he said, making his escape.

I wonder if Papa wants me to marry Albert? The disturbing thought suddenly arose. *Perhaps he hopes I will – just to make Mama happy?*

'I understood Albert intended to propose to you,' Martha said.

'You did?' Nia croaked, swallowing hard.

Her mother looked utterly crestfallen. Her shoulders slumped and she turned to pour out the fruit juice.

After listening to all Nia's news about Newport and the Goodmans, Martha brought the conversation back to the subject on her mind.

'So Nia. Let me get this clear. Are you telling me that Albert has said nothing to you at all about marriage?' The question was pointed and unavoidable, her eyes on Nia's face as she waited for an answer. Nia bit her lip.

'I didn't say that, Mama.'

The expectation flew back to her mother's eyes and she leaned forward, catching Nia's arm.

'So he has proposed? Has he, Nia?'

Nia drew in a deep breath.

'He asked me before we went away Mama,' she admitted slowly and reluctantly.

'That's wonderful . . .' Martha broke off, horrified, seeing Nia's closed expression. 'Oh, Nia! You didn't. . . ? How could you?' She shook her head and buried her face in her hands. 'How can you be so foolish.'

'Because I don't love him, Mama!' Nia's voice rose in desperation. 'I don't want to marry Albert. Never, ever!' She fled from the room and rushed up to her bedroom, overcome with anger, self-pity and anguish.

'It's not fair,' she yelled, frustrated. 'It is just not fair of Mama to do this to me. She's holding her illness over me like . . . like a threat! Oh, God. What can I do?'

A book of poems that Albert had given her was lying on her dressing table. She picked it up and hurled it across the room. It knocked against a jug of flowers, sending it smashing on the floor.

'Miss Nia! Miss Nia!' Bethan was tapping on her door, her voice urgent. 'Come quickly, it's your mother, miss. I think she's having one of her turns.'

Nia leapt up and rushed down the stairs, trailed anxiously by Bethan.

'Call my father. Hurry, Bethan,' she shouted as she ran.

Her mother was gasping when Nia reached her, her face pinched and grey. She looked all but unconscious, but fluttered her lashes when Nia took her hand and spoke to her.

'Don't get upset, Mama. Please don't worry about Albert. We'll work something out, you'll see.'

Her eyes flickered open. 'You . . . mean . . . ma. . . ?' she managed.

'Yes,' Nia said, anything to stop this attack progressing further.

A firm hand clamped on her shoulder and squeezed. She raised tear-filled eyes to her father's grim face.

'Thank you,' he whispered. He had brought Martha's medicine with him and he spooned few droplets on to her blue tinged lips.

'Can you try to swallow that, my love?'

Obediently Martha sipped at the spoon, swallowed a few drops more, then a second spoonful. Liam tenderly picked her up and carried her over to the *chaise-longue*, then covered her with a blanket.

'Try to sleep. Will you sit with her please, Bethan.'

He beckoned to Nia, who followed him out.

'I heard what your mother said . . . and your answer?' His voice held a question, his eyes sad.

Despairing, Nia shook her head.

'I had to. What else could I do, Papa? What could I say to her?'

He appeared equally shaken.

'I really don't know, Nia. I understand why you did it, and I'm grateful.' He began pacing around the room. 'But I thought you turned Albert down before you went away. Did he ask you again?'

'No. He told me then he was prepared to wait ... hoping I'd change my mind. I tried to avoid telling Mama this, but ...' She gave a sob and turned to her father, who hugged her against him. 'It's my fault! I started this off, I got cross with her. I couldn't bear anything to happen to her, Papa. Do you think I should marry Albert? Do you want me to?'

'No,' he said heavily. 'I don't think you should, my Nia. He is the wrong man for you. But we must try to keep away from this whole subject for a while, let things settle.'

Nia felt so helpless. 'Perhaps I could write to Albert and explain how things are? Ask him not to call for a while?'

'I doubt the man will understand.' Liam was sceptical. 'He loves you, he wants to be with you. You can understand that feeling well enough.'

'Yes, I'm afraid I do,' she sighed.

The following morning Nia wrote a letter of thanks to the Goodmans, then composed a second, long letter to Albert. Anxious for him to understand why she was asking him not to call in the immediate future, she discarded sheet after sheet as she phrased and rephrased her words. She explained about her mother's latest attack and how worried they were, and why nothing should upset her for a while.

> *... I hope you will understand that it is not you who is upsetting Mama, Albert, but it seems any excitement sets off ...*

She left the letter to reread again after lunch. Then, deciding she could improve it no further, she sent Bertie, the stable boy, off with both letters to be posted in Swansea.

Martha was much recovered in a few days, and although she made veiled references to the idea of Nia and Albert getting married she seemed content to leave it at that.

But Nia was not deceived, realizing that her mother now believed she would accept Albert's proposal. The problem had not gone away, had merely been postponed.

★

Madoc and Robert handed their hats to a maid.

'This way, gentlemen.' A manservant ushered them into the room where Mrs Trent was seated. 'Mr Robert Morgan and Mr Madoc Morgan,' he announced solemnly.

Mrs Trent rose, gliding over to them, making her way past numerous little tables covered in heavy chenille cloths, all crowded with assorted ornaments. The room was overpowered by red velvet and tassels.

'How lovely to see you both.' She extended a limp hand to Robert, her fingers were encrusted with jewelled rings. She continued on to Madoc, pausing before extending her hand to him. 'Madoc? It must be, though in truth I would never have known you. You have changed since I saw you last. I hear you have been playing the hero in the southern oceans.' She tapped him playfully with her closed fan, tilting her head on one side in a coquettish gesture.

Madoc's mouth tightened, but he forced a smile as he returned her greeting. He hated it when people made remarks like that; it made him feel like some character in a cheap novelette.

She threaded her hand through his arm, leading him to some chairs. Over her shoulder he could see Rob's amused glance. Madoc pulled a face behind her back as she sat down and turned towards Robert.

'Do sit down, gentlemen.' As both men took their seats she added: 'Lucy will not be long she – Ah! There she is.'

They both rose to their feet again as Lucy came through the door. To Madoc she appeared even more ethereal than he remembered. She was clad completely in black, which emphasized her translucent beauty: the enormous violet pools of her eyes, swimming in the delicate bones of her face, her pearly skin with the lustre of alabaster. Her expression was pensive as she crossed the room, her hooped skirt swaying gracefully from side to side as it swished across the carpet, her jet beads hanging to her waist and swinging in time.

Robert walked towards her, reached for her outstretched hand and raised it to his lips.

'Robert. I have been so looking forward to seeing you again.' Her voice was little more than whisper.

'Not as much as I longed to see you, Lucy. I have brought my brother with me.'

She turned to Madoc and stared up at him in surprise.

'Is it truly Madoc?' Her mouth opened a little and her eyes widened. 'Why! It is true then. You are now the image of your handsome father.'

Madoc gave a crooked smile. Warily, he took her proffered hand, careful to avoid squeezing her fragile bones and crushing them between his hard fingers.

'Lucy. I was saddened to hear of your great loss. It must have been a dreadful shock.'

'Yes. Thank you, Madoc.' Her brow wrinkled and instead of releasing his hand she felt it, turning it over to examine his roughened palm with interest, smoothing it with one soft finger. Embarrassed, Madoc wanted to snatch it away, which he couldn't do. It was the first time anyone had ever done that, though he realized that his hands were obviously not as those associated with non-seagoing gentlemen. As she released it, her eyes flashed thoughtfully up to his face again. 'Yes. It was a dreadful shock,' she continued. 'I am getting over it a little now, but it has been devastating.'

She sank down on to a settee and tapped the place alongside her with her fan. 'Sit here, Madoc. I want to hear about your trips around Cape Horn.'

Madoc took a deep breath, his glance flicking towards his brother, whose returning smile did not quite reach his eyes.

'I am sure you would be bored, Lucy.' He tried to walk past her.

'I assure you I will not be bored.' She caught his sleeve.

This was unexpected. Madoc had assumed she would be distantly polite to him as always – patronizing almost. Curling his fists to conceal the palms, he took the proffered place, throwing an apologetic glance at Rob, who studiously avoided it.

'Well? What have you to tell me?' Madoc's attention returned to Lucy, who was fluttering her fan beneath her chin and looking up appealingly from beneath her lashes. Against his will, he was stirred by her beauty, would like to have kissed those fair eyelids, that creamy neck, to excite her pale beauty into life. His lip turned up at one corner as he recalled those times when, alone in his bunk, he had fantasized about Lucy. And now here was the real woman, sitting next to him.

'What are you going to tell me?' she repeated.

'What do you wish to know? I am certain you do not want to hear about storms at sea.'

'I heard there was a fire aboard. That you risked your life pulling someone from it.'

'Where did you hear that?' He was shocked out of his composure.

Her laugh tinkled. 'A little bird . . . perhaps a seagull. Is it true?'

Madoc laughed, shrugging it off.

'You must not believe everything you hear; people say all sorts of things.' He threw an appealing look at Rob, who grinned unkindly.

She reached for his curled left hand, which looked huge in her small ones. A white scar was visible along the edge of the back of it, which she examined before turning his hand over. Madoc clenched it more tightly.

'I heard you were burnt. May I see?' Madoc looked away, keeping his hand closed. 'Please, Madoc. Surely that is not a lot to ask?'

His glance came back to her face, her hurt-little-girl expression, and he pursed his lips. Feeling absurd he allowed her to uncurl his fingers, revealing the puckered scar covering his palm and wrist, continuing up to disappear under the sleeve of his jacket.

'You did get burnt. It must have been painful.' She started to push up his sleeve to examine it further, but he snatched his hand away, rose to his feet and walked over to the window, aware of everyone watching him. He stared out at the grounds where two gardeners were working, his gaze wandering across the lush lawn to the ornate fountain in the centre.

'That's a lovely fountain,' he said, grasping for something to change the subject.

'We had it installed last year.' Mrs Trent came over and looked through the window with him. 'I am very pleased with it. Lucy said the Indian princes all have them in their gardens.'

Her words recalled the Indian servant's call to the office a week ago and Madoc realized that he had told no one about it.

'Would you like to see it up closer?' Lucy had appeared at his other side. 'I'll put my cloak on and we can walk out in the grounds.'

Madoc looked appealingly at Robert, who was lounging against the mantelpiece staring into the fire, his expression dispirited.

'Are you coming, Rob?' he called. 'Lucy wants to know if we would like to see the fountain up closer.'

'Why not.' Rob straightened and sauntered over. A slow smile crept across his face as he looked down at Lucy. 'Will you show me?' He held out an arm and, with a little return smile, she fluttered her fan at him and took it. Madoc was turning away in relief when Lucy reached out and took his arm as well.

As Robert had bowed to Madoc's preference for riding, the two men had ridden their horses over instead of bringing the gig. They trotted away from the Trents' residence, but once they were round the corner Robert reined in his mount, pulling her to a halt.

'What were you playing at, Madoc?' His face was tight and angry.

'Oh no! You can't blame me for that. I tried to walk away from her.'

'Huh! The big hero, returning from the South Atlantic. Can I see your scars, Madoc?' he mimicked.

'Just leave it drop, Rob,' Madoc exploded. 'I felt as ridiculous as you sound using that squeaky voice. Who told her about it anyway?'

'Certainly not me! I didn't know. You never told me you were a big hero—'

Madoc broke in with a string of profanities and kneed his horse into a trot away from Robert. He soon heard Robert following, close on his heels.

'Madoc. Wait! Madoc!'

Madoc's face was grim as he allowed Robert to come alongside.

'I'm sorry, old man.' Robert sounded contrite. 'I'll admit I was jealous. She seemed enthralled with the whole idea of your being a Cape Horner . . . and a hero!'

Madoc's mouth tightened. 'Oh, God! Not again, please! Can't we leave the subject drop?' He turned blazing eyes on his brother.

'All right. Point taken.' Robert never said another word all the way home leaving Madoc to his own thoughts.

Robert is annoyed, and who could blame him? Madoc thought. *Rob's fiancée, well almost fiancée, was flirting with me. And Rob is not used to this behaviour in ladies, certainly not used to taking second place to his brother – and with Lucy of all people! She could hardly bother to talk to me when we were young and now she reacts like this, mildly flirting with me. Not that it isn't pleasing – but not with my brother's fiancée. And it makes it damned uncomfortable as far as Rob is concerned. The sooner Nia returns home from Albert's the better, I don't think Robert is entirely convinced that I am not interested in Lucy.*

CHAPTER FOURTEEN

'Did you enjoy your afternoon?' Emily asked her sons as they entered the hall.

'Yes thank you, Mother,' Madoc replied. He returned Sîan's smile briefly as he handed her his hat and walked straight upstairs, taking them two at a time as he always did.

Emily watched him; he looks disturbed she thought. She turned to Robert as the maid vanished with their hats.

'Did Lucy not make him welcome?'

'On the contrary, mother. She was inordinately welcoming.' Robert's voice was curt, his mouth turning down. 'She seemed hardly bothered to talk to me.'

Emily frowned. Rob wasn't usually surly but in this case she could understand why. 'She was probably making an effort to be nice to him. After all—'

'Please! Don't patronize me, Mother. It was certainly no effort on her part. She was positively gushing. By the way, did you know your baby boy is a hero?'

Emily regarded him warily.

'You mean because he sails around the Horn?' she asked, wondering whether he was beginning to show resentment about not serving at sea.

'No! Something quite apart from that feat of endurance.' His tone was acerbic. 'Apparently Madoc pulled someone out of a fire on board . . .'

'A fire on board the ship? His ship do you mean? I haven't heard anything about that. Did *you* know about it?'

'Not until I heard it from Lucy. I have no idea how she heard, but it was obvious that she knew he'd been burned in the process. She seemed enthralled by the episode.'

'Robert.' Emily's stomach tightened, realizing how deeply upset he was. 'Madoc knows your intentions, I am sure he would never jeopardize those. Lucy has not seen Madoc since they were young, it's natural for her to make a fuss of him. She is being polite. You know she's not interested in him.'

'Really? That is not the impression she gave.'

Emily caught his arm. 'Do you believe Madoc encouraged this?'

Robert heaved a deep breath and, to her relief, shook his head.

'No. To be fair he didn't. He was embarrassed, if anything. Especially when she asked about this fire.'

'What answer did he give?'

'He changed the subject, but she took his hand to examine his palm. He was most unwilling to open it, but she more or less insisted. It *was* scarred, and it ran up his arm. Quite a nasty scar it looked to me.'

'How did he do it? I wonder if your father knows? Did you discuss it with Madoc? Later, I mean?'

'No. He didn't want to talk about anything to do with his journeys around the Horn. Got quite waxy with me in fact.' He gave a mirthless smile. 'I shall not stay for dinner, Mother. I'll get a bite to eat in town, and see if I can get a ticket for the theatre.'

As she walked back into the drawing room Emily heaved a sigh. They had been so wrong to take it for granted that Lucy would marry Robert – but they had always enjoyed each other's company, had seemed so well-suited. Everyone had been completely bewildered when she chose someone else.

'Please, God, don't let it happen again,' she murmured.

Lucy had been staying in London with her aunt when she met the rakish Randolf Chilcott. Dashingly handsome, charming, he had swept her off her feet. Now Lucy was free again, and from the way she had behaved with Madoc today it appeared that marriage with Robert was not a certainty this time either. Looking back at her own life, she recalled the women who had been attracted to David – and Madoc closely resembled his father, though he had a more open, less brooding manner.

She frowned, again considering whether Robert's damaged arm might be the reason Lucy had looked elsewhere. Rob was going to reach that conclusion himself if it happened a second time. He had never confided his thoughts to her, but as far as she knew he'd never reproached Madoc for the injury. But she knew that Madoc held himself responsible; another rejection would further torment him. This could easily cause friction between her sons.

She heard David's voice in the hall and rushed out to him, flinging herself into his arms with a radiant smile. He hugged her briefly, giving her a light kiss and she caught his hand, led him into the drawing room and pushed the door shut behind them. As soon as they were alone he drew her into his arms, kissing her with passion, pressing her against him.

'Did you miss me?' Her eyes were dancing and he grinned.

It was a ritual they practised. She invariably asked this question, knowing the answer, but she still wanted his reply.

'I missed you.' Pulling her to him, he kissed her again, then released her reluctantly as they heard Madoc tapping on the door.

'Did I hear Father's voice?'

'Come in, Madoc!' David reached for the handle and pulled open the door. They both ignored Madoc's knowing grin. Although David did not reveal his emotions freely, he never concealed his love for his wife.

'Good trip?' Madoc asked.

'Very successful.' David pulled a bottle out of his leather bag. 'Try this.' He took some crystal glasses from the sideboard and began pouring out some pale amber liquid. 'I brought a few bottles of this Madeira wine back with me. See what you think of it.' He turned, holding the glass up to the light before passing it to Emily.

'There's something I forgot to tell you,' Madoc said. 'It went right out of my head and I never mentioned it to mother. An Indian man called round to the office as I was locking up one night. An old boy, dressed in the full gear, complete with turban.'

'An Indian? Who was that?' David turned, holding the second glass of wine, his interested gaze on Madoc.

'Gave his name as Aseem. He said he used to be a servant to Prince Lokesh and the Princess Meena.'

Emily saw David start, slopping wine over the carpet. She laughed, but her smile dropped away at his shocked expression.

'You know this man?' Her face was alert. 'What did you say his name was, Madoc?'

'Aseem.' Madoc appeared slightly nonplussed. Apparently he had noticed his father's reaction too. 'He was an amazing old boy, very impressive. Richly dressed in traditionally Indian attire.'

'Do you know this prince, David?'

'Yes.' David had regained his composure and smiled, but his eyes were guarded. 'I went to his house a few times when I was a young lieutenant.'

'That's who Aseem asked for, Lieutenant Morgan.'

'What did he want?' Emily asked, still studying her husband, who turned away, wiping the glass and pouring more wine. He seemed to take a long time before turning back.

'He didn't say. He's coming back . . . sometime,' Madoc said.

'There we are. If he returns we shall find out what he wants.' David didn't sound concerned but something was worrying him.

'Is there any cause for concern about this Indian fellow?' Madoc asked his father. They were on their own, having a post-prandial brandy and a cigar.

David blew a cloud of smoke into the air.

'What do you mean?' He met Madoc's gaze. Madoc gave a little shrug.

'I received an impression that you were . . . let's say surprised when I mentioned this Prince.'

His father took a gulp of his brandy and smiled wryly.

'Then your mother will have received that impression too, she reads me like a book.' He swirled the liquid in his glass, watching it. 'I *was* . . . a little . . . taken back.' His eyes caught Madoc's and his mouth twisted. He reached forward to tap the ash off his cigar.

'You *are* concerned about this man?'

David took a deep breath and put his glass down on the table. 'A little. But don't tell your mother that.'

'She already knows.' Madoc was also uneasy; his father dealt with everything confidently. That anything could disturb him was completely outside Madoc's experience. 'She asked me about this prince when you went upstairs to change for dinner.'

'I expected that. What exactly did Aseem say?' David looked intently at him.

'Very little. He was extremely reticent, he didn't answer any question I asked him. He seemed anxious to see you soon.'

His father pursed his lips, looking pensive.

'To tell you the truth, he is coming back at three o'clock on Monday. I thought it more expedient not to tell Mother. But he was so anxious that I did make an appointment,' Madoc explained.

'I see.'

'Look, you don't have to meet this man. I can. . . .' Madoc broke off as David threw him a sardonic glance. 'Forget I spoke . . . Look, can I do anything to help? You're not in some sort of trouble?'

David snorted. 'Not with the law, if that's what you mean.' He leaned back in his chair, staring into the distance before his eyes came back to Madoc. 'But there is . . . there could possibly be . . .' He broke off rubbing a hand over his mouth. When he moved it, Madoc was chilled by his father's bleak appearance.

'You don't want to tell me?'

'Not unless I have to. But thanks for the shoulder.' He gave a frosty grin and walked out, leaving Madoc unsettled.

Bethan came into the drawing room bearing a letter on a silver tray.

'Please, Miss Nia, the stable boy collected the post from Swansea and Mr La Velle said this letter is for you.'

'Thank you, Bethan.' Nia took the letter from the tray. 'I expect it is from my friend, Amy.'

'I don't think so, miss. You often get letters from her and this isn't her writing.'

Nia laughed. 'Fancy you knowing that. If it's not from Amy, then I wonder who it is from? This is most mystifying.' She studied the writing on the envelope, which seemed vaguely familiar, then realized that it was Albert's. He had written on the flyleaf of the book of poems he had given her – the one she had flung across the room!

He must have sent a reply to my letter, she thought, tearing it open. It was from Albert, rather a poignant letter, saying he understood why she was writing and would comply with her wishes not to visit – until he heard to the contrary.

'. . . My father was anxious for someone from the firm to go over to France for about six months. He wants to establish a new business connection to purchase wine there,' he continued. '. . . My French is reasonable, so I offered to go, thinking this separation would give us both a chance to reflect on things. I hold great hopes that you may have reconsidered your answer to me, by then. Perhaps you might even want to come over to France for a holiday – with your friend Amy perhaps? You would be both very welcome. I will write to you once I am set up *there. Please pass on my best wishes to your parents and I hope your mother will soon be recovered. And please, please write to me, dearest Nia. I will be eagerly waiting for your letter. . . .'*

Distressed, Nia dropped it into her lap. Poor Albert. He deserved someone better than her, she thought. He should have someone nice and normal, someone like Amy. She would suit him admirably. Amy? Why hadn't she thought of her before? Maybe she could stimulate their interest in one another? It would have to be later on though, not just at present. At least she now had a valid excuse to offer to her mother for not seeing Albert to accept his proposal. In the meanwhile, they could only hope that her health would improve and that she would come to accept Nia's decision.

'David. Why are you concerned about this Indian man?' Emily was already in bed and David sitting on the edge of it, pulling off his elastic-sided boots. She knelt up as she spoke to him and she stared at him, her expression strained. He clenched his jaw, returning her gaze silently. 'I know you are worried.'

'I am not worried. It was just such a shock hearing his name after all these years.' His voice was relaxed but she could see his eyes, which she knew so well, dark blue, swirling with clouded emotion. 'I will be interested to meet him after all these years.'

As he saw that she watched him a shutter seemed to drop over his eyes, and he gave her a reassuring smile. A knot of worry tightened her stomach. She was not deceived; she hadn't seen that shutter descend to conceal his thoughts since before they were married. David revealed little anxiety about anything unless it affected her or the family. But this man came from before she met David. Could it be something to involve the family in some way?

'Please tell me, David. We have never kept secrets from one another.' She put her arms tightly around his waist from behind and rested her cheek against his back. 'Don't you trust me?'

He gave a smothered groan and turned, pulling her towards him, nuzzling his lips in her neck.

'God, I love you, Emily.'

'As if I don't know that.' She rubbed her cheek against his shoulder. 'Do you want to tell me what's wrong? I can't bear you to be worried.'

'I will tell you. Just let me see this fellow first and sort it out, then I'll tell you. I promise.'

Her eyes travelled over his face and she kissed him gently.

'All right. But don't forget you've made a promise.' She had to be satisfied with that.

CHAPTER FIFTEEN

MUSIC filled the dining room in Craig y Mor as a quartet played gently in the background. The long windows were thrown open to the light evening and the heady fragrance of honeysuckle drifted into the room, mingling with the perfume from roses arranged in bowls along the centre of the table. The oil lamps had not been lit this evening, instead flames from the softer lighting of candles, in a myriad of silver candleholders and chandeliers above, danced off the silver and sparkled in the crystal glasses on the table.

Madoc's eyes had been drawn to Nia when she first arrived. She wore a gown of deep-green silk, the colour enhancing her exotic beauty. He admired the smooth tawny skin revealed by the low off-the-shoulder neckline of her bodice, the slender column of her neck. Her hooped skirt was flattened at the front, but still billowed out behind her, ending with a suggestion of a trail.

He picked up his glass and leaned back in his chair, studying the mixed company around the table. Nia was seated on his right-hand side. Sitting opposite him Lucy had Robert on one side of her, Tom on the other. Madoc could see Lucy's frosty glance on Nia, who appeared not to notice and continued talking animatedly to Robert who was responding with equal enthusiasm.

Lucy turned her attention to Tom.

'What did you say your profession was, Mr La Velle?'

'I am hoping to be a lawyer, Mrs Chilcott. I'm in a practice in Swansea. With Pritchard and Tudor. You may have heard of them.' He dabbed his mouth with his linen napkin.

'That is an extremely useful profession, Mr La Velle. Much safer than going off to sea.' She darted a look at Madoc.

'Much safer.' Tom gave his lazy smile, glancing at Madoc.

'Why didn't you try something like that?' Lucy asked Madoc.

'Never even considered it,' Madoc drawled, his attention more on Nia and his brother, who seemed to be getting on too well.

'You enjoy danger?'

Madoc took a sip of his wine. 'I never think about it.'

'But surely you must? After all, with a fire on board. . . .'

'What fire?' Nia's voice broke in from his side. 'Did you have a fire on board?'

Madoc smiled at her. 'It was nothing and soon extinguished.'

'But you were burned rescuing—' Lucy began.

'Please, Lucy. Don't let's bring that subject up again.' He spoke softly, but there was authority in his voice, causing both Robert and Nia to regard him with surprise and Lucy's eyes to widen. This was a side to Madoc that they had not encountered before.

'Perhaps that is why you are not returning to sea?' Lucy's voice was deceptively innocent.

Madoc's head went up, his eyes blazing an emerald green.

'Are you calling me a coward?'

'I say, old man,' Robert began to protest, but Lucy put her hand on his arm.

'No. It is all right, Robert. I'm sorry, Madoc. I didn't mean . . .' Her eyes filled with tears and she rushed from the table.

'God!' Madoc whispered under his breath. He gritted his teeth, shaking his head.

'Did you have to upset her like that?' Robert glowered at him, rising to his feet.

'She did rather sound as though she was . . .' Nia's voice broke off uneasily as she saw Madoc's grim face.

Emily looked down from the top of the table with surprise.

'Is Lucy all right, Robert?'

'I'm just going to see, Mother.' He cast another disgusted look at Madoc and stalked out after Lucy.

Nia and Tom sat in uncomfortable silence, intent on cutting up their food. Madoc flung down his napkin and pushed his chair back.

'Excuse me, please.' He strode from the room as the rest of the guests looked over with surprise.

He stormed out through the back of the house, leaving through the servants' door. He went over to the stables, waving the stable boy away as he came towards him, and took a saddle down from the rack himself. He threw it over the animal as Nia appeared in the stable doorway, holding her skirt well up in both hands, away from the straw and mud. Madoc looked up at her, unsmiling.

'She is just the same bitch she always was,' Nia said.

'I'm just wondering if other people are thinking the same thing,' he pointed out.

'Don't be ridiculous! She said it quite deliberately; she wanted to rouse you. You were not paying her enough attention.'

He paused, his hand still on the horse's saddle, and looked at Nia in the lamplight.

'Why do you say that? You weren't listening to our conversation.'

Her eyes flicked away from his.

'No. But I did notice that she kept asking you questions and you barely replied to her. Were you trying to do the same thing with her?'

'The same thing? I don't know what you mean.'

'Trying to get her attention?'

Her dark eyes were questioning as he studied her; her spicy perfume filled the air around them and he longed to catch her in his arms again, to bury his face in those tempting breasts. *Nia, why would I want any other woman's attention?* But he did not express this question. He'd bared his feelings too freely already, now he had to be sure they were returned before he did so again . . . and he was not at all sure that Nia did return his love.

'Madoc. You're not going to let her think she has the better of you?' Nia asked. 'If you ride off now, she has.'

Madoc sucked in his cheek between his teeth, considering her words. 'All right.' He began taking the saddle off the horse again then bellowed for the stable boy to finish the job for him.

Lucy and Robert were seated in their places at the table. Lucy looked across at Madoc as they sat down.

'I'm sorry, Madoc. I didn't mean to upset you. I was only teasing. I didn't understand how strongly you feel about it.' She fluttered her fan provocatively as Madoc returned his attention to his now cold food. Aware of Nia casting him a sideways, assessing glance, he recalled his brother's words: *Nia regarded Lucy as a rival.* If only she thought enough of him to feel like that now, he thought morosely. Well at least Albert wasn't with her this evening. He wondered whether she would marry him.

When the party rose from the table the little quartet engaged for the evening began playing again, the pleasant sound drifting amongst the guests as they wandered between rooms, conservatory and garden or stood talking in little groups. Madoc was standing with Nia and Tom when Lucy, trailed by Robert, came up and threaded her arm possessively through Madoc's.

'I want to tell you how truly sorry I am, Madoc,' she said.

'I assure you, Lucy, there is no need. It is forgotten.' He tried unsuccessfully to free his arm.

'But you will show me the garden, won't you, Madoc?' Her eyelashes fluttered at him.

'I expect Rob will want . . .' he began, glancing at his brother, but Robert looked away, turning his back on them, addressing Nia.

'Will you walk in the garden with me, Nia?' Robert asked. 'We've had some additions to the artificial lake since you were here.'

Nia looked surprised, but could hardly refuse. Madoc glowered, but could do nothing other than escort Lucy.

'The lake is just perfect, your mother has such admirable taste,' Lucy gushed. 'And the garden has been extended greatly since I was here last. It must be years since.'

'Many.'

'You've changed too. But I always did like you, Madoc.'

He smiled, shaking his head.

'You never liked me.'

'I did. Truly.' She gave his arm a little squeeze and obviously realizing the inflexibility of the muscles beneath his jacket, squeezed it again, pulling an admiring face. 'You are so hard and strong, Madoc,' she whispered, snuggling up against his arm. 'So manly. I can understand you saving a man's life.'

Madoc went cold. This time he was certain she was flirting with him. By now he was used to women being attracted to him, but Lucy was his brother's fiancée; she should never be talking to him in this manner.

'A woman would always feel safe with you, Madoc. I know you could make a woman happy.'

Again he tried to ease his arm out of her grasp, but she clung tighter. Apart from actually wrenching himself free he was helpless.

'Lucy. You've promised to marry Robert,' he protested.

'I told him I would consider it. I made no definite promise.'

'He believed you did, Lucy.'

'I can't believe how much you resemble your father now, Madoc.

And I have never known a man adore his wife as much as he does your mother. Of course, she is still very beautiful.'

'She is.' He was relieved to change the subject and looked around hopefully for Robert. Seeing him sitting on a bench talking to Nia he began guiding Lucy towards them, but her feet dragged and she pointed in the opposite direction, towards the lanterns suspended in the little arbour of trees and shrubs.

'Aren't they lovely. May I see?' She took his hand, pulling him towards them. 'It's like fairyland.' She wandered further into the trees. 'Are they Chinese lanterns?'

'I believe so. I think Mother also has some Chinese fireworks arranged for later on.'

'I hope they are not firecrackers? I hate firecrackers, they frighten me.' She gripped his arm again with both hands. 'But I would never be afraid with you, Madoc.' She snuggled up to him, rubbing her head against his chest. She lifted her face. 'You may kiss me, Madoc. No one can see us here.'

He swallowed hard, looking down at her delicate features, very tempted to kiss those dewy lips.

'Lucy . . .' He groped for a reason to escape. 'I'll go and find out about the fireworks.' He almost managed to extract his arm from her grasp, but she stood head down, her shoulders drooping. Hearing a little sob escape her he hesitated.

'I love you, Madoc,' she whispered. 'Please, don't scorn me.'

He jerked away from her, dumbfounded, feeling like a traitor.

'Lucy you don't mean that. You're going to be sorry you said—'

She whirled away from him and raced back to the house as those she passed turned to watch her again in surprise. Robert shot up from the bench and stormed over, Nia close on his heels.

'What's wrong with Lucy now?' he demanded.

'How the hell do I know.' Exasperated, Madoc scowled at his brother. 'Stupid female,' he muttered.

'Were you being lecherous with her? Here in the trees.'

'No!' Madoc's temper was rising. 'I most certainly was not!'

'If you did—'

'I said I didn't . . . but what if I had?' Madoc taunted him. He was furious with Lucy and Robert was the obvious choice on whom to vent his fury.

Robert swung an incensed punch at Madoc who never even

attempted to dodge it. It connected on Madoc's cheek with a crunch, jerking his head back and knocking his teeth together.

'Feel better now?' Madoc jeered. 'Or do you want another go?' He held both hands out sideways away from him, invitingly.

'You swine, Madoc . . .'

'Stop it, Rob!' Nia pulled at his arm. 'Madoc wouldn't do that to *you*.' Her eyes met Madoc's glittering ones. 'Would you?'

'Think what you wish.' Rigid, Madoc glared at them both.

'I'm going to find Lucy.' Rob was struggling to recover his poise. He hesitated. 'I . . . I'm sorry, Madoc.'

Madoc turned his back on him and after a slight hesitation Robert stalked off. Madoc snorted, running a distracted hand through his hair, leaving it tumbling wildly over his forehead.

'Come and sit on the bench.' Nia took his arm. 'Come on! People over there are beginning to look at us.'

'Did anyone see what happened?' Madoc glanced around with concern, not wishing to embarrass his parents.

'I don't think so. I think they were watching Lucy.' She gave a little laugh. 'But your name is going to be mud now.'

'That'll be nothing new.' He fingered his cheek and grinned. 'Rob packs a good punch.'

A frog began croaking further along the path, then suddenly dived into the lake, leaving shimmering concentric rings.

'If you didn't proposition Lucy why did you let him hit you?' She must have realized he hadn't tried to dodge the blow.

'Did I?'

'You know you did.' She sank down on to the bench.

'I was just so furious with . . .' He broke off, shaking his head. 'And I felt guilty. Though I don't know why I should.'

She patted the seat alongside her.

'So what happened?'

He shook his head. 'I don't wish to talk about it.'

'It was the other way around . . . wasn't it? From what Rob suggested?' She was studying him perceptively.

He flashed her a calculating glance but remained silent, unwilling to admit it. Nia could always read him like a book.

'Why protect her? Everyone thinks she is so perfect.'

'But I would never want Rob to know.' Madoc was horrified at the thought. 'The man loves her. . . .'

'And you don't?'

He dropped his eyes away from her scrutiny, she saw too much. Perhaps it was better to let her believe that he did – for the time being. Leaning forward he put his elbows on his knees.

'She obviously returns your love . . . surely Robert should be told.' Her voice was distant.

'No!' He jerked up. 'She loves Robert, I'm sure she does. She was probably trying to lead me on to amuse herself . . . as she used to when we were young.'

Nia shook her head. 'I don't think so. You don't realize what an attractive man you have become, Madoc Morgan.'

'Don't be ridiculous. And you mustn't tell Rob,' he urged.

'I won't promise that. If I feel . . .'

'You must.' His voice rose and he sprang to his feet. 'Promise me, Nia. I wouldn't have admitted it otherwise.'

'Actually, you didn't.' Her voice was cool. 'All right, I promise . . . but I might speak to you again about this,' she warned him. 'I'm going to see what's happened.'

He watched her erect figure cross the lawn, her head held high, her movements graceful and smooth, no pretence or coyness in her bearing. He noticed a few heads turn to watch her; she certainly was dazzling.

I don't care what she looks like, I've always loved her. But I must know how she feels about me before I tell her. I can't take her response for granted, as I did before.

He lit a cigar as he walked along the path, around the lake, stopping to smoke it, his foot propped up on a stone urn. Thank goodness they could be natural with each other again. They appeared to have got over that awkwardness between them since he'd kissed her. He felt a stirring of desire as he relived that moment, longing to kiss her again until she begged for breath. He smothered a groan at the idea. It was so good to be with her.

I can tell her my innermost thoughts and know they are safe, he thought with a rush of tenderness towards her. *I'll start all over again, make her love me. Tomorrow. I'll call on her again tomorrow.*

He looked up to see Nia running back towards him.

'Madoc!' There was urgency in her voice. She reached him slightly breathless because of the tight stays she wore for fashion's sake. 'That heartless minx has just told Robert she will not marry him!'

'What?' Madoc's skin crawled, his stomach lurching. 'She would-n't—'

'She just has.'

'Why, for God's sake? How do you know?' He flung his cigar into the lake.

'I saw Rob going out. He was very edgy and bitter, very aloof. He said to tell you you have won, she wants to marry you!'

'What? How could she do that? God, why the devil didn't I take another ship? I should never have stayed at home.'

'Madoc. Did you mention marriage to her?'

'Only to remind her that she was betrothed to my brother.' His tone was caustic. 'I've tried to distance myself, tried to draw Rob to her each time she took my arm . . . though he has not helped.'

'What do you mean?'

'On more than one occasion he has turned his back and walked away, leaving me no choice but to escort her.'

'Yes, he did that this evening.' Nia's voice was thoughtful. 'It's almost as though he was testing you . . . or Lucy?'

'It wouldn't enter his head. He is besotted with her.'

'Well, I hope you're prepared.' Her voice was suddenly remote. 'She is coming towards us right this minute.'

'Nia. Don't go! Stay here!'

Nia raised her chin, her expression haughty.

'Am I to chaperon you with that little minx?'

Lucy came up, and darted a glance at Nia.

'Would you mind leaving us, please, Miss La Velle?' She gave Nia a sugary smile. 'I wish to talk to Madoc . . . alone.'

Nia hesitated, glancing at Madoc.

'Please, Madoc,' Lucy said.

His mouth tightened and he turned his head away.

'Please. Won't you let me make amends?'

His eyes flicked back to Lucy as Nia walked slowly away.

'How can you possibly make amends to Robert?' he retorted. 'How could you tell him you are going to marry me? We are certainly not getting married; you know that's not true.'

'But Madoc. I know you have always loved me.' Those violet eyes regarded him appealingly.

'You're wrong, Lucy. It's Robert who loves you.' He was wondering how he was going to reverse this impossible situation. Robert must not be rejected a second time. 'You have always been the only woman for Robert. He idolizes you, Lucy.'

'I do know that . . . but don't you see? I've already lost one man whom I loved. Now I must seek happiness wherever I can find it.'

'Robert will make you happy, Lucy.'

'But you've always loved me. It is true, isn't it?'

He shook his head, unable starkly to say: *No. I don't love you.* She was like a beautiful butterfly, so delicate and fragile, he was unwilling to hurt her.

'Lucy, I told you, I am in love with another woman.' He leapt to his feet. 'And I appeal to you not to reject Robert's love for—'

'And I beg you not to reject my love,' she gasped, giving a little sob. The light of spluttering torches near the lakeside revealed two huge tears sliding down her face.

Madoc turned away, not wishing to witness her pleading expression but she stood up and he tensed as she slid her hand through his arm again.

'Please. Don't let people see me crying,' she whispered, drawing him towards the trees again. 'I am so unhappy, Madoc.'

He stopped near the edge, angry and rigid.

'Look Lucy—'

'I do love you, Madoc. You stir me in the same way that Randolf did. In a . . . *certain* way.' Her eyes flicked up to his face.

He sucked in a breath.

'And I am certain you feel the same about me. Do you love me? Please answer me, Madoc.'

'I've already told you, Lucy. . . .' There was an expectant pause whilst he considered what reply he could give without offence. 'No, Lucy. I can't truly say I do,' he managed eventually. 'I don't love you. I think you are very beautiful but . . .'

'You are not telling me the truth,' she broke in.

'Lucy, it is the truth.'

'I appreciate the unselfish way you are protecting your brother's interests. But my mind is made up. When I take another husband, it will be you and no other.'

He didn't want Lucy. Had not the slightest wish to marry her – but how on earth could any man humiliate a woman by bluntly telling her that? He felt trapped, enmeshed in a net, and the more he wriggled the further he was bound.

'I will repeat, I love another—'

'You don't mean Nia?' Her voice was outraged.

Yes, he wanted to yell. *Yes, I do.* But he wasn't going to tell Lucy that before he told Nia.

'That is my business. I cannot marry you, Lucy. And I'll be going back to sea.' His voice was curt.

'I was married to a soldier.'

'And look what happened.' Madoc jumped on it. 'What if I were drowned? You wouldn't . . .'

She darted forward, winding both arms tightly around his waist, squeezing herself against him. Pressed close to her, he was very aware of those smooth breasts in her low-necked dress, and because her fashionable skirt was flattened in the front, she was pushed up against him. In spite of his intentions, he felt himself become aroused by the nearness of her soft body, the headiness of her perfume, and he jerked back out of her arms. But having been married, she was obviously fully aware of his arousal.

'You can't tell me you don't want me, Madoc.' She gave a knowing smile, her eyes flicking down for a brief moment at his trousers. 'I can see you do . . . just as much as I want you.'

He swallowed hard, felt himself blush, something he hadn't done since his youth.

'I don't want you, Lucy,' he muttered. 'I love someone else.'

'Then why won't you tell me her name?'

He shook his head.

'I believe you are making it up. And Robert will want me to be happy. It will be all right, you'll see.'

'I speak the truth, Lucy. And it will never be all right.'

'Where did Rob get to?' Emily enquired. Their last guest had left and she had come out into the conservatory. 'I haven't seen him for ages. Do you know where he is, Madoc?'

Madoc was slumped in an armchair, gulping down French wine, a half-empty carafe on the table alongside him. He cast a bleary look up at his mother and stood up, swaying slightly.

'I . . . don' know,' he slurred.

She flashed him a sharp look.

'You are inebriated. How dare you get into that condition here. How could you?'

'Sorry, M . . . other.' Madoc made an effort to pull himself together, standing up straighter. He was aware of both his mother and father regarding him with consternation.

'How did you get that awful bruise on your face? Did you fall over?' Her face was accusing.

David strode over and gripped his arm with hard fingers.

'Come on, man! What's got into you?'

Madoc swayed slightly towards his father.

'I'll tell you wh . . . 's . . . wrong. Lucy tol' Rob she's . . . she's not going to marry him,' he managed to get out.

Emily's face blanched.

'How do you know?'

'Because . . . because . . . stupid woman . . . said . . . sh'wants . . . t'marry me.' His face twisted. 'I tried . . . tell her. Don' know wha' . . . to do 'bout it.' He looked at his father, shaking his head.

There was a lethal silence, both of them staring at him.

'Rob knows this?' David asked harshly.

Madoc gave an exaggerated nod. His mother sank into a chair.

'Did you ask her to marry you?'

' 'Course not. Wha' d'you think I am? But Rob wo' believe it.'

'Come on!' David grabbed his arm, and led him to the door. 'We'll talk about this in the morning, when you're sober,' he said when they reached the hall. 'If this is true I can quite understand why you got drunk.' He began guiding Madoc on to the first step.

'I don' need a nursemai . . .' Madoc shook off his father's arm. Pulling himself erect, he held firmly on to the banister.

'Maybe it will all work out.' David's tone did not sound reassured as he watched his son.

CHAPTER SIXTEEN

MADOC opened his eyes and immediately shut them again, trying to block out the sunlight streaming in through the window. He turned on to his other side and groaned as his head began pounding again. He swallowed, pulling a face at the vile taste in his mouth. *Why did I drink so much?* Then his mind jerked into full awareness.

Oh God! Rob! he remembered. He sat up, wincing, clasping a hand to his head as he pulled back the bedclothes and put his feet on the floor. *What am I going to do about Rob?* he agonized, sitting on the edge of the bed. *What on earth am I going to say to him?* There was a tap on his bedroom door.

'Just a minute,' he called hoarsely, reaching for a sheet, not wanting that forward maid to come prancing in and find him naked. 'Who's there?'

'Your father.'

'Come in.'

'Good morning, Madoc.' His father studied his face with a hint of sympathy. 'You probably have no wish to discuss anything right now, but I'm afraid we have no choice.'

'I know that.' Madoc nodded, grimacing slightly as his head hammered. 'Let's sit down.' He pulled a sheet around him and staggered over to the window, bringing another chair with him for his father.

'Can you remember what you told us last night? David asked.

'I wish I could say no.' Madoc's face twisted. 'But I can remember only too well.'

'You told us Lucy said she wants to marry you . . . is that correct?'

'Yes.'

'But you didn't propose to her? At least that's what you indicated last night.'

'Of course not! Apart from her being Rob's . . . well . . . betrothed, I don't want to marry the blasted woman.' His voice rose slightly. 'How do you tell a woman that?'

'Difficult.' David's eyebrows rose. 'You tried?'

'Yes. Not in those words. I said something about her being betrothed to Rob, that Rob loved her. I told her I'm in love with someone else. But she insisted I was making it up . . . for Rob's sake.'

'So she believes you agreed to this . . . let us say . . . betrothal?'

'Like hell, I did!' Madoc protested. 'I definitely said no. I told her I couldn't marry her. Oh God! Rob will think it's my fault.'

'Why did she get the impression that you were interested in her? We must understand, Madoc.'

Madoc leaned back tilting his chair off the floor on to two legs, staring up at the ceiling.

'Madoc?'

His chair came down with a bump and he grimaced, putting a hand to his head again.

'You believe me, don't you?'

'Do you need to ask? But we all have to ask ourselves how she got this impression.'

Madoc groaned. 'She said I've always been in love with her.'

'You gave that impression at one time.' David smiled grimly.

'Maybe I did once. I suppose I imagined I was . . . when I was young. But not now. Lucy's beautiful, but not for me. . . . Never.'

'There is someone else? You weren't making it up?' His father's frank gaze was on him and Madoc gave a twisted smile. 'Perhaps I can hazard a guess. . . ?'

'Who else?'

'I thought as much, by the way you looked at her when they arrived. She's a lovely—'

'I don't care! It wouldn't matter to me what she looked like.' Madoc sighed. 'She's just . . . Nia. She'll never really change.'

His father gave an understanding nod.

'You say Lucy actually told Robert their betrothal is off?'

'So Nia said. I had no idea Lucy was going to say anything to Robert. Nia saw Rob going out, she said he was very upset. I never saw him after he left us by the lake. He was already riled up with me . . .' Madoc broke off, deciding he could hardly explain to his father that Lucy had more or less made advances to him.

'That's how you got that bruise? From Robert?' David's eyebrows rose. 'God! That's not like him, he must have been riled.'

'He was. But I don't want him hurt again. And he'll never be able to understand ... I'm sure I wouldn't be able to.' He ran distracted hands through his tumbled hair. 'What a mess.'

'I agree. What are you going to do about it? You do intend making the situation clear to Lucy?'

'Yes! Though how in hell, I have no idea. She just won't listen. And what about Robert? How can I make it clear to him?'

'Unfortunately I don't think you will. If you want to reassure him you'll have to convince him that Lucy has changed her mind ... again. Has decided she wishes to marry him after all ... and not you.'

Madoc perked up.

'You think he might? If I can convince Lucy that I don't want to marry her?' He pulled a face at the idea. His father allowed himself a grin.

'You shouldn't let yourself get into these situations. Were you perhaps a trifle amorous towards her?'

'No! You might say the opposite. She ...' He broke off with an intake of breath.

David's eyes widened, then he gave an understanding grin.

'I see. Well ... I must admit that once happened to me too. With another young woman, not with your mother,' he supplied hastily, seeing Madoc's questioning expression.

'Then at least you can understand the situation.'

'When are you seeing Lucy again?'

'I never want to see her again! But I suppose I'll have to in the circumstances. Not today though, I heard her say she was going on holiday today, with her mother. To stay with relatives in Bath. I don't know when she'll be back.' He thumped his fist down on his knee. 'The stupid woman. I want it all cleared up now.'

'At least you'll have plenty of time to work out what you are going to say ... to her ... and perhaps more important, to Robert.'

Madoc nodded glumly.

'It's Nia I want to talk to. I don't know what her feelings are about it, or towards me, she didn't seem very interested in me, to tell you the truth.'

David raised an eyebrow.

'You think she will accept this fellow Albert?'

'I don't know. This damned episode won't help, will it? What does Mother think about it? Does she think it's my fault?'

'I ... don't think so. She did question whether it could have happened because you drank too much. . . .' Seeing Madoc's horrified expression he went on quickly: 'But she understands that you would never deliberately hurt Robert. None of us wants that.' He got to his feet and walked towards the door. 'I'll try to explain to your mother that it is a misunderstanding, that you did not propose to Lucy. At least I can save you that ordeal.'

Madoc had not had such a hangover for years. Eventually surfacing he went downstairs.

'Is my brother at home?' Madoc asked Sîan, who was crossing the hall.

'No, sir.' She gave him a flirtatious look from under her lashes. 'He came home earlier, but after washing and changing he went out again.'

'Did he happen to mention where he was going?'

'I believe he said he was visiting, sir.'

Madoc had to be satisfied with that. His parents knew nothing more than that Robert had come home and had gone out again without speaking to either of them.

Robert strolled in around midday, coming into the main drawing-room where the family had gathered before luncheon.

'Good-morning . . . or is it afternoon? Mother, Father.' He gave a slight jerk of his head at Madoc and greeted his mother with a light kiss on the cheek. 'I hope you did not mind my leaving the party early?' Emily looked up at him anxiously, but he appeared to be his normal self and quite in control of his emotions. 'I was finding certain female company rather wearing, to be truthful.'

'Were you? I . . . I see,' Emily returned as Madoc hastily held the *Cambrian* newspaper up in front of his face.

'I have been doing some serious thinking.' Robert went over to the sideboard and poured himself a sherry as the family waited for him to continue. 'I am not at all sure I want to marry Lucy.' Madoc lowered the paper to regard his brother more clearly and Robert looked over at him, giving a brief smile. 'That should please you, Madoc,' he said pleasantly.

Madoc said nothing, nonplussed at this turn of events. How should he manage this? he brooded. After already deciding to convince Robert that Lucy had had second thoughts, he could hardly tell him that he was not interested in the woman. That would defeat the whole plan. He put the paper back in front of his face.

'Where have you been this morning?' Emily hazarded. 'I believe you came home before breakfast and then went out again.'

'To tell you the truth, Mother, I went to pay Nia a visit. I thoroughly enjoyed her company last night and I am to meet her again this afternoon. We are going for a trip up the river. A nice day to be on the water.'

Madoc dropped the paper again, staring at his brother. Did he understand how Madoc felt about Nia? Was he doing this deliberately?

Madoc had admitted to an interest in her, but Robert could not know the extent of his feelings when he didn't even realize it himself. Their father had guessed, but he hadn't told anyone, not even Nia. And as far as Robert was concerned, he had always wanted Lucy.

'You don't mind, old man?' Robert looked at Madoc. 'Not that it matters anyway.' He gave a sardonic grin.

Madoc swallowed hard, fighting back the retort which rose to his lips. Seeing his father dart a glance his way, Madoc walked out, unable to remain with Robert without giving the game away. Robert must not find out at this stage, he vowed. He must clear things with Lucy first. The infuriating woman, why did she have to go to Bath now? He could visit her, he pondered, scratching his chin.

He wandering aimlessly out towards the stables where he found Idris, the groom, talking to Sîan. She fluttered her lashes coyly at him.

'Good morning, sir.' She dropped him a curtsy. She was smiling, her bold eyes still on his face as he nodded acknowledgement.

'Good morning, sir,' Idris echoed. 'Are you looking for a mount?'

Sîan gave a suggestive snigger and Madoc frowned, glaring his disapproval at her.

'If you please, Idris.'

'Before luncheon, sir?'

'Yes. I think I'll give luncheon a miss.'

'Lunch! Goodness! I'll have to go. I'll be late.' Sîan hurried away, deliberately swinging her hips, making her hooped skirts swing from side to side as Idris watched her admiringly.

Because Madoc had been away for so much of the time ever since he was a boy, on occasion Idris had difficulty in placing him as one of the masters of the house. Idris still remembered back to the time when he'd been a stable boy, sitting on the yard wall talking to Madoc. A boy always in hot water.

'Pretty, isn't she?' Idris turned to look at Madoc.

'She knows it too well.' Madoc turned towards the stables.

'She's yours for the taking . . . sir,' Idris said slyly. 'You're a lucky sod . . . really soft on you, she is.'

Madoc spun back, his face hardening.

'That's not my inclination, Idris. I don't hold with seducing the maids.' His tone was harsh.

Idris's smile dropped away.

'Sorry, Mr Madoc, sir,' he stuttered 'I didn't mean any harm. I was just thinking—'

'And *I* think we'll leave it there.' Madoc's expression was wintry. 'My horse!'

'Yes, sir.' Idris scuttled into the stables as Madoc waited outside, his mouth turned down.

God! I hope he doesn't believe I would do that, he thought, unsettled, remembering Nia's words about the subject.

Madoc rode over to Mead Rise stables, arriving just as the family was sitting down to luncheon.

'That's all right,' Madoc told the maid who was about to go in to announce him. 'Don't disturb them, I'll wander around outside for a while.'

The maid came hurrying out to him as he leaned on the fence.

'Sir. Mrs La Velle is asking if you would like to join them for luncheon?'

He hesitated. 'Is Miss Nia at home?'

'Yes, sir. But she is not dining with the family; she had a bite to eat earlier. She has gone up to change. She is going for a cruise up the river.'

'Then please tell Mrs La Velle I will wait here, thank you. You might tell Miss Nia I am here,' he added with a smile.

'Yes, sir.' She beamed back at him, bobbing a curtsy, her face flushing a rosy pink.

He wandered into the stables where a young lad was polishing tackle, the smell from the pot of beeswax alongside him strong in the air. When he saw Madoc he leapt to his feet, touching his temple.

'Did you want to see the 'orses, sir? I'll call—'

'Don't disturb yourself, lad; there is no need to call anyone. I'm not in a hurry.'

The boy eyed him uncertainly, the harness and cloth still in his hands.

'You carry on, I'll talk to you as you work.' Madoc pulled up a wooden box and sat near to where the boy was working.

'Oh, sir. Don't sit on that!' The boy was horrified. 'I'll fetch you a proper chair, like.'

'Don't worry yourself. I am quite comfortable on this. How long have you been here?' he added, as the boy seemed about to dispute his words.

'Only a few months, sir.' His eyes wandered lovingly over the horses in the stalls. 'I loves workin' with 'em, I always wanted to, like, but never thought I'd 'ave the chance.'

'Well you have come to the right stables, Mr La Velle is the best.'

'I knows that, sir,' the boy said with fervour. 'He's wonderful with the 'orses.'

'Where are you from? The village?'

'No, sir. From Swansea. I'm a norphan. My uncle put me into sweepin' chimneys but Mr La Velle bought out my indentures from my master.' He gave a chirpy grin. 'This is much better.'

'I'm sure it is.' Madoc's face was serious as he thought about all those other captive children climbing up chimneys, getting smothered with soot. 'How did he realize your interest in horses?'

' 'Cause I was givin' one a drink. In a coal-cart, 'e was ... and 'e was awful 'ot.'

Madoc grinned. 'Good for you, lad. What's your name, by the way?'

'Bertie, sir,' he said, grinning back. 'It turned out good for me anyway.'

'Good afternoon.' said a voice. Madoc looked up to see Nia and hastily rose to his feet. 'I didn't expect to see you here. I thought you would be visiting Lucy.' Her voice was aloof.

'Shall we go outside?' His glance flickered to the boy, who was listening with interest.

'Very well, though I haven't long.' She flashed him an enquiring look. 'Did you know I am to go on a river trip with Robert?'

'Yes.'

'I found he's uncommonly nice, when you get to know him. I've discovered I enjoy being in the company of gentlemen.' She gave a mischievous smile at Madoc's glower.

'Do you?' Madoc grunted.

'And I never realized how charming Robert can be because I was always taking your side against him. . . .' She gave a little laugh, as though amazed at such naïvety. 'He seemed to keep himself remote from me when we were children and I never had that much to do with him . . . apart from him bossing us about.' She pulled a face. 'Now you seem to be the one bossing people about.'

'Me? What do you mean?' He was flabbergasted. 'I don't boss—'

'Well, you put Lucy in her place last night.'

'I did *what*? When? I don't remember.'

'When you virtually told her to shut up.'

'I certainly did no . . . Oh! I see what you mean.' He was taken back. 'I didn't think I was putting her in her place.'

'We all did. Most impressive. It showed you're used to giving orders. I believe Lucy liked it though.' She laughed. 'I think she likes men to be the strong, commanding type.'

Madoc pondered on her words.

'And you don't?' His glance returned to Nia, hung on her lips as he recalled again that kiss.

She evaded his remark.

'I believe she goes for the dare-devil types too. Tell me about the fire.'

'Not you as well? Why does everyone want to know about the bl . . . dashed fire?' he growled.

'Because, apparently, you were a hero.'

'Rubbish. I pulled someone out, but they would have done the same for me.' His face was disgusted.

'That is a typical Madoc remark. How did it start?'

'We must have had wet coal underneath. The top layer certainly wasn't wet. Both Captain Davies and I examined the load. The dealer must have put dry coal on top of wet. That's extremely dangerous.'

'Why would that cause a fire?' She looked puzzled. 'I would have thought . . .'

'Spontaneous combustion.'

'I see.' She nodded, without understanding. 'You managed to put it out though? Were there problems?'

'We put it out.'

'But there were problems?'

As he shrugged he noticed Robert walk into the yard. Madoc tensed as he came over. Robert raised his eyebrows.

'Madoc. What are you doing here?' he drawled. 'I had expected you to be at Lucy's . . . But of course. She was going away this morning, I must admit I had forgotten. So you decided you would visit Nia instead?'

Madoc saw Nia flash him a searching glance, her chin lifting and her mouth turning down.

'Not at all. I came to see Nia bec—'

'Never mind, Madoc. Another time,' Nia broke in. 'I'm afraid we'll have to leave you now. We don't want to miss our steamer. I'm sure you would find it very dull.' There was ice in her voice. She beamed at Robert. 'Have you brought the gig, Robert? Or shall I ask Bertie to get ours out?'

'No need. I have ours. Whenever you are ready, my dear.'

With a nod at Madoc Robert tucked Nia's arm into his own and they turned away leaving Madoc glowering after them. Why the hell was Rob taking Nia out? he wondered. He had never been interested in her before. And worse still, Nia had made it obvious that she was thoroughly enjoying his company. She seemed happier with Rob than she was with himself, he reflected.

CHAPTER SEVENTEEN

MADOC had another restless night deliberating and worrying about Nia, Lucy and Robert, and also about his father. The Indian would turn up on the morrow, he reflected. He expected that his father was thinking about the same thing. He was up early on Monday morning but when he went for breakfast he discovered that his father had already left and that Robert had taken the early steam packet on a business trip to Newport. David was to have gone but he had arranged for Robert to go instead. Madoc wondered whether he wanted him out of the way before this Indian man arrived.

Unable to concentrate in the office, Madoc watched his father covertly all the morning. He certainly was preoccupied, unable to settle down to work. He noticed him light a second cigar, a habit he rarely indulged in, sucking in great gulps of smoke. Seeing Madoc's eyes on him he walked towards the door.

'I'm popping to the Mackworth.' He offered no explanation.

'The cap'n is in a mood today,' Russel said. 'He nearly bit my head off just now.'

'Did he?' Madoc said, but he had already noticed.

'It's not like him unless he has good reason. Did you see that that old Indian fellow was hanging around again?'

'When?' Madoc was suddenly alert.

'This morning. I saw him and I was going to call you, but the next minute he'd vanished.'

'I didn't see him.' Madoc wondered where he was gone. Evidently he was making sure that David was here before he turned up for their appointment.

'I feel as if he's watching the place. I find him a bit spooky.'

Madoc laughed. 'Spooky? You need to get around the world a bit, Russel.'

'It's all right for you. You've been off everywhere on your travels . . .'

'Nothing stopping you.'

'Suppose not.' A thoughtful look crept over Russel's face. 'To tell you the truth I have been thinking about it. I'd like to talk to you about it sometime.'

'Are you serious?' Madoc was surprised. 'We'll talk about it over a pint of ale sometime, if you like.'

'I'd like that. Though I think my young lady would murder me if I did go. You'll be captain on your next trip, won't you? Would you have room on your ship for me?'

Madoc regarded him pensively.

'If you really mean it . . . but give it plenty of consideration. It might be good pay but it's damned hard work, mind, with not much comfort.' He laughed. 'That's a misleading statement. With no comfort. We'll talk it through.'

David had not returned by midday and instead of going off for his luncheon Madoc strolled down to the wharf, ostensibly to talk to a few sailors on the Morgan ships in dock, but in reality keeping a look out for the Indian. His father reappeared as Madoc was becoming concerned that he would not be back in time, and was in his office when the Indian returned. Aseem came into the big outer office where Madoc was hanging around waiting for him. He walked over to Madoc, salaaming.

'Good afternoon, sahib. Captain Morgan is here?'

'Yes. He is back. He's expecting you.'

'Will he be seeing me now?'

'I'll just ask if he is ready for you,' Madoc answered hastily.

He walked along the corridor and entered his father's office, pulling the door to behind him.

'He's here. Do you want him in yet?' he asked as David looked up.

'Yes. Of course,' said David smoothly, but Madoc was aware of the slight lines of worry etched around his mouth, making him look older than usual. 'Show him in, please.'

'Do you want. . . ?' Madoc broke off as David lifted his brows.

'I think I can manage on my own, thank you, Madoc.'

Madoc walked back to the outer office and beckoned to Aseem

from the door.

'This way, Mr Aseem.' As he spoke, Madoc was startled to see a woman appear from behind the Indian. Although a voluminous cloak enveloped her, he could see she was an Indian woman, her flowing sari was just visible, her head was bowed modestly, her hand was holding up the cloak to cover most of her face. He sucked in a breath. God! Was this why his father was worried?

Aseem ushered the woman ahead of him towards Madoc, her anklets tinkling as she came.

'May I present the Princess Charu, Mr Morgan.'

A trace of musky perfume teased his nostrils as the woman raised her head slightly without meeting his glance. Madoc gasped, his own eyes widening when they caught sight of hers. They were a vivid, arresting blue, the exact colour of his father's, the iridescent sapphire and silver threaded sari enhancing their colour, startling against her perfect tawny skin.

'Mr Morgan.' She performed a salaam.

'Princess.' His voice was strangled as he bowed his head. Aware of the staff looking on with interest, he glared around at them and they immediately began scratching away or turning papers, busy with their work. 'Won't you come through, please.'

He led her along the passage and into his own room, which inter-connected with his father's.

'Mr Morgan, sir. I am the daughter of Prince Sagar and Princess Meena.'

Madoc swallowed hard. 'I see.' He was torn, uncertain whether he should take her into his father or go in and warn him first. He was relieved of this decision however, as his father opened the door.

'Where's . . .' David pulled up abruptly as he noticed the woman. She bowed her head over her hands, then raised it to give him a view of her face. Madoc saw him suck in a deep breath, holding it, his mouth dropping slightly as he let it out, closing his eyes for an instant. Recovering himself quickly, he pulled himself upright, his expression detached, and bowed to her.

'Mistress. Captain David Morgan at your service. Please come in.' His voice was remote. Holding his hand towards his open door he nodded to her elderly servant. 'Good to see you again, Aseem. Thank you, Madoc.' He ushered them into his room and closed the door.

'Captain Morgan. May I present Princess Charu. The daughter of Princess Meena.'

'I am very pleased to meet you, Princess.' David touched his hands together, slightly bowing his head over them. He was surprised how naturally the action came after all these years. 'Please do sit down.' He pulled out a chair for her. 'And you also Aseem.' He forced a smile. He was aware of a pulse throbbing in his throat. 'How can I help you?' He forced his voice to be detached, though his stomach churned.

'You can help me . . .' she began, only to pause, lifting her eyes lifting briefly to meet his before dropping them again. David half-smiled, aware that for a woman to make eye-contact was considered disrespectful in her culture. 'I hope you do not think I am taking liberties?' she began again hesitantly.

David was at a loss to know what to reply. *This woman must surely be my daughter . . . God!*

'Perhaps if you finish telling me.' His voice was gentle, his thoughts becoming more coherent as he took control of his chaotic emotions.

'You remember my mother? Princess Meena?' Her eyes flicked up again, and he realized that they were filled with anxiety.

'Of course I remember her. Very well,' he acknowledged quietly. *How could I ever forget her*, he thought?

Relief flooded her face and she let out a little sigh.

'She always remembered you, Captain. Always.'

David looked away, unexpectedly filled with sadness. Poor little Meena, he thought, running a hand through his greying hair.

'My mother is ill. Very ill.' David saw tears glinting in her downcast eyes. 'She wants to see you again, Captain. Very much.'

David swallowed hard.

'I'm afraid that is impossible. I cannot travel to India. . . .'

'There is no need to go. My mother is here . . . in England. In Southampton. My father died last year. My brother is now the ruler and he has a wife alongside him. So my mother is free. She would love to see you again before she dies.'

David pursed his lips.

'You know she is . . . dying?'

Charu nodded. 'She has the lung fever. I do not think she will live much longer. Will you see her?' She raised her eyes, this time frankly meeting his. 'Please. I am beg—'

'Yes,' he interjected, before she could add more. 'I will come.'

'Thank you.' She salaamed to him gracefully.

'Princess Charu. Who is your father?'

She made no reply for a moment.

'You are my father, sahib,' she said softly.

David slumped back in the chair at her words. Why had he asked her? But then he'd never have known he'd had a daughter all these years. A daughter he knew nothing about.

'But only my mother, and Aseem, know. My fath ... Prince Sagar always believed I was his daughter....'

'I see. Did no one remark on the colour of your eyes?'

She nodded gravely. 'Everyone, Captain. But only to say how unusual, how beautiful they are. There is a history of light-coloured eyes in my fath ... Prince Sagar's family. It comes from a northern concubine, many years ago.'

David scratched his cheek. How convenient, he thought wryly. What would have happened to Meena and Charu, his daughter, otherwise? He was suddenly chilled.

'You closely follow your mother's looks. She was very lovely.'

'Thank you, Captain. And she always told me about my beauti-ful ...' She shook her head, correcting herself, '... my handsome father,' she continued. 'Now I can see for myself. Thank you for asking....'

'No!' David held up a hand, then reached both of them towards her. 'Thank you for telling me, Charu.'

She took them, bowing her head low over their joined hands and David dropped his own head briefly.

'Prince Sagar and my mother had three sons, so there is no worry about lineage. And you will come to Southampton soon?'

David's frowned, his mood plummeting.

'I shall have to make arrangements. I will let you know tomorrow.'

'Thank you. I will send Aseem to hear from you. I am returning to my mother before then. There is a train later today. Aseem will await you and bring you to her hotel.'

'You are not travelling alone?' His voice expressed concern.

She threw him her brilliant smile again.

'No. My maid and a bearer will be travelling with me, Captain.'

'Excuse me one moment please, Princess.'

Madoc's father came out and sat down on the corner of Madoc's desk, his head bowed. Madoc got up and shut the door to the corridor.

'You all right?' he asked.

David looked up, his face bleak.

'You've probably guessed.'

Madoc remained silent.

'She's your sister,' David growled. 'I didn't even know of her existence. I was young.' His voice held a defensive tone that Madoc had never heard before.

'I understand completely.'

'I don't know if you can really ... the circumstances. ... But I doubt if your mother will understand ... I never want to hurt your mother, Madoc. You know how much I care for her.'

'She knows that well enough. Surely she'll understand? After all it was years before you even met her ... wasn't it?'

'Of course it was!' David barked, cold steel flashing from his eyes. 'But how am I going to explain a daughter to her?'

'Do you need to?'

'I promised I would explain everything to her. She knew I was ... concerned about something.'

'Well you can tell her about Aseem, but surely you don't need to tell her about ... Charu. Can't you say—'

'But I do. Apart from promising her an explanation, there are complications. Meena, Charu's mother, is dying. She has come over to Britain hoping to see me before she dies. ...'

Madoc thumped the desk and swore in his best seaman's language.

'That does complicate matters,' he agreed. 'I take it this woman,' he nodded his head at the office, 'knows she is your daughter? She told me her father was Prince Sagar.'

'She knows, but her father didn't.'

'What! With eyes like those? Surely Indians all have dark eyes?'

'Not always. In the north, light eyes are not unknown. And apparently Prince Sagar has some history in his family of blue eyes appearing from time to time ... a throwback to a European concubine.' David gave a mirthless laugh. 'Which rather let us both off the hook, as it were.'

Madoc grinned. 'I wonder how many times those throwbacks were held responsible for the same reason? Did this Sagar fellow know about you?'

David shook his head.

'No. Meena and I met several times, before she was married. The first time at her father's home, then afterwards at a friend's home. But she was already betrothed and about to be married to Prince Sagar. It had been arranged when they were children. She hated the idea of spending her life in the zenana. She begged me to take her away.'

Shocked, Madoc was lost for words. At last he stuttered:

'Did . . . did you . . . consider it? Marrying her I mean?'

David shook his head sadly.

'No. But she was so gentle and lovely in all ways. Both innocent and sensual at the same time, as their culture requires. Far removed from that of European ladies. She arranged for me to be smuggled into her. I was young and didn't really consider the consequences. Poor little Meena.' He paused, 'I had yet to meet your mother . . . if I had, this conversation would not be taking place.'

Madoc shook his head.

'You had better be careful which way you put that to Mother. I am sure she's not going to like it.'

'You think I don't know that? She will not accept any of this easily.'

'What will you say?' Madoc asked sympathetically.

'God only knows.' Absentmindedly, with one finger David traced a deep scratch on the mahogany desk.

'Will you tell her about this woman? The one who is dying?'

'I will have to visit her. I cannot refuse her that.' He faced up to Madoc. 'Could you?'

Madoc blew out a breath.

'I can see your predicament. You will just have to . . . to clear it with Mother, in some way. She is sympathetic, I'm sure she will . . . understand. . . .'

As the words left his mouth he felt that she would not. His mother was understanding, was sympathetic. But she loved his father with a single-minded passion. He came first in her life, came before either himself or Robert; she would be insanely jealous to think that her husband had loved another woman before her.

'Not easily I think. But I owe it to Meena at least to visit her before she dies.'

'What if it's a trick? What if she hopes to lure you back to her charms?' Madoc was wary about this unknown woman

'No, Madoc. She wouldn't be capable of such deceit.'

'She did it once. She deceived her prince.'

His father's expression was dispirited.

'It is my fault that you regard her in such a light. I believe she loved me, Madoc; she would have died had she been caught. She wanted to give up her royal status and marry me.'

'I'm sorry. I didn't mean to disparage her, Father. I suppose I don't want to think of her in a rosy light. I wanted to compare her un-favourably with Mother,' he admitted.

His father nodded.

'So what are you going to do?'

'I don't know. I have promised to let them know when I can travel. I must speak to your mother first.' David's whole demeanour was downcast. His head drooped, his shoulders slumped. He put his hand on the doorknob. 'You had better come in and meet . . . your sister,' he said quietly.

Madoc entered the room to find Charu looking eagerly towards the door, only to avert her eyes as they entered.

'Charu. I would like you to introduce you to your half-brother, Madoc,' David said.

Madoc walked over to her, meeting her glance as she darted a swift peep at him, but she lowered her eyes, bowing her head over her hands. Madoc took her hands in his, raising them to his lips.

'Greetings, sister. I am pleased to make your acquaintance.'

Her smile lit up her face and he was dazzled by her serene loveliness.

'I also am more than pleased to meet you,' she whispered, in her heavily accented English. 'I have often wondered if . . .' She let the sentence trail off as her glance searched his face, making minimum eye contact. 'You are truly your father's son.' A delightfully wicked smile crept over her face. 'Except for your eyes, of course. They are not his.'

'No.' Madoc returned her smile. 'But yours are.'

She bowed her head, salaaming prettily.

'My mother often told me this. Now I can see it for myself.' She flicked a sideways look at David. 'I can see my very handsome father as my mother described him to me.' Nodding her head at Madoc she added, 'And in his son I can see him as a young man.'

★

David slumped back into his chair after seeing his two visitors to the door and heaved a huge sigh, running distracted hands through his hair.

'God! Now what do I do?' he groaned to himself.

CHAPTER EIGHTEEN

IT was all so long ago now, David mused, his thoughts travelling back through time and distance to the sub-continent of India.

INDIA 1820

He was leaning on the rail of the British East India ship the *Jewel of India*, looking down at the scene below. The overpowering smell of rich spices permeated the air around him, filling his nostrils, clinging to his clothes, his skin. So used to it was he that he hardly noticed it, any more than he paid heed to the cacophony of sounds resounding everywhere. Arguing voices, the splash of oars in water, lowing cattle, dogs barking, children's shrill tones, seamen calling in various languages, the creak of his ship's timbers as she sat at her moorings, and the water slapping against her hull.

'Sahib! Sahib! You are wanting fresh oranges?' Drawn up alongside them was a small home-made boat, made out of old planks of wood. A ragged urchin was standing in it, holding a basket of oranges up towards the crew of the *Jewel of India*. Many of her sailors were hanging on to the side of the ship, bargaining with vendors for their various goods.

His attention was caught by an ornate barge sculling past, its canopied seat curtained to hide the occupants from view. One of the moguls, he decided, watching it with interest. As it passed close by he caught a glimpse of a girl inside, her breathtakingly beautiful features unveiled in the cloister and anonymity of her enclosed conveyance. Even as he watched, her enormous kohl-darkened eyes met his gaze for a brief instant, holding it audaciously. He smiled at her, giving a nod of appreciation; daringly she returned his smile before raising her veil to cover her face. She darted another glance over her shoulder as the barge skimmed on its way.

'Lieutenant Morgan, sir,' a voice sang behind him.

As David turned towards the seaman, upraised voices and a resounding crash drew his attention back to the water. A gaff-rigged craft had collided with the barge containing the girl, severely damaging it, and capsizing it, flinging its occupant into the filthy harbour water. Her scream rang out shrilly, only to be broken off as the water swept over her head, her arms flailing wildly as she was pulled under by the doomed boat. A jabber of shouting Indian voices filled the air and one of the men from the barge, clinging to part of the floating wreckage looked up at David.

'Help! Please help my mistress, sahib. I cannot swim,' he shouted out hoarsely in broken English before letting go of his lifeline to sink under the water after his mistress.

Without stopping to consider the consequences David flung off his jacket and leapt into the murky water, wise enough not to risk diving into all the debris beneath the surface. On surfacing, he swam the few strokes needed to reach the capsized vessel before swimming down under the water where he had seen the girl disappear. It was impossible to discern much in the foul water but he was just able to make out a slight form tangled with debris. He grabbed it firmly and pulled the girl to the surface. At the time, he was not aware of the cheers from his shipmates above, though later he recalled them. Her body was limp in his arms, her dark hair in tendrils around her waxen face as he held her against him, marvelling once again at her beauty, as her veil had been lost in the water. Small vessels converged around them, many eager hands reaching to take her from him, but he was reluctant to release her into their care until he knew where she was going. Two of the seamen from the *Jewel of India* dropped into the water alongside him, safely relieving him of his burden, as others hung over the side of the ship to receive her from them.

'I've got her, sir.'

David then upended, swimming down under the water after the servant. Grasping the struggling man, he brought him back to the surface, quite happy to hand *him* over to the reaching hands.

'Sahib. Sahib.' Treading water, David looked towards the source of the voice, finding that another ornate barge had pulled up alongside the *Jewel of India*. A richly dressed Indian, obviously high-born, was addressing him from his secluded seat. 'Please, sahib. May I have a word with you.'

David swam over to it and held on to the gunnel as its occupant leaned through the curtains towards him.

'I owe you my daughter's life, sahib,' he said softly. 'They have taken her on to your ship. May I come aboard to see her?'

'Certainly. I'll get the men to lower a ladder.'

He had no need however, as the rope ladder had already snaked down into the water. As he gripped it he looked up at the faces lining the rail above, calling down raucously to him, and he grinned, returning their greetings with a wave. With both David and a seaman holding their visitor's arm, they assisted him to get a foot on the ladder and take a firm grip, before allowing him to ascend to the deck.

'Bring that other man as well,' David instructed, indicating the servant who had jumped in to rescue his mistress.

The girl had regained consciousness and was sitting on deck on a stool, her head drooping. Enveloped in a blanket, she held one corner up to shield her face from the view of the fascinated seamen.

'She seems all right, Lieutenant Morgan,' one of the midshipmen said to him. 'She vomited up a lot of water.'

'Just as well.' David grimaced, wiping his own lips with his equally polluted shirtsleeve. 'That water is disgusting.' Her dark eyes lifted, scanning his face for a brief moment before dropping decorously as he followed her father over to her.

She raised her palms together in front of her face, still holding the blanket, and dropping her head over them whispered:

'Thank you, sahib. I owe you my life.'

David straightened, inclining his head in a formal nod.

'My pleasure, mistress.'

The rescued servant was standing anxiously nearby, water dripping into a muddy pool on the deck.

'May I present the Prince Lokesh and his daughter the Princess Meena, sahib,' he said.

'Lieutenant Morgan, at your service, Sir. Ma'am.' David nodded to each of them again. 'Can we offer you the hospitality of our ship, sir? The captain is not aboard at present, he has gone ashore, but—'

'Thank you, Lieutenant, but I will take my daughter home as soon as possible,' the prince broke in.

'Certainly, sir. Do you need us to ferry you across the harbour?'

David's eyes strayed to the girl who was sitting with downcast eyes.

'Thank you, but no. We will easily fit into my barge. . . .' Prince Lokesh paused. 'I will be inviting you and your captain to dine at my home. Aseem will return.' He indicated the wet servant.

'Aseem showed great courage going into the water when he is unable to swim,' David said, smiling at Aseem.

'I would gladly give her my life, sahib,' Aseem replied gravely, salaaming with his palms.

'He is a loyal servant,' the prince observed dismissively.

David watched them as they were ferried across the harbour, his thoughts filled with the girl's beauty.

The following day David tapped on Captain Blake's door in answer to his summons.

'Come.'

David entered to find Aseem already standing in the captain's spacious cabin.

'Good morning, sahib.' Aseem bowed over his hands.

David greeted his captain and returned Aseem's salutation.

'We have been invited to dine at the Prince Lokesh's palace this evening, Lieutenant Morgan. It seems you played the hero yesterday.' Captain Blake allowed himself a restrained smile.

David laughed.

'Hardly, sir. Apart from the ordeal of entering that foul water. May I enquire after the health of Princess Meena, sir?'

'How is the young lady?' Captain Blake asked the servant.

'She is feeling much better, sahib, thank you. The physician has been giving her a dose of medication . . . to clear the bad humours from her system.'

'I have written a note of acceptance for us both.' The captain was handing the envelope to Aseem. 'Please attend at the change of watch this evening, Lieutenant Morgan.'

David's pulse gave a little surge of pleasure at the thought of seeing the princess again – though would he see her? He was aware that high-born Indian ladies were kept in purdah, away from the eyes of men.

But surprisingly Princess Meena was present when they entered, sitting on silken cushions on the dais with her father. Their feet echoed on the marble-floored room, their swords bumping against their sides as they approached across the huge room towards the prince and his daughter. Meena's dark eyes flashed briefly at David before dropping discreetly away, and although her face was veiled, he had to make a conscious effort not to stare at her, visualizing her loveliness as he had seen it yesterday.

They dined on an assortment of Indian dishes, with another appearing each time David thought they had finished. Meena did not join in the conversation with the men, keeping her eyes averted throughout the meal, though David caught her looking at him once when he glanced at her.

'Meena is the only surviving child of my favourite wife,' the Prince explained. 'She died last year, making Meena very precious to me.' David felt his anger rise on Meena's behalf when the prince added: 'Even though she is only a woman.'

His glance went back to her at the hurtful words and he caught her eyes dropping away from him again.

After their meal, as they were escorted back along endless corridors, the captain walking ahead, Aseem appeared at David's side and pressed something into his gloved hand. With the merest suggestion of a nod at David's start of surprise, he hurried away. Curious, David was impatient to get back aboard the ship, dying to know what it could be. Once safely on his own he examined the missive. He straightened out the scrap of hand-made scented paper; it proved to be a note printed in ill-formed English letters.

'Meet me please Aseem will come Meena.'

My God, he thought, grinning widely. The little hussy. I always thought Indian women were inhibited. He showed the letter to another officer on board, his close friend, Claude Rick, who pulled an appreciative face.

'Sounds promising . . . but I'd be wary if I were you. You could end up to your neck in trouble.'

'Possibly,' David agreed, scratching his chin contemplatively, though his eyes danced.

But sure enough, when he went ashore the following day with Claude, Aseem seemed to materialize alongside him, salaaming.

'Greetings, sahib.' His glance strayed to Claude.

'Hello there, Aseem,' David replied. 'You go on ahead, Claude. I'll follow on after you.'

Claude smothered a grin and nodded, walking away.

Glancing around to make certain he was unheard the Indian asked: 'You are coming with me, sahib?' When David nodded Aseem sucked in a breath. 'I am giving you warning, sahib. My young mistress is . . .' He paused, searching for the English to express what he wished to say. Not finding it he shook his head and continued. 'She sees no danger. Your life is in danger if you come with me.'

David studied the man and after making sure they were alone he said:

'You mean you are taking me to see her? And that is strictly forbidden.'

'Exactly, sahib.' Worry-lines furrowed the man's brow. 'It is very much forbidden. You are both in much danger. I have tried my best to . . .' His voice trailed off and he shrugged. 'The princess is very indulged by her father but if he heard about this . . .' He sucked in a breath, letting it out in a rush.

'Are you trying to tell me to refuse?' David was flooded with disappointment.

'I am telling you nothing, sahib. The princess wants to see you. She will be very unhappy if you do not come.' Aseem's voice was resigned.

'Then we can't let her be unhappy, can we, Aseem? Where are we going?'

'To the house of a very great friend of hers. I will walk ahead and you will follow me, sahib.'

David soon lost his bearings as they went down one narrow alley after another, until they arrived at a door opening directly off the street into the side of a large house. Aseem pushed it open and slipped inside without looking in David's direction, but left the door ajar. With a quick glance around David entered the doorway after Aseem, following him through shaded corridors until they reached a small courtyard.

Windowless walls completely encased the courtyard and a small fountain bubbled into a pool at its centre, pleasantly cooling the air. David stood near it, holding his hand beneath the water and dabbing a little over his perspiring face as he glanced around him. A small tree, full of fragrant blossom, overhung the pool and a few songbirds sung sweetly from a cage suspended from its branches. One corner was canopied with brightly coloured silk hangings and in the shade beneath it stood a low couch, piled high with soft cushions; a small sandalwood table placed near it held a bowl of fruit and plate of little cakes. As his eyes alighted on a second low door in the wall with a screen of fretwork set into the wood, Meena came through it, her face veiled.

She seemed to glide rather than walk towards him and he bowed politely to her as she reached him, holding out her hand. He took it, raised it to his lips and kissed it, his fingers caressing her soft brown ones.

'Princess,' he murmured.

Ignoring convention this time, she stared openly at him, her eyes huge and dark.

'I was afraid you would not come.' Her voice, husky and sensuous, trembled slightly.

'I wanted to come.' He held her glance. 'I longed to see your beauty again.'

She sucked in a breath, hesitated, then raised her hand, dropping her veil, allowing him full view of her radiant face.

'You are gorgeous,' he breathed.

'What is gorgeous?' she asked uncertainly.

'It is another word for beauty. Extra beautiful.'

'And I want to look at your beauty also.'

He laughed. 'I have never been called beautiful before,' he said with a grin.

'That is wrong?' she asked anxiously. 'Is a man not also beautiful?'

'It is not a word used about a man,' he conceded.

'Please. What is that word?'

'I would much rather discuss you. But aren't you afraid? Entertaining me here unescorted . . . and without your veil?'

She dropped her eyes.

'Perhaps. You are also in much danger.' Her expression was suddenly anxious. 'Your life would be ended if they caught us.'

'It is worth the risk.' He touched her cheek with his hand.

She caught his hand and kissed it and he lifted her chin, gently lowering his lips to hers.

She clung to him as he lifted his head, her hands reaching up to touch his face, tracing the outlines of his mouth with her fingers.

'You *are* beautiful,' she insisted. 'Never have I seen a man with such beauty. With eyes like precious sapphires.'

Holding hands, they sat on the low wall around the pool.

'You must tell me about your home. About England,' she demanded.

'I am not English. I am Welsh.'

'But you are on an English ship?'

He had to explain to her, tell her about Wales, and in return she told him about life in the zenana.

'I hate it,' she sighed. 'All the time I long to be free. Not to be imprisoned for ever.' She waved her hand at the cage in the tree. 'Like a bird in a cage. Perhaps in the next life I will be born a man. Then I will be free.'

'I am glad you are not a man.'

She giggled, leaning forward, was touching his lips with her tongue when a bell tinkled discreetly, just outside the door where David had entered.

She pulled back with a sigh.

'That is Aseem. I will have to go. You will come again?' she pleaded.

'I will,' he promised.

They met several times after that, always on their own in the same courtyard. On the last occasion he told her that his ship was sailing the following day.

'Take me with you,' she pleaded. 'I love you. I do not want Prince Sagar, the man I am promised to. I want to be with you.'

'I cannot do that, Meena.' His voice was gentle. 'I am in service with the East India Company. I have little money and no property of my own. You are a princess, I could not support you.'

'Then make love with me. Just once before you leave me. Please!'

Tempted, David was torn with indecision. She was so seductive, so cajoling. But it was so wrong, terribly wrong. He would probably never see her again and she was already promised to another man.

'I cannot do that, Meena. And your husband would know. . . .'

'In the zenana . . . I learn ways to hide that. Please!' she whispered again. 'Something I can remember for the rest of my life . . . in the zenana,' she coaxed, knowing his sympathy for her way of life. 'Like a bird in a cage, forever looking through bars at life outside.'

He sighed, moved by her words, then took her in his arms, kissing her, running his hands over her body, before lifting her, gossamer light, and carrying her over to the couch. As he laid her there, she slid out of her sari and lay there naked, her skin smooth and sleek as silk, as she watched him undress, her eyes hanging on his rippling muscles.

He leaned towards her and her eyes sparkled with delight as she caught her fingers in the dark hairs curling on his chest.

She gave a delighted giggle and rubbed her cheek sensuously against it.

'I love this hair here. You are so beautiful, my David. So beautiful.'

As he took her gently in his arms, holding her close, she nibbled at his earlobe with sharp little teeth, then released them to whisper in his ear.

'I love you, my David, and for the rest of my life I can remember this wonderful moment.'

CHAPTER NINETEEN

THERE was a tap on the door and David started guiltily, as if the intruder could read his thoughts. Emily popped her head around the door and he leapt to his feet, wondering whether she had seen his visitors leaving.

'Hello. I came into town shopping and thought I'd pay you a visit.' Her smile faded. 'Are you all right?'

'Yes. Of course I am,' he said a trifle testily.

Her chin lifted. 'I am sorry I asked.'

'Sorry, my dear.' He came around the desk and went to kiss her, but she offered him her cheek.

This was not an auspicious start. He pulled up a chair for her.

'Are you sure you wish me to stay?' she said tartly. She regarded him curiously for a moment, then sucked in a breath. 'That Indian has been here, hasn't he?'

'Yes. Yes, he has been here.' Instead of returning to his seat he prowled around the room, running a distracted hand through his hair. *Now what do I tell her?* He stared blindly at the barometer on the wall, aware that she was watching him.

'He has obviously upset you. Are you going to tell me what he wanted?'

What if it breaks up our marriage, destroys our wonderful trust? Resigned, he turned back to her, then saw the strained lines around her mouth, the anxiety on her face.

'Emily, my love. Forgive me.' He gave her a hug, held her close. 'One moment. I'll tell Madoc we are not to be disturbed.'

He banged open his office door, pushing it behind him, and stalked over to Madoc, who wore an alarmed expression.

'I didn't have a chance to tell—' Madoc began.

'Doesn't matter. I don't want to be disturbed for a while.'

Back in his office, he pulled his chair alongside Emily's as she regarded him warily. He took her hand, holding her gaze purposefully.

'I have something to tell you. . . .' he began, his voice firm now he had reached a decision. 'I know you are not going to like—'

'David,' she interrupted, 'you don't have to tell me anything, unless you wish to.'

'No. I must tell you! Please, Emily. You have a right to know. After all these years you know the strength of my love for you.'

'You have no need to remind me, I've never doubted it.'

'If anything I love you more now than the day we were married.' His voice rang with passion. 'So . . . today I have just. . . .' He broke off, swallowing hard. 'Let's start again. Years ago, when I was a very young man . . . in India, I met a young woman. . . .'

'A woman!' Emily gasped. Her colour seemed to drain even as he watched.

'She was a high-born Indian princess. . . .'

'Oh, God! No!' Her voice shook and she covered her face with her hands, muffling her words when she asked: 'Were you in love with her?'

He smothered a groan, his own face feeling stiff and taut. When he didn't answer she dropped her hands to look at him.

'Were you?'

'No. But I was a little infatuated by her beauty,' he admitted with reluctance. 'You must remember it was years before I met you. . . .' His voice trailed off and he rubbed a hand across his chin, his shoulders slumping. 'Emily. I swear, you are the only woman I have ever loved. Truly loved,' he said in a low voice, looking squarely at her. 'Since I've met you all other women pale in comparison.' He reached for her hand, finding it icy as he enveloped it in his own.

She gave a smothered whimper, pressing her lips together.

'You do believe me?'

'Of course I do.' She flung herself into his arms, hugging him tightly. 'I should know by this time.'

'Thank God.' He gathered her towards him.

She managed a weak smile.

'But now you have to tell me the rest,' she said, realizing that there was more to follow.

He nodded, but she didn't flinch when he said:

'Today I discovered I have a daughter.'

'A daughter.' Her voice wobbled slightly but her expression was matter of fact. 'That must have been a shock for you.'

He gave a grimace.

'I could put it more strongly. Ever since I knew Aseem had been here I've been worried sick about hurting you.' He took her hand again, still cold.

She nodded, her face earnest.

'But there's more? Otherwise why did he tell you about her now? After all this time.'

David tensed. 'My . . . she came with him.'

Emily closed her eyes briefly.

'Your daughter? Why?'

He took a deep breath.

'Her mother is dying. She . . . she—'

'For heaven's sake, David, tell me it all!' Emily burst out.

'Her mother has come to Britain . . . hoping to see me again before she dies,' he finished with a rush.

'What?' She was indignant. 'She's not expecting you . . .' She paused, studying his expression. 'You have already said you'll go.'

He nodded.

'I could hardly do anything else, Emily.' His eyes met hers. 'I felt I owed her that much.'

She bit her lip as she nodded.

'Yes. I suppose you do,' she agreed in a choked voice. She pulled his handkerchief from his top pocket to dab her eyes. 'Well at least *I* have you, and not that . . . that princess. You can tell me about it when we get home. Can't you finish early and leave Madoc to cope?'

Flooded with relief he slumped back against the chair.

'I certainly can. Thank you for understanding, Emily,' he said softly. 'Most women would not.'

She managed a smile.

'They don't have you for a husband.'

He smiled at her.

'Come on! I'll tell Madoc we are going.' He held out his hand and she took it firmly.

With Emily's agreement, David found time to travel to Southampton during the week and accompany Aseem to the private infirmary where Meena was staying. He was greeted by Charu, her expression a mixture of joy and sadness.

'Greetings, Captain Morgan,' she murmured, bowing her head over her touched palms. 'I am glad you came today. I was worried my mother would not last until you came. She knows you are coming.'

David returned her greeting and leaned down to kiss her cheek. His stomach felt strangely jittery, apprehension being an unfamiliar emotion.

'Then it is as well I came today. Where is she?'

'My mother is in the next room.' She pushed open the door to the adjoining room. 'Please. You go in. I will wait here.'

He nodded and walked towards the bed as the door closed behind him. The tiny figure hardly raised a mound under the bedclothes and he approached cautiously, almost on tiptoe. He stood looking down at her, his face solemn. The arm lying outside the bedclothes was insect-thin. Her face was sunken and yellow, appearing almost transparent; dark stains bruised the skin beneath her eyes. As if she felt his presence, her eyes fluttered open and seeing him, came alive.

'David. My beautiful David.' Her voice was so quiet he had to lean close to her to hear what she said. 'I knew you would come.'

Her hand felt birdlike as he took it in his.

'Of course I came.'

'I am . . .' She stopped, sucking in a few gasping breaths.

'Don't talk. I'll sit here with you.'

'No! I must. I want . . . to thank you . . . for our daughter. I've been happy . . . even in the zenana. I have my . . . our Charu. She was my life. Always.' She gave a little sigh, her lids drooped shut, and she drifted off again.

Dejected, David pressed his lips together. Poor little Meena. He sat there quite some time, but she didn't open her eyes again. He heard a tinkle of anklets and realized that Charu was standing alongside him. He stood up, their eyes meeting, hers bright with tears.

'Thank you for coming, my father,' she whispered, bowing over her hands. 'Now she can die happy.'

'And thank you for bringing me. I feel . . . better to know she has had your love and company all these years. What will you do? When. . . ?' He didn't finish the sentence.

'I am going home. I have two children. My husband does not know why I am here. He thinks it is for treatment for my mother.' Seeing his questioning look she continued. 'He is a good man, he treats me well.'

'I am glad to hear that. Is it possible for you to write to me, Charu? Or will it be too difficult? I wouldn't want to cause you any problems but I'd like to keep in touch with you.'

Her face lit up, her eyes glowing, and she nodded gracefully. 'I would like that too. It is possible. Where will I send the letter?'

'To the office of Morgan Shipping. I have a card.' He felt in his breast pocket then handed her a card. 'I will reply to whatever address you supply.'

'Maybe one day we will meet again?' she whispered.

'Maybe.'

His confession behind him, Emily's love as firm as ever, and his poignant visit to Meena now past, David felt his life should be back on an even keel. But during the following weeks he became increasingly concerned to notice that Robert was forever in Nia's company. Albert appeared to have taken a back place, and on asking Robert about him, David learned that Nia had turned down Albert's marriage proposal, and that he was now living in France. Nia was now hoping to encourage a romance between him and her friend, Amy.

Madoc, usually so approachable, prowled around like an injured lion, snapping and growling at everyone. Everyone kept out of his way, except Robert, who seemed positively to welcome Madoc's aggression, confronting him head on in all situations. David understood that Madoc had no way of retaliating, as he felt Robert was justified in harassing him. Madoc would have been quite as challenging had the situation been reversed.

'Are you listening to me, Madoc?' David heard Emily ask.

'What did you say?' Madoc dropped the net curtain he had been holding aside and turned to his mother.

'You haven't heard a word I said. Are you feeling unwell or just being impolite?'

'I apologize, Mother. I was thinking. And I am perfectly well, thank you.' He gave a stiff nod and stalked out of the room.

David watched him go, empathizing with his younger son, so evidently eaten up with resentment.

Emily frowned as the door shut behind him.

'I don't know why Madoc is so grumpy lately. You think he'd be in a better state of mind, being engaged to Lucy.'

'I did explain about that to you, Emily.'

'You mean about him not proposing to Lucy?'

'Yes. I do mean that. It wasn't Madoc's doing.'

'I still can't understand how it could happen. Women do not proposition men . . . anyway Robert seems to have accepted the situation. I think he's getting over Lucy's betrayal very well.' Emily looked pleased. 'I believe he is getting fond of Nia.'

'You do?' He was alarmed at this new turn.

'I'm glad. I was so worried about him at first, thinking he was bottling it all up; after all, he doesn't show his feelings the way Madoc does. Yes. I do believe Robert is recovering.'

Madoc showing his feelings? David stared at her, lost for words. This was a difficult one to cope with. He didn't want to offer any further disclosures about her sons, it would only add to her concern; and Madoc was successfully managing to hide his true feelings, even if everyone did wonder why he was so bad-tempered.

'Nia is a delightful young woman. She would make a lovely wife, don't you think?'

David spun back to her.

'You don't mean for Robert?'

She frowned at him. 'Why do you say that? You like Nia.'

'She would make Madoc a better one.'

'Well, it can hardly be Madoc now.' She held up a newspaper, rustling it crossly.

'Emily. I told you Madoc has no wish to marry Lucy. He does not love her.'

'Are you implying that he is in love with Nia?'

'I am not implying anything,' David hedged, uncomfortably.

'But obviously you think he is?'

He drew in a breath, his face unreadable.

'Well? Do you?'

David turned away, unwilling to answer her, aware that her eyes were boring into his back as he left the room.

'If you will excuse me. I am going to have an early night.' Madoc rose from the table after dinner. Robert had already departed to take Nia out for the evening.

'You don't want a brandy with me?' His father held up the crystal decanter as Emily took her leave.

Madoc shook his head. 'I don't think I'd be very good company.'

'I would enjoy it better than being on my own.' David was being persuasive.

'Oh, very well. Just a quick one then.'

He sat down again as his father picked up a brandy goblet and began pouring. Madoc's eyes widened as David handed him a large measure.

'Are you trying to get me drunk again?' He laughed bleakly.

'It might help.'

'Nothing will help. Only getting that stupid woman reconciled with Rob.' He squinted up at his father, who was still standing and pouring himself a drink. 'Do you think Robert is getting interested in Nia?'

David drew a breath through his teeth.

'To be quite honest, the thought has crossed my mind.'

Madoc closed his eyes, running both hands through his hair.

'God! I'm between the devil and the deep. I can hardly show him I care when he believes I have the woman I've always desired. And, however much I'd like to, I can't tell him I don't want Lucy, otherwise he will realize that I was the one who ended it. Not her, as we wish him to think.'

'You're right.' David added water to his own brandy, offering it to Madoc who shook his head.

'It's obvious he is as bitter as hell with me . . . which as far as he is concerned is fully justified. I'd be the same.' He gave a derisive snort. 'Let's get it straight. I *am* as bitter as hell about Nia.' Madoc gulped down a mouthful of brandy, then a second. 'The thing is, I feel so helpless and I'm not used to that. I am used to being able to sort out my problems . . . and suddenly I can't.' His voice ended on a helpless note. 'There is not a single thing I can do without injuring Rob. And I've done too much of that already.'

'Your mother . . .' David began, trailing off.

'What? What were you going to say?'

'Your mother thinks Rob is interested in Nia,' David finished.

'Dammit!' Madoc gulped down the rest of his drink and leapt up.

'Do you want another brandy?'

'No thanks. I think I'll go for a ride and get some fresh air.'

Madoc changed into a pair of lightweight trousers and a thin linen shirt. It was a warm evening, the sun was low in the western sky, staining the clouds a peachy pink. He rode up over the headland, wanting to look out over the water. Colour from the sky was melting into sea, reaching fingers of molten gold towards the land.

He must not feel resentful towards Rob. It was not his fault. He was not to know that he was upsetting Madoc . . . or did he? For days the idea that Robert did know had been gnawing at him like a voracious worm. He had rather seemed to be flaunting Nia at him, Madoc deliberated. Almost as though she were a prize to be won.

He had hardly slept properly for nights, imagining them together. His main worry was that Nia seemed to be revelling in Robert's attention. Was she in love with Rob? Had Robert fallen under Nia's spell? Either thought was intolerable.

How had he got into this mess? What if Robert decided he preferred Nia? If he were in Robert's place he wouldn't want Lucy back. Not in a million years. Madoc reined in Storm, his stomach churning as he at last faced up to reality. His mother and father were already considering the notion that Robert was falling in love with Nia and, as far as Robert was concerned Madoc had the woman he wanted. And, even worse, Nia seemed to be falling for Robert's renowned charms.

'Nia is a superb horsewoman,' Robert remarked casually at breakfast the following day. He lifted the lid off a chafing dish on the sideboard, helped himself to smoked haddock and glanced at Madoc when he passed no comment. 'Don't you think so, Madoc?'

Madoc gave an evasive grunt without looking up from his plate, not wishing to be drawn into a conversation about Nia.

'Do you know, I realize that she is much more fun to be with than Lucy.' Robert put his plate on the table and gave a deceptively innocent grin to Madoc as he reached for the butter.

His mother glanced at Robert, frowning a little, then her eyes flashed back towards Madoc, who studiously kept his own on his plate. His knuckles were white as he gripped his knife and fork tightly. After taking one or two more sawdust-tasting mouthfuls Madoc clattered his cutlery on to his plate and threw down his napkin. His mother looked up in surprise.

'Excuse me, Mother, Father.' He nodded to them, pushed himself to his feet and stalked out, leaving them all staring after him. He was very aware of the smirk on his brother's face.

CHAPTER TWENTY

'YOU seem to be seeing quite a lot of my sister.'
Tom and Robert were riding their horses towards the woods on their way to play cards with a friend, their usual Friday evening occupation.

'She is remarkably entertaining company,' Robert said. 'I find her fascinating, very unlike many women. And who would have imagined that Nia could become such a beautiful woman?'

'I must admit that did surprise me.' Pondering on Robert's remarks Tom gave a little frown, rather concerned about the way things were developing between Nia and the two Morgan brothers. Perhaps on the surface she appeared very much a lady, but in reality he didn't think Nia was any different from what she had been as a child. And though she was shunning Madoc, professing more interest in Robert, Tom believed that this was a strategy of some sort, that Madoc still held Nia's heart.

'To be quite honest, Rob, I imagined Madoc would always be the only one for Nia.' Tom shot a little glance to judge Robert's reaction and saw his mouth tighten. 'She idolized him. And she was so defensive. A real little wildcat as far as Madoc was concerned.'

'Wasn't she just.' Robert pulled a disapproving face. 'Madoc was such a little ruffian, and if I dared to criticize him in Nia's hearing she would be on to me in a flash.'

Tom nodded. 'She would. Madoc included Nia in too many of his escapades for my mother's peace of mind; I don't think he even considered her to be a girl. Though, saying that, he was always ready to take the blame for everything.'

'Huh! Madoc never cared a whit about anything.' Robert was dismissive. 'He was forever in hot water at school. I used to get quite embarrassed by it at one stage."Mad" everyone used to call him.'

179

Tom laughed. 'Suited him perfectly. But, being Madoc, everyone likes him. He is open and friendly with no regard for the conventions.'

'Not so open these days.' Robert's tone was acerbic. 'After what he did with Lucy.'

'But are you really sure he did?' Tom darted a glance at Robert. He had heard another version of that tale, though not from Madoc.

Robert's face darkened, his eyes narrowing.

'He knew she had accepted my proposal. I could hardly believe that he would go behind my back and—' He broke off to duck his head under a low branch that overhung the path.

Tom was sorry for him. Though he liked Madoc, he had never been closer to one brother rather than the other when they had all been children but, being of an age with Robert, he'd felt more inclined to think of himself as Robert's friend not Madoc's. He regarded Robert thoughtfully. Robert was not one to display bitterness, but it came through quite clearly. Tom's family had been amazed when they heard that Lucy was going to marry Madoc. Personally, Tom thought Madoc and Nia were ideally suited, as did his father, who had seemed disappointed by the news. His mother said she wasn't surprised, she had always maintained that Nia was reaching beyond her station in life.

He smiled to himself at that idea, which he and Nia found highly amusing; neither of them felt inferior to anyone and their father certainly never had. Their education, first with the Morgan boys then later at school and college had instilled confidence into them. Mixing with the children of gentlemen and the newly rich middle classes, amongst whom they included themselves, had assured them of acceptable behaviour and good prospects.

'So is it true about Lucy and Madoc?' Tom asked, wanting to hear Robert's views on this subject. 'Are they truly betrothed?'

'I have no idea.' Rob was deceptively aloof. 'As far as I know Lucy has not yet decided to take another husb—' He reined in his horse as they came to a tree lying across the path. 'Good heavens. How did that come down? There's been no storm.'

Both men dismounted and walked over to the tree. Many big branches stuck up in the air, making it impossible for a horse either to jump or to walk over it.

'Perhaps we can drag it to one side.' Tom studied the obstacle objectively. Belatedly he remembered Robert's disabled arm and realized that he would have difficulty in pulling it. He glanced around. 'Or we can push a path through there.' He pointed off to the side with his riding-crop.

'Yes. I think we can get through there.' Robert walked over to examine the undergrowth, only to pull up, startled, as men appeared from amongst the trees on either side of them. He regarded them in astonishment, as they were all wearing home-made hoods over their heads.

'What the devil . . .' Tom began.

'Robbers,' Robert yelled, throwing a punch at the nearest man who had reached out to grab him. It connected with a satisfying crunch on the man's jaw, sending him reeling back with a curse as Tom struck out with the riding-crop in his hand, slashing it hard across the face of the next assailant, who gave a shriek and held his cheek with both hands. Warily eyeing one of the other ruffians, Tom brought his crop back for another stroke as a man approached him, when a cudgel blow from behind hit him squarely over the head. He buckled at the knees as lights flashed across his vision.

Vaguely aware of Robert grappling with the other men, Tom was struggling to rise to his feet when two pairs of hands grabbed his arms in vicelike grips, yanking him erect. He blinked at their owners dizzily, trying to clear his head.

'Now we got you, gypper,' a rough voice sneered. 'It's 'bout time you 'ad a lesson in manners.' On this last word the huge man in front of him brought a hard fist thudding into Tom's stomach, doubling him up in agony on his knees once more.

'Stop that!' He heard Robert shouting, as he also struggled to free himself from the men restraining him. 'If you want our money, just take it. Leave—' Robert broke off with a grunt as a fist thumped against the side of his head.

The men pulled Tom up to his feet. Still gasping to recover his breath, he faced up to them, still held firmly on either side by two men.

'What is your business with me?' he snarled, not willing to be cowed. 'You are liable to get yourselves transported with this behaviour. You'll be in serious trouble.'

'Oh yeah? 'Ow will you know who it is then?' the biggest of them taunted. 'You can't see our faces, can you.'

Tom studied the brutish form towering in front of him, the broad, over-muscled shoulders, the man's ungainly stance.

'I don't need to see your face, I know who you are. You're the prize-fight—' was all he managed to get out before the man brought his fist back and punched him straight in the face. Unable to avoid the blow Tom felt his nose crunch under it and blinding green stars with flashing lights seared across his vision, tears springing to his eyes from the impact.

'I warn you,' Robert's voice bellowed across. 'We'll see you all in gaol. Release him this instant.'

Groggily Tom looked over at Robert, also held by two men, one of them twisting his withered arm distressingly high up behind his back. His face was white and contorted with pain; Tom knew Rob was incapable of moving his arm in that direction.

'You shurrup . . . cripple,' Bull jeered. 'Or we might just let ew go . . . then we'd see 'ow you manage in a fight.'

'Let me go then, and I'll show you cowards. Let me go, right now.' Robert was still struggling to get himself free. 'You're brave fellows in a gang aren't you?'

'Tie 'im to a tree.' Bull waved an arm. 'Let 'im watch. That'll take them Morgans down a peg.' He gave a snigger. 'I always liked doin' that. Let's go further into the woods first, we don't want no company, do we, boys?'

'Do you want the 'orses brung too?' one asked.

'Yeah. Fetch 'em. Someone might come past and see 'em.'

'Nice 'orses. We'll get a tidy penny for 'em.'

'No we won't,' Bull asserted. 'We'll 'ave to leave 'em. Pity . . . but if we sells 'em someone might get to point us out, like. We do' want no comebacks. We can pinch what money they got though . . . le's get 'em deeper into the woods.'

They were engulfed in shade as the foliage from the branches met above their heads, shrouding the path beneath in deep shadow. Tom and Robert struggled, pulling back as the gang manhandled them, half-stumbling, half-dragging them further into the thicket as they pushed a way through the undergrowth. Branches lashed and tore at their faces, snagging and lacerating their skin as they were thrust into them. Tom closed his eyes, trying to turn his head aside, afraid he might be blinded by a sharp twig.

When they reached a little clearing, deep inside the woods, Tom saw them wrench both Robert's arms roughly behind him; he saw him flinch, smothering a gasp of pain. Robert's face was deathly pale as he scowled fearlessly, for once his temper thoroughly aroused.

'Don't let him talk you into believing you can get away with this,' Robert bellowed, his eyes flashing fire. 'You men are fools to let your-selves be led by that idi—' He broke off with a grunt as a fist rammed into his kidneys.

Tom's attention came back to the leader, Bull, standing in front of him.

'You forgot you was a gypper, didn't ew?' He put his face so near to Tom that he could smell his vile breath, see the rotten stumps of broken teeth in his mouth. 'Forgot your place in life, you 'ave . . . gypper.'

Tom jutted his chin defiantly but felt his stomach curl with fear as he went icy-cold and the hairs on his arms prickled. Panting slightly he licked his lips, realizing there was nothing either he or Robert could do to prevent this nightmare really happening. Nobody was going to stop these bullies carrying out their unnamed threats . . . and to think that he and Robert had laughed when Madoc had warned him. Bull stood before him, an ugly sneer on his mean little mouth, visible below the hood, his eyes glittering through the slits in the hood.

'Oright. Strip 'im.'

Feeling slightly sick, Tom sucked a deep breath in through his nostrils as two of them roughly yanked his jacket down over his shoulders.

'Look! Think again. You've made a terrible mistake.' Robert's voice was hoarse as he called out to them. 'I don't know who you think this man is but I'm telling you he's a prominent lawyer in Swansea.'

The men paused indecisively, looking to their leader.

'He is, I tell you,' Robert yelled. 'He's a lawyer in the practice of—'

'Do you think per'aps . . .' one man began in a nervous voice.

'Shove somethin' in 'is mouth to shut 'im up,' Bull snarled.

'You'll be in grave trouble. I warn you, you'll live to regret—' A piece of grimy rag was rammed into Robert's mouth ending his flow of words.

Bull nodded at his henchmen, who were all grinning again now, delighted to see one of the gentry humiliated.

As the ruffians got his jacket-sleeve off his right arm, Tom swiftly pulled his arm up to attack the man who was leaning forward holding the jacket. Tom chopped hard down with his elbow on back of his assailant's head, dropping the man to his knees as Tom tried to shake his other arm free of its sleeve.

'Watch 'im!' he heard someone shout.

Vicious punches began raining upon his body and under the assault he felt his senses swimming.

'That's enough!' Bull screamed. 'I don' want 'im knocked out. But don' leave 'is arms go again.'

Now, holding his arms firmly, they grabbed handfuls of Tom's fine linen shirt, tugging at it, ripping it to tear it off him without freeing his arms. He swallowed hard, a band of fear tightening his chest as he saw Bull hold out his hand and someone place a whip into it. They tied his hands together, then threw the rope over a branch of a tree and yanked his arms high in the air above him. Tom's breath was coming in rapid pants as his glance hung on Bull, following him with his eyes as far as he could as he walked round behind him.

He heard Robert's muffled protests and then the whistle of the whip rushing through the air. Bracing himself, he gritted his teeth, waiting, and felt it come down across his back, biting agonizingly into his flesh. He bit back the whimper that rose in his throat and clamped his teeth on his lower lip, determined not to give them the satisfaction of hearing him cry out. He heard the whip sing out again to rip into him a second time. As it seared and burned across his back he and felt his lower lip split as he bit down on it again, swallowing his cry.

Madoc was in the stable yard when a dishevelled Robert came tearing up to Craig y Mor, his horse lathered and trembling. It was completely alien to Robert either to be in disarray or to treat a horse in such a manner and Madoc and Idris watched in amazement as he flung himself off his animal.

'Saddle me another mount . . . two mounts,' he gasped to Idris. 'And hurry! Madoc, I want a word with you . . . in private.' He grabbed Madoc's arm and hustled him out of hearing distance.

Realizing his urgency Madoc complied, puzzled. Then he noticed the bruises and scratches on his brother's face.

'What the hell happened to—'

'It's Tom,' Robert said tersely. 'Those thugs carried out their threat
... with a vengeance.'

'Thugs? What thu— You. . . ? Oh God! You mean Bull? Did his
cronies attack. . . ?'

'Yes . . . though they were masked. They bull-whipped Tom. . . .'

'I'll kill the bastards!' Madoc punched the fence and let off a string
of obscenities. 'How badly is he hurt?'

'It looks pretty bad to me.' Robert's face was ashen. 'I tried to
prevent it but I was about as useless as a child with this.' He thumped
bitterly at his withered arm with his good one. 'It took me ages to free
myself from the rope they tied me with.'

Madoc looked down at the ground, understanding his brother's
humiliation; the familiar guilt overwhelming him once more.

'He doesn't want to show anyone so I came for you.'

'Where is he? And where are we going to take him?'

'I don't know.' Completely distracted, Robert's voice shook. 'I don't
know. He can't go home, he doesn't want Liam and Ellen to know.
Where can we take him?'

Madoc rubbed his chin.

'How about Elwyn's? He'd keep it secret if I asked him.' Elwyn had
been a village friend of Madoc's since childhood and they had met
often since he'd been home. A fisherman, he was married now and
lived in the hamlet of Pentrebach. 'With the tide at this stage, he's
probably fishing. But probably his wife will be home . . . they have a
new baby.'

'All right. We've got to take him somewhere. Come on! Please
hurry!'

'Can he ride?'

'Lord! I don't know.' Robert rubbed a shaking hand over his
bruised face. 'I didn't think of that. What if he can't?'

Madoc looked grim. 'We can take the gig.'

'No. It's deep in the woods, we'll never get it through.'

'Well then I can put him up in front of me.' Madoc had been hesitant to suggest it in case his brother might feel further belittled.

'Why not?' Robert's shoulders slumped. 'I surely cannot hold him.'

Madoc noticed Robert nursing his withered arm with his other
hand; evidently it had been hurt in the skirmish. Idris, his curiosity
evident, had the two horses ready.

'Was it footpads, Mr Madoc?'

'Er . . . yes,' Madoc agreed hastily.

'Do you want me to come with you?'

'We'll manage thank you, Idris.'

'Then do you want me to inform the constable?'

'No! No thanks. And I'd be obliged it you don't mention this incident to anyone. Not anyone,' Madoc stressed.

Idris looked surprised.

'All right, sir. I won't tell a living soul.'

'Thank you. I'm obliged.' Madoc nodded at the groom. As he watched Robert mounting, he realized that he was finding it difficult but Madoc pretended not to notice, neither offering assistance nor passing any comment. Robert had been humiliated enough as it was.

Tom was far into the woods, lying on his face, covered lightly by his torn shirt. Madoc lifted it to see his back and swore under his breath, appalled by the raw weeping weals criss-crossing Tom's back.

'The bastards. I'll get them for this, Tom. I know at least three of the cowardly—'

'We don't need heroics,' Robert broke in hotly. His lip curled. 'What do you think *you* can do on your own?'

Madoc puffed out his lips, not saying any more, willing to keep his thoughts to himself for the time being as he concentrated on helping Tom.

'We should have brought some salt with us,' Madoc remarked.

'Salt?' Rob gasped. 'That's a harsh cure.'

'An effective one though . . . after a flogging.' His voice was impassive.

His brother's eyes widened in realization.

'You've seen one?'

'As a boy, in the Mediterranean.' He knelt down and lifted Tom's arm gently over his own shoulder.

'Sorry about this,' he said softly, when Tom groaned. 'Brace yourself now. I'm going to get you up. I'll be as quick as I can.' Tom whimpered slightly as he hoisted him to his feet.

'I'll be all right,' Tom croaked, but his legs buckled as he tried to free himself from Madoc's support. His face was like alabaster and Madoc took his weight again.

'Lean on me for a minute, just to give yourself time, man. Can you manage your horse?'

'Yes . . . I . . . I don't know,' Tom admitted weakly.

Tom smothered another groan as Madoc lifted him effortlessly up in his arms on to his own horse, Storm, where Tom half-slumped forward over the animal's neck.

'Just watch he doesn't slip whilst I mount,' Madoc said to Robert.

Still holding Tom with one hand, Madoc leapt easily up behind him supporting the smaller man against him with one arm as they made their way out of the woods.

'It might be a good idea if you were to find Nia,' Madoc suggested. 'I'll go.'

'Nia? Bring a lady to this situation?' Robert was horrified. 'Don't be rid—'

'She's the best person to deal with this. She's never taken fright easily, Rob.'

'Do you want me to bring Nia?' Robert asked Tom, unconvinced.

'Yes,' he whispered.

Without another word Robert turned his horse and left, leaving the other two men to proceed slowly, Tom's horse tethered on a rein behind.

Elwyn's wife answered Madoc's knock. Her eyes widened as she saw Madoc supporting Tom, standing at the doorway.

'What happened to him?' She scanned Tom's battered face. 'Has he been in a fight?'

'Sort of. Can we come in please, Nesta?' Madoc asked.

'Oh, yes. Of course you can.' She ushered them into the one big living room where they sat Tom down on a stool. 'Do you want him to lie on the bed, Mr Madoc?' She had not known Madoc previously and was still in awe of her husband's friend from the quality.

'Come on, Nesta. Let's forget the mister bit, shall we? I thought we were friends.' He took a deep breath, looking down at Tom. 'Would you rather lie on the bed, Tom?'

'I'm fine here,' Tom murmured weakly, slumped forward with his arms on his knees.

'I'm sure Elwyn's got a drop of brandy, somewhere.' Nesta dropped down to kneel on the flagged floor to search in a wooden chest. 'He got it from a Frenchie boat.' She pulled it out, holding it aloft triumphantly. She poured a generous amount into a pewter mug and held it out to Tom. Her anxious glance lit on his broken nose, the dried blood covering his face, his tattered shirt. 'I'll get a wet cloth for that,' she said.

Madoc followed her into the lean-to outhouse.

'Are you hurt . . . Madoc?' she asked looking at the blood staining the front of his shirt.

'No. It's Tom's blood. Nesta. What I'm going to tell you I'd like you and Elwyn to keep to yourselves, please.' He went on to explain briefly what had happened.

'How could they do that?' Her eyes were full of horror. 'Do you know who they were?'

'They were masked, but I know who they were. Bull's gang of cronies.'

Nesta pulled a face. 'The prize-fighter. He's a horrible man.' She glanced at Tom. 'Poor thing.' She didn't know him but she'd heard Madoc and Elwyn talking about Tom and his sister from when they were children. 'We'll have to do something about his back as well then, won't we?'

'My brother's gone to bring Nia back.'

'Who's Nia?'

'Tom's sister.'

'His sister?' she gasped. 'Should she see him like that?'

'She's a good healer. . . .' Madoc began.

'A healer? Of course! I know who you mean now. I remember the gypsy girl. Everyone used to talk about her years ago. Is she the same one?'

Madoc smiled. 'You won't recognise her as the gypsy girl now.'

Nesta dipped a tin into a barrel of water, scooped some out and poured it into a bowl. She took it into the living room, dipped a cloth in the water, then washed the blood from Tom's face with it. When she had finished this she wrung the cloth out again, then held it to his nose. As she was doing this there was a tap on the door. Nesta dropped the cloth back into the bowl and she ran to open it. She ushered in Nia and Robert. Nia rushed over to her brother, her face pale and drawn.

'What have they done to you?' she wailed, throwing herself down on her knees beside Tom.

Tom managed a weak smile. 'It's not as bad as it looks. You'll soon see me right.'

She lifted the remnant of the ragged shirt off his back and bit her lip.

'Why you?' she whispered, blinking back tears. She looked up at the others standing around her. 'Where's my bag?'

Robert placed the battered leather bag he'd been holding on to the scrubbed wooden table as Nia rose to her feet. She began taking things out of it and placing them on the table.

'Can I get anything, miss?' Nesta could not reconcile this elegant creature with the gypsy girl she'd known before.

'Yes, please. Will you bring me a pitcher of water and I also need some boiling water separately?'

When Nesta came hurrying back with the boiling water Nia poured it on to the herbs she had already put into a cup, leaving them to infuse whilst she took more things from her bag. Then she added a little cold water to this brew and held the cup to Tom's lips.

'This will deaden the pain,' she murmured, kissing the top of his head. 'I think we will have to straighten your nose first.'

'Yes. Can't spoil my beauty.' Tom tried to joke.

Madoc saw her press her lips together, but she didn't trust herself to reply.

Madoc and Robert left the women to their ministrations and went outside to sit on the edge of a stone horse-trough. It was close to the river which flowed over the nearby waterfall, and Madoc picked up a handful of small stones which he threw at a branch floating down with the current.

'I'll get those bastards for this,' Madoc snarled to Robert, his face harsh. 'Just you see.'

Robert glared at him.

'Two of us couldn't manage, but you can take them on single-handed, I suppose?' He pulled a belittling face. 'You have to play the big hero again, don't you?'

Madoc frowned, taken back by his brother's vehemence.

'Are those just words, Rob? Or do you really mean that?'

'Why do you doubt me?'

Madoc stared at him for a moment, studying his face. Then he realized that he was very worked up and in an emotional frame of mind.

'Rob. I can understand you being upset—' he began.

'Upset! So *I'm* upset, am I? Poor Robert is upset ... but tough Madoc will take care of it.' Robert clenched his fist, looking ready to hit Madoc. 'I can't believe you are saying this! But there, you've always been irresponsible and reckless, ready to do the first thing that came into your head regardless of its consequences.'

'Rob, that was when I was a boy—'

'Yes, it was. And if you hadn't been such a little hooligan I would-n't have got this crippled arm,' Rob burst out.

Madoc felt as if he had been punched hard in the solar plexus. His mouth dropped and he sucked in a breath, stunned by Robert's words. He turned and stalked away, unwilling to show Robert how badly his words had affected him.

'Christ!' The blasphemy escaped from his lip as he stared blindly up at the sky. For all these years Rob had maintained that it had been his own fault, Madoc reflected. Said he'd goaded Madoc into it – and now he'd admitted his true feelings. He must have always thought this, probably believed his arm was the reason for Lucy's marrying Randolf Chilcott. No wonder he was bitter!

'Madoc!' Hearing Nia's call he turned. Robert was standing near her and they were both looking his way. He took a deep breath, trying to compose his expression and his emotions as he approached them.

'How is he?' He avoided his brother's eye.

'He'll be all right ... though he will always bear the scars. Both physical and mental.' Nia was dispirited. 'I have managed to reset his nose, I don't think it will be crooked ... at least I hope not. It's so unfair,' she burst out. 'When he has never even considered his Romany blood ... barely acknowledged it even.'

'Is Nesta willing to let him stay here for a while?' Madoc asked, remembering he hadn't asked her.

'Perfectly happy. She doesn't mind ... I don't think she believes it's true,' Nia said softly. 'That we are half-gypsy,' she supplied as Madoc looked questioningly at her.

'That's not what I meant,' Madoc objected. 'About being half-gypsy.'

'As if it mattered to anyone other than us,' said Nia, downcast.

Madoc looked at her, aching to take her into his arms, to comfort her, to kiss away her misery. But it was not him she wanted. His eyes wandered to his brother, trying to will him to comfort her instead – even though the idea of Robert holding Nia in his arms was like a knife cutting into his flesh.

As if reading his thoughts, Robert put his arm around Nia's shoul-ders, hugging her against his side, looking down at her with affection. Nia smiled up at him tremulously, unshed tears shimmering in her eyes. Not wanting to watch, Madoc looked away, gritting his teeth. So he didn't see the longing in Nia's dark eyes as they looked over at him, reaching out to him, only to dull with despair as he walked away.

Over at the river, he continued his aimless throwing of the pebbles that he still held in his hand, wishing he could discard his problems as easily.

'What will you tell your parents?' Madoc asked, eventually turning back to them.

'I hope we won't need to tell them anything. He doesn't always come home. Sometimes, when he has a case on, he lodges at a house in Swansea for a whole week or more. They won't be worried or anything.'

Madoc's brooding eyes hung on Nia. What if they had attacked her? His skin crawled at the very idea, leaving him vulnerable and terrified. *I must watch out for her. If they ever harm her I'll kill them,* he vowed. *I'd gladly face the hangman for her.*

'Mama and Papa don't see him undressed,' Nia continued. 'As long as they don't see the scars on his back we can pretend it was footpads.' She reached a hand up to Robert's face and Madoc was once again suffused with an overwhelming jealousy. 'I'd better put something on those bruises too.' She turned away to fetch her bag.

As if he felt Madoc's cold eyes on him Robert glanced over at him. His gaze met Madoc's, his expression became shamefaced, and he took a few steps towards him.

'Madoc. I'm sorry. I spoke in haste. I—' he began as Nia left them. He was beginning to recover his normal aplomb.

'I think not. You have every reason to make your assumption,' Madoc finished softly.

'But I didn't mean it. Truly I didn't. You will forgive my slip of the tongue.' Robert was ill at ease. 'I was irate . . . not with you . . . but I lashed out at you in the heat of the moment.'

Madoc nodded impassively, hiding his hurt from his brother.

'Forget it was said.' But Madoc realized that he could never forget; the words had driven yet another insurmountable barrier between them. After the troubles he had caused Rob, how could he ever tell Nia he loved her, when Robert loved her too?

CHAPTER TWENTY-ONE

MADOC crouched low over his horse, pushing him to the limit, galloping along the hard sand of the beach as if he were trying to outrun a hurricane. Realizing that the horse was tiring he reined in and flung himself off, patting the animal's heaving sides. He was filled with remorse when he found that Storm was sweating.

'I'm sorry, boy.' He stroked his velvet nose. 'I am punishing you for my own emotions. I'd better let you cool down.'

The horse whinnied softly, nuzzling his nose against Madoc, searching for the sugar-lumps he always carried when riding.

'Here we are, Storm.' Madoc found one and offered it to him, allowing him to take it. The soft mouth was gentle on his palm, before nuzzling his pocket for a second lump which Madoc supplied.

He trudged listlessly towards the sea, the horse's reins held loosely in his hand. Staring out at the horizon, he wondered whether he should sail with another ship until the *Gower Girl* was ready. He clenched his jaw, his face pensive and morose.

He couldn't stay here. So close to Nia. Torturing himself by knowing she was with Robert. He'd had a lucky escape, ending up with Nia rather than with that treacherous Lucy. He closed his eyes. How the hell had he ever got into this mess? It would be easier to be miles away, where he couldn't see Nia to have his mind set in turmoil.

He had tried to put her out of his mind, filling it with anything else instead. But the harder he tried the more she invaded his every waking moment. He'd loved her since they were children, would love her for ever. He was still astonished that he hadn't realized it. Lucy was so superficial, possessed of surface beauty only, with no thought for anyone other than herself, not like Nia.

What if Nia were simply sorry for Robert because he'd been hurt and she was trying to console him? His mood lightened at the idea.

So, once Lucy was back with Robert . . . no, that wouldn't hold water. It was evident that Nia was enjoying Robert's company and he hers. *Oh God! I've lost her!* He raised his face skywards, not even seeing the seagulls wheeling above, their plaintive calls echoing his misery.

He'd go back to sea as soon as he could, he decided. Then he'd be so occupied he wouldn't have time to think. With luck, Lucy would find someone else and he wouldn't have that problem to solve.

The horse had cooled down a little now, so Madoc pulled off his boots and stockings and led the animal into the sea. As usual when on his own, Madoc had scorned a jacket and was riding in his shirt-sleeves, but his trousers quickly soaked up water as both he and Storm splashed along through the shallows.

He remounted and turned Storm towards the far margin of the beach, continuing to the little copse of trees. Sunlight shed dappled light and dark shadow across his face as the horse plodded through the trees until they emerged near an isolated cottage that stood along-side the path, where Madoc knew there was a horse-trough. Madoc dismounted and, still barefooted, his feet coated with sand, he led Storm over to it, allowing the horse to drink before he re-mounted and continued on his way, his boots draped over the saddle in front of him. On reaching the cliffs, he rode listlessly, his head dropped on to his chest.

'Madoc! Hey, Madoc!'

He looked up, catching his breath when he saw Nia cantering towards him, Laddie running alongside, tongue lolling. This time, though, she was playing no grand lady but wore a cotton skirt and a plain blouse, and was sitting astride her horse as she used to do as a child, her skirt and petticoats bunched up around her thighs. Her hair was loose, and, tumbled in a dark cloud around her shoulders. Memories of so many times when he had seen her like this came flooding back as he reined in, waiting for her. He smiled, watching her, loving her.

'Hello, Madoc.' She drew to a halt alongside him. 'I thought Nesta said you were going fishing with Elwyn.'

'I changed my mind.' His eyes wandered over her face, her huge eyes black as midnight, her generous full-lipped mouth. His whole being ached to take her into his arms, to make love to her. It would be wild and passionate with Nia – she was all fire and vitality. His mouth twisting, he dragged his gaze away and caressed her horse's muzzle, feeding him a sugar-lump too, then throwing one to Laddie.

'Have you been to see Tom?' he asked. 'How is he?'

'He is coming on well. His back has almost healed now. He told me you've been calling regularly to see him.'

They urged their horses into a walk, side by side.

'I feel responsible for him getting set on like that,' said Madoc dispiritedly.

'You warned Tom. Why should you feel responsible?'

'It's just that I know what Bull is like. I should have—'

'Tom and Robert know what he's like, too.'

'But they never got involved with him as boys the way I did.'

'You mean they never got beaten up by him . . . like you did.'

He shrugged. 'I should have gone for them before they had a chance. I still intend to. He's not getting away with it.'

'Madoc. Don't be a fool. Bull is—'

'A big, slow-witted—'

'. . . professional prize-fighter,' she broke in. She reined in her mount, putting a hand on his arm as he drew up alongside her. 'Madoc. Just leave it be. Please. It's bad enough having Tom hurt, without—' She broke off, pressing her lips together.

Do you care about me, then? The words remained unspoken, but Madoc was longing to ask them. He felt as though a rope was wound tightly around his chest, restricting his breathing. He looked down at her hand on his bare forearm, wanting to lift it up to his lips. But he didn't. Glancing up at her again, he found she was studying him intently and he swallowed hard, looking away in case she could read his love for her written on his face.

They drew up near the edge of the cliffs, right above their child-hood 'secret' cove, and looking down at it. To a casual onlooker it appeared to be inaccessible except from the sea.

'Let's climb down to it, shall we? To our secret cove.' Nia's laugh bubbled out.

Madoc forced a wry smile, still afraid that he might give himself away, but reluctant to pass up any opportunity of being with her.

'Why not?' His glance flicked over her clothes and footwear. 'If you can mange to climb in that skirt. And I'll bet your feet are gone soft.' They had always climbed barefooted.

'I did it often enough in a skirt when we were children. And I have not gone soft,' she flashed back.

Madoc threw her a grin, his misery easing.

'But you were not a high and mighty lady then,' he taunted.

She tossed her head, not deigning to reply, and jumped off her mount, tying the reins over a gorse bush as Madoc followed suit. She pulled off her shoes and stockings, leaving them by the bush, and then hitched the hem of her skirt up into its waistband revealing firm brown calves and slim ankles. Laddie looked up at her eagerly.

'No. You stay!' she told him. 'Guard the horses.'

His ears drooped, but obediently he lay down beside the horses, his head on his paws, his eyes following them.

They climbed down easily, the familiar hand- and footholds seeming to come to them naturally. When they reached the sand below they crossed the tiny cove towards the water, their feet leaving two rows of footprints in the unmarked sand, which was always hard and damp as the cove was completely flooded by each tide. The ozone smell was strong: big waves were thundering on to the beach, exploding into a froth of creamy surf before dying out in the shallows where Madoc and Nia paddled. Madoc's trousers were already soaked up past his knees and though Nia held up the hem of her skirt it was dipping into the water and was soon just as wet. With a grin, Madoc bent down, scooped up water in both hands and threw it over her.

'You beast,' she shrieked, quickly returning his action. In no time they were both completely drenched, laughing aloud like the children they had once been.

'I'm going in for a swim.' Nia began undoing the buttons on her blouse and Madoc drew to a halt, his heart beginning to thud. Nia began splashing back towards the sand as Madoc stood motionless, staring after her in an agony of indecision.

God! Now what was he going to do? he thought, his jaw clenched. He watched her pull off her wet blouse then step out of her long skirt and petticoats and turn back towards him. She was wearing no corset, only her lawn undershift and drawers.

'Come on! What are you waiting for?'

Yes, what? his mind screamed. He took a stumbling step towards her as she entered the water again, her face alive with mischief. Reaching her he stopped, his eyes wandering down over the clothes clinging wetly against her, at her nipples standing in peaks, the shadows of their aureoles dark beneath the cotton, at the dark triangle at the top of her thighs. His wondering gaze came back to her face, hung on her lips, those luscious ruby lips.

'God, Nia,' he groaned, putting his hands on her shoulders, his fingers digging into the creamy flesh. With a little whimper she leaned towards him, holding up her face, her lips parted, her eyes dark and luminous. He lowered his mouth to hers, salty from the sea, pulling her closer as her lips eagerly explored his, returning his kiss. The world seemed to stand still around them, the roar of the waves, the screaming of the gulls, faded into nothing. He was isolated with Nia. Aware only of her lips on his, her tongue exploring his mouth, her body in contact with his, the swell of her soft breasts pressed up against him through the thin cotton. Wonderful, exciting Nia – he loved her, the only woman in the world. He slid his arms around her and lifted her, her arms clinging around his neck, his mouth still on hers as he carried her up the beach. Raising his lips from hers, he dropped to his knees on the sand, lowering her gently to the ground in the shelter of the rocks.

'I love you to distraction, Nia.'

'Do you? Do you really love me, Madoc?' she whispered.

'I love you. I'm wild about you.' His tongue traced a path down her neck. On reaching the base of her throat his fingers slid towards the top of her chemise, and paused, curling away from temptation. She reached up her hand and pulled down the low neckline, baring her breasts.

'You are so lovely, Nia.' He buried his face in the valley between those superb swelling orbs, soft, yet firm as ripe peaches, nuzzling at them. His mouth slid towards one brown nipple, taking it in his mouth like a luscious grape, teasing it with his lips before taking the other, sucking at it. His hand slid up her leg, exploring that delightful valley between her thighs, his body responding, his erection pressing against her as she arched her back towards him, moaning softly, both her hands tugging at handfuls of his wet hair.

'I love you,' she whispered, her lips against his throat.

'I've always loved you, Nia. I've been insane with jealousy seeing you with . . .' He broke off, horror sweeping through him. Robert! Robert loves her! Nia is Robert's woman – not mine!

'Oh, my God! What am I saying?' He sucked in a shuddering breath, managing to pull away from her. He had no right to say these words.

'What do you mean?' Nia's eyes jerked open. 'You said you loved me? What's wrong with that?'

'Because I've no right to tell you that.'

'Why? Why not?'

'Because I can't marry you. . . .'

Nia gave a loud gasp. Twisting, she rolled on to her knees, brought her arm back, then slapped him with the full strength of her arm across the face, her face torn with grief.

'I hate you, Madoc Morgan,' she shrieked. 'I hate you! I always thought you were so wonderful ... but you're not! You're not even man enough to make love to me.' She leapt to her feet and raced away from him along the beach. He sprang up and chased after her, catching her arm and spinning her around to face him, trying to hold her in his arms as she struggled and fought to get away, raining punches on his face and arms.

'Nia. Listen. Please listen to—'

'Stop it! I hate you!' She pounded both her fists against his chest, tears flowing down her face as she flung her head from side to side, trying to escape from his grasp. 'Let me go!' she gasped. 'Let me go! You said you would never force a woman. . . .'

He released her abruptly, exhaling a sighing breath and she turned away from him, her face buried in her hands.

'God, Nia. Give me a chance to explain—'

'I don't want to hear anything,' she shrieked on the top of her voice. She clamped both hands over her ears. 'Leave me alone! I hate you! I hate you!' She began crying hysterically, loud, uncontrolled sobs shaking her body.

Helpless, his chest heaving in great gulps of air, Madoc scrubbed distracted hands though his wet hair, feeling almost like crying himself. Beside himself with grief and frustration, he turned on his heel, and ran towards the water. Wading out, he dived under the waves and swam out strongly to sea, kept on swimming.

CHAPTER TWENTY-TWO

A s Madoc ran away from her, Nia, aware of him moving quickly, opened her fingers to see where he was going. A ripple of alarm shuddered through her as he threw himself into the sea and swam out, kept on swimming. Swift panic jangled her nerves.

'Come back,' she whispered, her hands flying to her mouth. 'Madoc. Please come back!' Her eyes fixed on his diminishing form, she sank down on to the wet sand, her legs doubled up under her. 'Come back. Please come back,' she kept repeating under her breath like a mantra.

The sun had now sunk below the skyline, leaving a warm glow across the horizon as he swam towards it.

He said he could not marry me, she considered bitterly. *I never thought Madoc would care about my gypsy blood. Not Madoc of all people. Mama was right!* Tears poured unheeded down her cheeks, dripping off her chin on to her chest. Shivering, she clutched her arms around her body, her teeth chattering as much with fear as with cold as she tried to keep her eyes on the tiny speck in the water that was Madoc; but eventually it was lost to her sight. Desperately she screwed up her eyes, shading them with her hands as she scanned the darkening sea. She let out a sigh of relief as she thought she found him, until the speck flew up in the air and winged further out to sea.

Her shivers becoming more violent, she got up to look for her clothes, which she found swirling around in the encroaching tide. She tried wringing the water out of them, then, pulling a face of distaste at their sodden state, pulled them on nevertheless.

Shall I fetch someone to look for him? she wondered. A sailing boat could cover a lot of water quickly, there is plenty of breeze. But he'll come back soon, he can't go much further. Her face crumpled and she sobbed again, softly this time, slow tears of misery gradually trickling their way down her cheeks.

'He loves me. He said he loves me,' she whispered under her breath. What had he said? 'I love you to distraction', those were the words he used. She drew the words around her like a warm blanket, shutting out more unpleasant thoughts. How long she sat in a stupor she didn't know but she heard a dog barking, voices calling from the cliffs above.

'Nia. Nia. Are you down there?'

Papa! Goaded out of her inertia, she got stiffly to her feet, noticing that the tide was almost lapping up to where she was sitting, creeping very near to the foot of the cliffs. Wearily she made her way across the beach. Cupping her hands around her mouth she answered the repeated call.

'Yes. I'm here, Papa. I'm all right.'

Laddie raced over to her, leaping up and licking her face, and in the gloom she was able to make out the figure of her agile father scaling down the rocks towards her, accompanied by Bertie, both of them carrying lanterns. She bent down to give the dog a hug, then, feet dragging, she went to meet them as they reached the sand.

'Nia. What are you doing down here?' Gratefully, Liam gathered her against him, hugging her tightly. 'I've been worried sick about you.' He broke off, feeling her clothes. 'What have you been doing, girl? You're soaking wet. Someone saw your horses up on the cliffs. . . .'He glanced around him. 'Isn't Madoc with you?' His voice was harsh.

'He was. He swam out to sea,' she said tremulously, tears threatening again. 'I've been waiting for him to come back.'

'What do you mean, come back?'

'He hasn't come back,' she whispered.

'Are you trying to say he might have drowned?'

'No!' She shook her head violently. 'Don't say that! Please don't say that.' She began to cry again. 'I don't know.'

Liam strode towards the sea, holding the lantern aloft, waving it from side to side as he peered into the dusk. He was turning away when Nia saw something moving towards them in the water.

'Is that him? Is it?' As the moving shadow drew nearer, almost faint with relief she whispered: 'Thank God! It's Madoc.'

Struggling against the breakers washing over him, exhausted, Madoc waded from the waves, his head drooping, and collapsed on to his hands and knees in the shallow water, his chest heaving.

'Are you all right, man?' Liam was walking over to him. 'Do you need a hand?'

Madoc shook his head.

'No. All . . . right,' he gasped. 'Just winded.'

Nia was longing to reach for him, to touch him, but never moved as they were held motionless, like a tableau, waiting for Madoc to rise.

He pushed himself up wearily to his feet, still gasping, and looked at Nia, who was standing rigid, beside her father.

'Sorry,' he gasped, leaning forward to rest his hands on his knees as he tried to recover his breath. 'I frightened you.'

'You frightened me too,' Liam snarled. 'You should have had more sense . . . leaving the horses there like that. Didn't you think we might wonder what had happened to you?'

'I'm sorry,' Madoc repeated.

'Have you taken advantage of my daughter, Madoc Morgan? What did you bring her down here for? I don't trust you with her.'

Madoc pulled himself upright but remained silent, mouth set, still breathing hard.

Liam grabbed the front of Madoc's sodden shirt, twisting it in his fist as Madoc eyed him impassively.

'Papa. Stop it! He has done nothing.' Nia caught her father's arm, hanging on to it as he tried to shake her off. 'Please listen, Papa.'

'Have I your word you've not taken advantage of her?' Liam was still holding Madoc's shirt. When Madoc still didn't answer, Liam took a pace closer to him, reaching his face up towards Madoc's. 'If I thought. . . .' he began in a threatening tone.

'No, Papa! He didn't. I wanted him to . . . but he wouldn't. He wouldn't. . . .' Distraught, she broke into a fit of hysterical sobbing.

Liam's hand dropped and he stared at her, speechless. He chewed his lip, his glance going to Madoc, still silent, still stony faced.

'It looks at if I owe—' Liam began.

'No. This is my fault,' Madoc insisted. 'I should never have brought her down here.' He sighed. 'You need not worry, her maidenhood is intact, so let's drop this. I think you'd better get her home as soon as possible. She must be very cold.'

Liam looked at Nia; violent shudders were shaking her body, her teeth were chattering. He took off his jacket and helped her to put it on, putting his arm around her shoulders as they made their way back across the beach. Madoc was still watching her, and as they reached the foot of the rocks she turned to look back at him, her eyes desolate.

Upon waking on the following day, Madoc's mood was at first euphoric, so different from his depression of the previous morning. *Nia loves me*, he thought. *She loves me!* It being a Sunday, he allowed himself the luxury of lying in bed, thinking about her. She had said she loved him, had she meant it? Or had she simply been over-whelmed with passion? He was well aware that despite popular supposition a woman could, and did, feel desire as much as a man, could equally be carried away with her body's demands.

He managed to assure himself that she spoke the truth and was revelling in that consolation until his thoughts returned to his brother. Whichever way he looked at it he couldn't dismiss Robert from the equation. If he was in love with her, how could he let him suffer again on his account? He'd already caused him enough damage.

But did Robert love Nia, or was he using her to get his revenge on Madoc? Did he suspect that Madoc didn't love Lucy? Madoc was ambivalent on those points. But what about Nia? Didn't what she wanted count?

Yes! Madoc answered his own question. If Nia loved him they must be together, whatever the consequences. Nia and he belonged together.

'Nia,' he said, savouring it. He was aroused by the thought of those sensual moments they had spent together, and he rubbed a hand across his face. Pulling away from her at that stage was the hardest thing he had ever done in his life; he had almost failed. He groaned at the memory.

The sooner he got Lucy and Robert back together the better for all of them, Madoc decided, debating the tricky problem of how to accomplish it. In the meantime, he would tell Nia how much he loved her, explain everything, and ask her to marry him. Pleased with that idea he leapt out of bed.

Standing in the hall at Mead Rise Madoc looked eagerly towards the door through which the maid had disappeared. His heart plummeted when Martha came out instead of Nia, her face set, her stance rigid.

'Nia does not wish to see you.'

'Martha. Please ask her if she will spare me but a few minutes.'

Martha's eyes narrowed.

'Madoc, can't you understand what I am saying? Nia does not wish to see you. In fact, Liam and I do *not* want you calling here . . . pestering her.' Her voice dripped ice.

Madoc sucked in a sharp breath, his chin jutting at her words. Recovering himself, he nodded, adopted a stern expression, his stance erect.

'I am sorry I have troubled you, Mrs La Velle.' His voice was clipped. 'Would you please give Nia my . . .' He hesitated before adding softly: 'My love.' Turning on his heel, he stalked out.

Nia, who had been listening behind the door, gave a smothered gasp. She grabbed the door handle and wrenched the door open, but her mother was barring her way when she tried to leave the room.

'Excuse me, Mama. I must speak to Madoc.' She tried to push past her but Martha grabbed her sleeve.

'He's gone, Nia. Don't go chasing after him.'

'He loves me, Mama. I heard him say so.'

'And you told me he said he cannot marry you.' She kept a tight grip on Nia's arm, led her into the room and closed the door firmly. 'Do you want to be some man's trollop?'

Nia's eyes flashed fire.

'This is my life, Mama. You did what you. . . .' Her face was anguished. 'I love him, Mama. I love him.'

'Nia. Please do not upset me. Don't run after him.'

Madoc rode away in turmoil, despair, anger and resentment fighting for supremacy. Riding aimlessly, he eventually found himself in the vicinity of the fishing village, Llanmor, and Bull's treatment of Tom sprang into his mind.

'Right! Let's find you, Bull. Let's get that settled, anyway.'

After winding his way down through the narrow road that twisted its way past the church and through the village he arrived at the harbour. Empty baskets stood on end to dry, emitting a strong salty smell which hung in the air, combining with other odours, the overriding ones being those of tar and rotting seaweed. A few men in heavy woollen jerseys seated on some upturned casks were busy repairing their nets. One of them raised an arm to Madoc, others nodded. Here and there women bobbed curtsies, stopping to watch as he rode past; some of the younger ones flashed smiles at him. One, more brazen, threw him a kiss, then stood hands on hips, her admiring eyes following his path. Madoc acknowledged them all, touching his hat with his riding-crop. Storm picked a path amongst the litter of ropes and nets, and Madoc dismounted outside the Nag's Head tavern, tied up the reins and ducked his head to enter through the low doorway. A few customers lounged around inside where a stale smell permeated the low-ceilinged room, of sour beer coupled with unwashed bodies and tobacco smoke.

'Good to see you, Madoc.' The landlord approached him and, after wiping his hands in a grubby towel held out one of them. 'I haven't seen you here for a long while.'

'I don't get this way often. Good to see you again, Bart.'

'You finished with the copper-barques now, have you?' Bart asked.

'No. My ship is in for refurbishment.' Madoc looked around the room. 'Bull around anywhere?'

'Bull? What do you want him for?'

'I've got a debt to pay.' Madoc's expression was grim. He put some money on the counter. 'Porter, please, Bart.'

'You have a bet on him?' Bart turned on the tap and drew ale from a wooden cask set up behind the counter.

'Any idea where I might find him?' Madoc took a sip of the beer, wiping the froth off his lip with his fingers.

'You could try his mate's. You know, Dick Maddis?'

A spark of interest lit Madoc's eyes.

'Yes. I know him. Do you know where he lives?'

'Just down the road by there.' Bart nodded his head, as he slopped a wet cloth across the splintered counter. 'Right next door to the baker's shop, he is.'

'Who else does he hang around with?'

Madoc listened intently as Bart reeled off a few names, all of whom he knew. Madoc downed the rest of the porter and made for the door. He turned back before he left.

'Bart. If you see Bull, will you tell him I was looking for him.'

Untying Storm, Madoc led the horse along the road, then stopped to secure him again under the sign for the baker's shop. There was only one house immediately adjoining the shop and Madoc knocked on the door. He tensed, fists clenched, as he heard heavy footsteps approaching. The door was opened by Dick Maddis, looking bleary-eyed and half-asleep.

Madoc grabbed him by the shirt-front and thumped him hard in the stomach. As the man doubled forward with a groan, Madoc pulled his arm back and punched him as hard as he could in the face, feeling the bones crunch under his fist. As the man let out a scream of agony and collapsed to the flagstones another figure appeared behind him.

'What the hell—' he began.

Recognizing him as another of Bull's cronies Madoc stepped over the prostrate Maddis and felled the other man with a single blow. Yanking him roughly to his feet, Madoc punched him again then head-butted him before releasing him, allowing him to fall on top of Maddis. Breathing hard, Madoc waited cautiously in case Bull followed. He never appeared but a slovenly woman came out, her hair in disarray, her mouth dropping open with astonishment.

'Hey! Wha's you' game?' she screamed. 'Wha' you doin'?'

'Paying a debt.' Madoc pushed at one of the men on the floor with the toe of his boot. The man stirred, groaning, then seeing Madoc standing there, peered fearfully up at him, raising a protective arm.

'Remember me? Madoc Morgan? Do you?' he snarled when the man didn't answer.

'Yes. Yes, sir. I remembers you.'

'Right! In future you and your cronies keep away from my family and friends. You know what I mean?' Madoc swore, taking a threatening step towards the man when he didn't answer.

'Yes sir. I knows what you mean,' the man howled.

'Don't forget it then! You touch any of them again and I swear I'll bloody kill you. Who else was in that gang that attacked my brother and his friend?'

'I dunno.'

'I think you do. You'll give me their names if you know what's good for you.' Madoc kicked out hard at the nearest man's legs as he cowered away from him.

The two men stuttered out a few names and Madoc nodded.

'Right. I know two of them live here in the village. Where will I find them? Ron Fisher for a start . . . you might as well tell me first as last.'

Dick Maddis blurted out an address but said the other man was with Bull.

'So where do I find Bull?'

' 'E's not here. 'E's gone to Neath . . . 'E's fighting this weekend.'

Disappointed, Madoc scowled, then chewed at his cheek thoughtfully.

'Right! Then tell Bull I am challenging him to a fight.'

'A fight?' The man gasped. 'You and Bull? You don' mean a proper fight?'

'That's right. A proper fight, so no one else can jump in and help. Just him and me. All right?'

'All right. I'll tell 'im.' The man was looking up at him openmouthed with astonishment.

After rooting out a surprised Ron Fisher and meting out a similar punishment, Madoc returned to the tavern before leaving the village. He looked around at the few men still near the counter.

'Back then, Madoc. Same again?' Bart asked.

'Please.' He threw some money on the counter and turned to face the others in the bar. 'I want you all to know I have challenged Bull to a fight....'

'Bloody hell, man,' Bart gasped, horrified. 'You can't fight him.'

'Why not?' Madoc eyed the man belligerently over the top of his tankard.

'He'll bloody kill you. After all, you're gentry—'

'So you think that makes me soft or something?' Madoc looked around at everyone present. 'Does it?'

'God, no! I'd be the last person to say that about you, Madoc. 'Specially a veteran Cape Horner, like. It's just that ... well. ...' His voice trailed away and he looked around for support from the other men in the room.

'It's the only way I can be certain his cronies won't join in,' Madoc said. 'This is between me and Bull and no one else.' He strode out of the room, leaving them all staring after him.

God. Now what have I done? Madoc's stomach churned as he rode home and he gave a rueful grin. Well, at least he would have more chance without all his chums joining in – or tying me up, like Robert and Tom were. Madoc pulled a face. He thought it was a pity that he'd never spent time in the Orient, as his father had. He would have to ask the old man about some of those oriental fighting moves he used to show them when they were young.

'Mr Madoc, sir.' Jenkins, very much on his dignity, approached him as he walked in through the front door. 'There is a visitor, sir. He left his card.' He handed it to him.

'Lord Marks?' Madoc puzzled, reading the card. 'I wonder what he wants? Did he ask for my brother, Jenkins?'

'No sir. He did not. Mrs Morgan is not at home, but Lord Marks said he would wait to see the captain. He is in the drawing room. A letter has also arrived for you, Mr Madoc.'

'Thank you, Jenkins.' Madoc's heart surged with hope, thinking it might be from Nia, but as he turned the scented envelope over in his hands he groaned. Smelling of violets, it must be from Lucy. It was. She had written a brief note with profuse declarations of her love and saying she had arrived back at her parents' home the previous evening and was looking forward to seeing him. As he crumpled it savagely, he noticed his grazed knuckles and went to wash them before going in to their visitor.

'Good afternoon, Lord Marks.' Madoc strode over to shake the outstretched hand of the old man, the blue veins prominent through his wafer-thin skin. 'I am Madoc Morgan, the younger son of David and Emily Morgan, sir. I am pleased to make your acquaintance. I trust you have been served refreshment?' Madoc could see the tray on the little rosewood table beside him.

'I have, thank you, my boy.' Even though the man's voice was quavery, it was still authoritative. His shoulders were stooped and, as if his neck were immobile, he seemed to tilt his body, rather than his head, to look up at Madoc. 'Sit down, fellow. You are towering above me.'

'Is it my brother, Robert, you were seeking?' Madoc asked as he took the seat beside his visitor.

'No, your father.' The man's faded eyes were intelligent as they studied him intently. 'You say you are the younger son? Will your brother be home soon?'

'I'm afraid not. He is away for a few days. But I believe you have already met Robert. I know he has spent some time at your home as a guest of your niece. Is her name Caroline?'

'Robert? Hmm? Robert Morgan?' Lord Marks pondered. 'Yes, I believe I do recall the young man. Tall, blond, good-looking? That the one?' There was a twinkle in the man's shrewd blue eyes. 'But I did not realize he was David's son. Yes, he has been a houseguest of my great-niece, Caroline, a few times. She likes handsome young men. She lives with me

'So Robert said.'

'I do not think I have ever met your father, though?' Lord Mark's expression was alive with interest. 'But I did know your grandmother. You resemble her you know.'

'My grandmother?' Madoc said with surprise. 'I never knew her, sir. She died not long after my father was born.'

'So I heard. She was exceptionally lovely. Very lovely. . . .' The old man's voice trailed off, his eyes seeming to look into the past, and he shook his head. 'Sad.'

He's a funny old boy, Madoc thought, wondering what to say to him.

'Did you say your great-niece lives with you?' Madoc wanted to make conversation with the man.

'Yes. She is my ward. Caroline's grandmother, my sister, also lives with me. Caroline's parents died.' His eyes gleamed again. 'I have had great fun indulging her . . . I could never do that with my son when he was that age, of course.' He sighed deeply.

'Your son no longer resides with you, sir?'

Lord Marks shook his head sadly.

'It grieves me to say I no longer have my son or my grandson, Charles. They died in the jungles of Africa last year. Very intrepid, both of them, with a great sense of adventure. Still I suppose it runs in the family, I was like that when I was young.' His eyes studied Madoc again. 'I understand you have a sense of adventure, Madoc.'

Madoc gave a puzzled smile.

'I have been told you sail around Cape Horn in a copper-barque. Is that true?'

'Well . . . yes. I do. How did you know that, sir?'

'I have been making enquiries,' Lord Marks said enigmatically. 'About your family.'

'I think that is my father in the hall now.' Madoc had heard David's voice. 'Excuse me, sir. I'll tell him you are here.'

He left the room, and quickly explained to David that they had a visitor. David shrugged in surprise.

'I wonder what he wants?'

'You don't know him, then?'

'No. I've never met the man.'

Once introductions were over and they were all seated again, a glass of Madeira in their hands, Lord Marks gave a little smile, his gaze firmly on David.

'Well? That's what you are both too polite to ask. What does this old fossil want here?'

'Not at all, sir,' David assured him. 'We are pleased to make your acquaintance.'

'And I am more than delighted to make yours . . . David.' The faded eyes gleamed again. 'I have had diligent enquiries made, I know just about all there is to know about you and your family. You see . . .' he paused, as if for effect, before stating: 'I now know you are my son.'

'What?' David gasped. He had been on the point of placing his glass on the table; now he banged it down hard and stared at the older man in astonishment. 'I think a mistake has been made, sir. That can't be true.'

'Why not?'

'Because I . . . I. . . .'

'Your mother never told you the name of your father?'

David shook his head. 'She died when I was still a baby.'

'As far as I can make out, other than your grandfather she told no one that I was your father. Not even me. Your grandfather took her to Scotland for the birth and it was duly registered there . . . records were in force earlier in Scotland. My name was clearly recorded as your father.'

'It was? Good Lord! Why didn't she tell you?'

Lord Marks smiled ruefully. 'Because I was already married . . . though as yet without children. But as I have been telling Madoc here, my offspring are now deceased, leaving me, so I believed, without a direct heir to carry on the title. Now I have found one.' He beamed widely, revealing worn teeth, stained with age.

'You mean me?' David shook his head. 'I don't want it.'

Lord Mark's face fell.

'But you are my son. You must carry on the line.'

'Why did you never follow this up before?' David challenged.

'Because I had no idea that I had another child. I really did not know. Your mother certainly never told me she was carrying my child. Then she got married and went off to live somewhere in England. She died not long afterwards and we never met again.' He paused for a few minutes, staring into the past again. 'It was only when I began trying to find out where my son had disappeared to in Africa that enquiries further afield led to the discovery of an illegitimate child.'

'You may have others,' David put in shortly.

'No. I was not a promiscuous man, David. Your mother and I were truly in love.' His faded eyes peered at David. 'Have you never been tempted by Eve?'

Madoc sucked in a breath as his father's gaze dropped to the floor.

'I notice you are not answering that question,' Lord Marks said shrewdly.

There was silence for a few pregnant moments, each man considering his own temptation.

David gave a resigned shrug. 'So what are you leading to, sir?'

'I want to declare you officially my son and heir . . . with whatever legal implications that entails.'

'I don't know that I want any of it . . . but I will need time to talk it over with my wife and family. It involves their lives too.'

'Of course. I understand perfectly.' He chuckled. 'There are not many men who would turn down a chance to become a lord.'

'There is another problem,' David said slowly. 'I would not want to give up my name of Morgan. My mother's name.'

'Will you excuse me, gentleman?' Madoc said, rising to his feet. 'I have another engagement.'

'I have enjoyed meeting you, grandson,' said the old man, 'and look forward to doing so again.' As Madoc walked towards the door he heard Lord Marks continue: 'Even if you want the title to by-pass you, your elder son may wish to inherit it, David. He should be given the opportunity as well, don't you think?'

That's it! Madoc was elated as he mounted the stairs. *If Lucy knows that Robert will one day inherit a title she will wish to marry him*, he gloated. He would go and see her that afternoon, and make sure to let it 'slip' about the title. When Robert returned on the morrow he would not know that Lucy had heard about the title.

CHAPTER TWENTY-THREE

'COME in.' David looked up from his books as Madoc pushed the library door shut behind him.

'I need a bit of help,' Madoc said.

'What sort of help, Madoc?' David pushed the papers littering the desk to one side. 'Why don't you sit down and tell me about it.'

Madoc slumped into a chair, his elbows on the desktop. He gave an apologetic grin. 'You are not going to be pleased.'

'Try me.'

'I've challenged Bull to a fight. A professional fight. . . .'

'What?' David leapt up, knocking the pile of papers on to the floor. 'What the hell did you do that for? Are you mad?'

'Seems like it.' Madoc bent down to retrieve the scattered papers.

'What on earth possessed you to do it?'

'I'd better explain.' Madoc went on to tell his father about the attack on Tom and Robert.

David was appalled.

'That's when Rob said he'd been set on by robbers? I can understand your wish to retaliate but ... look, bare knuckle fighting is illegal now. I could get the fight stopped.'

'No!' Madoc shook his head. 'I trust you not to do that.'

'I should have known better than to suggest it to you.'

David was sorry he'd mentioned it; he should have done it without asking Madoc.

'So what help do you want from me?'

'Teach me some of those oriental fighting kicks you learned in the East. The ones you showed us when we were children.'

David laughed. 'If I can remember them.' His laughter fell away at the implications. 'When is this fight to take place?'

'I don't know. I went to Llanmor on Sunday and—'

'Sunday?' When Madoc said nothing, a suspicion crept into David's mind. 'May I ask if Nia has anything to do with this?'

'Nia? God, no! Well . . . sort of, I suppose.'

'Are you going to tell me?'

'Well. I wanted to sort a few things out, so I called round to her home. . . .' Madoc told him about his visit, his voice rising as he said: 'She wouldn't even see me . . . I was so incensed I just rode without noticing where, then I found myself near Llanmor. . . .'

'And decided to vent your wrath on those sadistic bullies.'

'I intended to get them anyway, but Robert had been so. . . .' He didn't elaborate. 'Would you have allowed them to get away with it if it were your friend and brother?'

David avoided answering.

'But to challenge Bull?'

'That is not what I intended. But I was on a short fuse, and when he wasn't there. . . .' Madoc laughed, his green eyes dancing. 'I got three of them anyway. And I know who the others are.'

'Pity. In that case we had better start as soon as we can.'

Madoc grinned. 'You will show me, then?'

'Against my better judgement. You were house boxing champion at school, weren't you? You will need all your skills to dodge those sledgehammer fists of Bull's.'

Madoc looked interested.

'Have you seen him fight?'

'A few times.' David's stomach turned at the thought of his son receiving those sickening blows. 'We shall have to practise away from your mother's eye. She will raise Cain if she finds out.'

'What about the old stable? The one used as a storeroom. She doesn't go across there, does she?'

'Good idea. And I'll find out whether Bull is fighting anywhere in the area and we can go along and study his methods.'

'That would be a help. I'm glad you understand.'

'Madoc. Is there still bad feeling between you and Rob?' David thought this was the reason for Madoc's smouldering aggression.

Madoc gave a mirthless smile and shrugged.

'Try and get it settled. It is worrying your mother.'

Madoc raised his brows skywards. 'Very well,' he sighed.

★

Madoc rode over to the Trents' home, determined to sort it out with Lucy. Under no circumstances could he ever marry her.

Mrs Trent's greeting was muted when the maid ushered him in.

'Ah, Madoc. I am afraid Lucy is indisposed.'

Madoc's spirits sank. Was he never to settle this problem?

'I am disappointed that Robert is not with you.'

'Was Lucy expecting to see Robert?' Madoc's mood rose. Perhaps she was already having second thoughts. 'He's at Beechwood, making final preparations before moving in.'

'Is he? We stayed there with him. And I was looking forward to seeing Lucy go to live there with Robert.'

Madoc nodded politely, wondering what was coming next.

'If you don't mind my speaking truthfully . . . I feel Lucy made a grave mistake. She became confused at your mother's dinner party. She has been under a great strain, as you can imagine.'

'Yes. I can understand that, Mrs Trent.'

'She and Robert were made for one another . . . don't you agree?' She fluttered her fan at him, waiting for his reaction.

'I do agree. You think Lucy still wishes to marry Robert?'

'Well now. I realize that you would be bitterly disappointed. But I am sure you wish for her happiness.'

'I want her to be happy. I would rather be told the truth, Mrs Trent. If Lucy wishes to marry my brother I prefer to know.'

'I believe she does . . . I'll admit she is still very confused. . . .'

'It is probably for the best. Robert would prove a far better husband than I.' He must steer this conversation around to Lord Marks, he thought. 'Why don't you ask Robert to call on Lucy?'

'Yes. I'll see if I can get her to do that. Thank you for being such a gentleman, Madoc, and accepting gracefully.'

Madoc was shamed by her words, but he reassured himself by thinking it had been Lucy's fault in the first place. He smiled.

'There will be much for Robert to celebrate, what with the title. . . .' He broke off abruptly, but Mrs Trent pounced on it.

'Title? What title? What do you mean?'

'I should never have mentioned it, Mrs Trent.' He tried to look suitably concerned. 'For the present it is a family secret.'

'But you can tell me. After all, we are to be family.'

Madoc looked uncertain.

'I don't know. I should not have said anything. Robert hasn't even heard about it himself yet. . . .'

'I promise we will give him no inkling that we know.'

'But if Robert finds out. . . .' Madoc was beginning to enjoy himself.

'You have my solemn word,' she said insistently.

'Well . . . my father, or perhaps Robert, is to inherit a title.'

'A title?' she squeaked, her voice rising. 'What sort of title?'

'He's to become a lord, I can say no more than that, Mrs Trent. I've told you more than I should already.'

'This is so thrilling.' She was breathless with excitement. 'And as the elder son Robert will eventually. . . ?'

'Inherit? Naturally. But please remember he must never hear that I told you. You have given your solemn word.'

'I promise, Madoc. But am I allowed to tell Lucy?'

Madoc pulled a doubtful face.

'Well . . . as long as you impress the need for secrecy on her.'

'She will never mention the title. I'll get her to write Robert a note. Please, in the meantime, tell Robert that Lucy wishes to see him.'

Madoc left in high spirits. He was relieved to receive a letter from Lucy later that day asking him to forgive her. She said she hoped he would understand. Forgive her! That would take a lot of doing.

A few days later, hearing his brother's voice, Madoc went to greet him, determined that he was going to end this feud.

'Welcome home, Rob. Good to see you.' Madoc stuck out his hand. Robert hesitated, then took it.

'You too, Madoc.' His voice was neutral.

'I thought you were returning earlier. Lucy is home.'

'Oh yes.' Robert appeared uninterested. 'Do you remember I stayed at Lord Marks' home a while back and met Caroline, his great-niece? Well, I spent a few days at the property adjoining Beechwood. Caroline was there too.' He raised appreciative eyebrows. 'It was most enjoyable.'

'That's a coincidence. Father has some astonishing information about Lord Marks.'

'What information?' Robert asked curiously.

'He'll have to tell you himself. But I have some other news.' Madoc tried to look suitably downcast. 'Lucy has broken our betrothal. She wishes to see you, Robert.'

Robert frowned. 'What can she possibly want with me?'

Alarm bells jangled. This was not the right reaction.

'I believe she wishes to apologize. She is hoping you will forgive her indiscretion; she sent their groom with a letter for you.'

'Did she?' Robert smiled without sympathy at Madoc. 'Getting a taste of your own medicine now, then.'

Madoc was relieved. That had worked anyway.

'Where is everyone?' Robert asked.

'The old man has gone to see Liam about a carriage-horse.'

'Speaking of Liam, how is Nia? Have you seen her lately?' Rob's eyes were boring into Madoc's.

'Yes.' Madoc tensed. 'I met her on Sunday . . . out riding.'

'You haven't seen her since?'

'No.'

'I'll probably ride over there later.' Madoc felt his resentment building up again, aware that Robert was studying his reaction. 'You are glowering at me as if you were about to object.'

Madoc clenched his jaw, biting back a remark. Robert gave a wolfish grin and made for the stairs.

'Listen Rob . . . what exactly are your feelings towards Nia?' he called out.

Robert spun back to face him.

'My feelings? I find the woman absolutely fascinating, if that's what you mean. I believe she is getting quite fond of me, too.' Laughter rippled through him as if he found it highly amusing. 'Don't tell me you're jealous.'

Madoc clenched his fists, taking deep breaths to control his rising temper. Robert continued to laugh as he went up the stairs.

Robert was enthusiastic about the proposed new title when David told him about it at dinner.

'But that's splendid. Congratulations. A great boost for us.' He held up his glass. 'We must drink a toast to the future Lord. . . .'

'No,' David frowned. 'It brings its own problems. . . .'

'Like sitting in the House of Lords.' Robert was gleeful. 'I can just see you parading around in your ermine.'

David and Madoc both laughed.

'Frankly, I can't,' David admitted. 'In fact I said as much to Lord Marks. . . .'

'You mean "my father", don't you?' Robert threw back his head, shaking with laughter. 'The sly old codger, fancy not telling you. And I've been to his home, I wonder if he knew I—'

'No. He didn't know I was his son until recently.' David told Robert the story. 'I wanted to talk to the family about this title.'

'What do you think about it, Mother?' Robert asked.

Emily glanced at David.

'You father is not happy about it.'

Robert's face dropped.

'I thought you'd be enthusiastic.'

'I must admit I am . . . a little. On your behalf. It would be your title as well, one day.'

Robert shrugged, but he half-smiled.

'To tell you the truth, Robert, I wanted to turn it down,' David said. He glanced at Robert. 'I was hoping the title could pass directly to you.'

Robert gasped, his normal self-assurance lapsing as he flushed slightly.

'I . . . er . . . I don't know what to say,' he stammered.

'Well, apparently I have no choice in the matter,' David said. 'So I suggest we go to visit Lord Marks together and discuss it further with him? Will you come?'

'Yes, I would like it, very much.' Robert said, looking pleased.

The following day Madoc and his father had arranged to rise at six o'clock to practise in the old stable.

'We'll try out a few moves,' David suggested. 'Just to get you used to the idea of kicking someone. Like this, see?' He brought his leg up sharply, catching Madoc unawares with a blow in the ribs with his booted foot.

'Ouch!' Madoc had leapt back but not quickly enough. 'Yes. I see.' He rubbed his ribs, eyeing his father warily.

'Or this.' David held his hands up in front of him, palms facing each other, weaving them slowly in front of Madoc's eyes. Madoc was watching his father's hands when David kicked him again, on the knee this time, making Madoc leap back once more, wincing.

'Hell! I thought you were going to show me, not attack me.' He laughed ruefully.

'Just getting you in the mood and keeping you on your toes.'

After a few more examples David began teaching Madoc one of the moves, showing him how to bring his leg up at an angle, using the outer edge of his foot to make contact, and using the strength of his thigh muscles. Madoc soon became proficient at leaping out of reach of his father's feet and at kicking the bale of straw he held up for him as a target.

'I think you are getting the idea,' David puffed. He collapsed on to a wooden box and leaned his head back against the wall.

'Perhaps we should leave it for now,' Madoc said, with sudden concern, realizing that his father was getting too old to be doing this. He rested his arm against the wall, wiping his face in an old towel hanging from a hook, as both men were soaking with perspiration.

Before he left David got Madoc to suspend a bundle of straw from a rope attached to an overhead rafter.

'Practise kicking it, and getting it again as it rebounds. Move it about to get used to different heights. We'll try again tomorrow.'

'What are you going to tell Mother? She will wonder what you're doing.'

'God knows,' his father groaned.

Madoc had bathed and changed and was coming down to breakfast when he met Robert coming out of the dining room.

'Did you see Nia yesterday?' Madoc asked him.

'No. She was out. Her mother said she has gone to stay at a friend's home.'

'You don't mean Albert?'

'No. Not Albert. A lady friend.' Robert smirked at Madoc. 'You didn't tell me Nia doesn't want to see you.'

'What's so amusing?' Madoc scowled at him.

'Your nerve. You make advances to Lucy and then expect Nia to come running.' He began walking past Madoc.

'I did not make advances to Lucy. Anyway, I thought Lucy had decided she wants to marry you. . . .'

Robert paused, staring at Madoc then adopted his sardonic expression.

'Me? Am I supposed to be pleased? Am I supposed to rush thankfully back into her arms?'

'How the hell do I know?' Madoc yelled, his temper snapping. 'I thought you loved the wretched woman?'

'Pity you didn't consider that before sneaking up to seduce her behind my back. Playing the big hero,' he snarled.

'I did no such thing. I don't want her. The only woman I want to marry is Nia.' Madoc closed his eyes as the words left his mouth, realizing that he had spoilt it all. 'Oh, God!'

'Don't be a fool. You can't marry Nia, she is half-gypsy.'

As the words left Robert's mouth Madoc hit him, flooring him with a single blow and causing him to knock his head against the newel post, just as their mother came into the hall.

'Madoc!' she shrieked. 'What do you think you're doing?' She rushed over to the unconscious Robert and knelt beside him, lifting his head on to her lap. Her eyes flashed fire up at Madoc. 'He's unconscious. Get him up from the floor!'

Madoc hoisted Robert up none too gently, slung him over his shoulder, carried him into the drawing room, and dumped him on to a settee. His mother grabbed his sleeve as he turned away.

'Please wait, Madoc. I'd like a word before you go.'

Madoc was tempted to ignore her, but respect for her won. He stood unrepentant, arms folded across his chest, looking dispassionately at Robert as his mother sent a maid for water.

'How could you do that, Madoc? You knocked your own brother unconscious. Do you really hate him that much?'

Madoc pursed his lips and made no reply.

'Please tell me, Madoc. I'd like to understand.' Emily's bewildered eyes were fixed on him.

'I'm sorry I've upset you, Mother,' he said reluctantly. 'But he insulted the woman I love.' His voice rose to a snarl. 'I bet father would hit someone if they ever insulted you.'

Emily frowned uncertainly.

'Do you think that, perhaps, you got it wrong? He probably didn't mean—'

'He meant it all right.' He eyed Robert grimly as he sat up, looking dazed. 'Will you excuse me now please, Mother?'

'But aren't you going to. . . .' She looked from one son to the other, neither of whom looked ready to apologise. 'Very well.'

'What happened?' Emily asked Robert, as he got up unsteadily, straightened and brushed at his clothes.

'I'm not really sure, Mother.' He fingered the lump on the back of his head tenderly. 'But I don't think Madoc should be going on those Cape Horn ships. He is quite uncouth these days.'

Emily bristled. 'But what did you say to him? He said you insulted— Whom did you insult?'

'I didn't insult anyone.'

'He thinks you did. What exactly did you say? About whom?'

'This is ridiculous. He said something about marrying Nia. . . .'

'Nia? He wants to marry Nia?'

'That's what he said. And I said he couldn't marry her. . . .' His voice trailed off uncomfortably.

'Be . . . cause?' She dragged out the word.

Robert exhaled a breath of exasperation.

'I said not to be a fool. He couldn't marry Nia because she is half-gypsy.'

'Robert. No wonder he was angry. What on earth did you say something like that for? Were you deliberately provoking him?'

'No, Mother.' His voice was clipped.

'You meant it?' She regarded him with horror.

He hesitated momentarily.

'Well it's the truth. She is half . . .'

'Oh, Robert.' Her tone was despairing. 'I never thought one of my own children would be prejudiced like this.'

'I am not prejudiced; it's a fact. Nothing can alter that, however much Nia plays the lady. I like—'

'I cannot believe that you are saying this. And I don't ever want to hear you express such an opinion in front of me again. If you feel like that please keep your thoughts to yourself.'

Emily rushed up the stairs to look for David. He was in his dressing room and turned in surprise as she burst in.

'David. Madoc just hit Robert. Knocked him unconscious. Now he's rushed off in a temper.' Shaking, she sank on to a tapestry-covered chair. 'I can't bear it when they quarrel like that.'

'What happened? Did you manage to find out?'

'Yes. Apparently Madoc said he wants to marry Nia. Did you know that? And Robert said he couldn't marry a gypsy.'

'No wonder he hit him. He loves her desperately, Emily.'

'I didn't know. I thought Robert was getting fond of her.'

'I think Robert has been trying to make Madoc jealous.'

'I'm sure he wouldn't do that.' Emily gave a deep sigh. 'Though as far as he is concerned, Madoc stole his fiancée.'

'Quite. So neither of them is really to blame. It has been a point of bitter strife between them for a while. All we can hope for is that it can all be settled as soon as possible.'

'I think you are getting the hang of it now,' David said with satisfaction. 'Bull is going to get a shock when he feels your boot in contact with his ribs.'

They were both pleased with the way Madoc was improving in the unfamiliar Oriental form of fighting. Apart from practising kicks, he had also been punching at a leather-covered sack, packed hard with sand and hung from a rafter, and for the last few mornings David had been actively trying to punch and kick Madoc, who managed to dodge most of his blows. Madoc had acquired an assortment of bruises and a slightly blackened eye in the process, which he had had difficulty in explaining away to his mother.

However, word about the fight had got around, and Russel Sutton approached Robert in the office.

'I say, is it true? About Madoc having a fight with Bull?'

'What do you mean?' Robert said, wondering whether anyone had found out about Tom and himself being attacked.

'I heard Madoc has challenged Bull to a professional fight.'

'Don't be ridiculous. Madoc would not. . . .' Robert's voice trailed off and a horrified expression crossed his face.

'He hasn't said anything to you, then?' As Russel spoke Madoc came through the door and they turned to stare at him.

'What's wrong? Have I got my coat on inside out or something?'

'Have you challenged Bull to a fight?' Robert's voice was tight with anger.

Madoc's gaze swung between the two men.

'Who told you?'

'It's all around town.' Russel was astounded. 'It's never true, then?'

Madoc gave a nonchalant shrug.

'I suppose it was bound to come out.'

Robert sucked in an exasperated breath.

'You stupid fool. You deserve all you get.'

'Thanks,' Madoc said mildly. 'I am glad I have your support. It's nice to know your family is behind you.'

Russel moved away, not wanting to be involved. Everyone at the office knew that Robert and Madoc were at loggerheads.

'How could you do such a thing?' Robert demanded in a low voice. 'It is not appropriate behaviour for a gentleman.'

'That's all right then, you can leave it all to a rough seaman, can't you?' Madoc's eyes were hard, green chips of jade. 'I don't care whether you approve or not, Robert. Tom is my friend as well as yours . . . even if he is half-gypsy.'

Robert gasped and the area around his lips went white. He turned on his heel and marched off.

David had posted a letter to Lord Marks and the family was invited to spend the weekend at Bath, to settle the matter of the inheritance. Madoc declined the invitation, and Emily thought it was better for Robert and David to go on their own. Legal formalities were dealt with, acknowledging David as the lord's son.

Robert had been delighted to be reunited with Caroline; each time they met he was the more attracted to her and she made it clear that she liked him. They decided that they wanted to spend more time together, and Robert was invited to return for a few more days. He could talk of no one else on their journey home on the train.

'You sound extremely fond of Caroline?' his father said.

'I am more than fond of her, Father.' Robert's happiness was obvious. 'And I am happy to say my feelings are reciprocated.'

'And are you interested in this young woman as a wife?' his father asked carefully.

'Most definitely. Next weekend, I intend to ask Lord Marks for her hand. She is sure he will approve.'

'That is the best news I have heard for a long while.' His father gripped his shoulder. 'She is a lovely young woman, Robert. I would think she'd make you the perfect wife.'

'I believe so. Wait until Mother knows.'

'And Madoc,' his father put in quietly.

'Why Madoc?' Robert's smile dropped away. 'He has little regard for my welfare.'

'I think you will find you are wrong.' David's lips were tight. 'Now that you are no longer interested in Lucy, I think there are a few points we should get straight. . . .' He went on to explain to Robert exactly what had happened between Lucy and Madoc and the dilemma Madoc had faced.

Robert was aghast.

'You mean to tell me it was all her doing? Madoc never proposed to her?'

'Precisely. Madoc couldn't believe what Lucy had told you. He only wanted Nia, he never wanted Lucy.'

'He did at one time,' Robert insisted.

'He believed that at one time. But not since he met Nia again, I assure you. He was appalled by it all, and has been sorely tried by this situation.' David went on to explain how Madoc had carried on with the pretence hoping that Lucy would regret her impulse. 'He wanted to work out a solution to salve your feelings.'

'Poor devil. I have been deliberately trying to provoke him with Nia. And in animosity I've said some awful things to him. I felt I hated him at times.'

'You are probably experiencing a little of what Madoc has also felt at times.'

For the rest of the journey Robert pondered over how he could straighten matters between himself and his brother. Once home, he tried to act as though everything was normal, but he could see that Madoc was still morose and unhappy. On seeing him making his way around to the stables, Robert followed him.

'Madoc,' Robert called. About to tighten a girth, Madoc paused, glancing up. 'Wait a moment, will you please.' Madoc waited, his hand on the saddle, as Robert crossed the yard. 'I wanted to catch you on your own.'

Unsmiling, Madoc looked back at the girth he had been tightening. 'What for?'

'I want to know whether you will accept my apologies?'

'Your apologies?' Madoc raised a sardonic brow.' What for?'

'For being such a prig and for accusing you unjustly about Lucy.' Robert was flooded with embarrassment. 'Father told me about it on the way home. I'm sorry. I didn't know what had happened, or how awful you felt.'

Madoc gave a barking, mirthless laugh.

'No. I don't suppose you did.' He shrugged. 'But you weren't entirely to blame. I would have been just as furious if the situation had been reversed.'

'And another thing. . . .' Robert paused uncomfortably. 'I am deeply sorry concerning what I said about Nia.'

Madoc's mouth tightened and he jutted his chin, his eyes becoming a swirling mossy green.

'What I said is unforgivable. Unfortunately I cannot retrieve what has been said. My only excuse is, I was trying to rile you.'

'You managed that all right.'

'That doesn't make it acceptable. I really am most—'

Madoc held up his hand. 'No need for any more apologies. I'd rather try to forget about it . . . I am not sorry I hit you though. You deserved that one.'

Robert managed a return smile.

'I understand. I wanted to try and straighten things between us; there has been too much bad feeling . . . and it appears it was mostly my—'

'I thought we were going to forget it.' Madoc led Storm into the yard, reached his foot up to the stirrup, but turned back as he was about to mount. 'You didn't go to see Lucy afterwards?'

'No. I had already decided to put her out of my mind before I received her letter. There was no chance of reconciliation.'

'I'm glad. She is not good enough for you. She will never think of anyone other than herself.'

'You are sincere about that, aren't you?' Robert looked thoughtful. 'As it happens, I've found the woman I want to marry.'

'Caroline?'

Robert nodded. 'My feelings are reciprocated.'

'Lucky you,' Madoc said under his breath.

Robert caught what he said.

'Madoc.' He was hesitant. 'Have you told Nia how you feel about her?'

Madoc looked down, kicking his toe against a mounting-block, obviously wondering what to say.

'She doesn't want to see me.'

'Oh yes she does,' Robert said softly. He crossed the yard, leaving Madoc staring after him questioningly.

★

Madoc sat outside on the stone bench, looking out at the artificial lake where wild ducks had settled and were now bobbing about on its surface. Seeing him there they paddled over hopefully, quacking. That was when it had all gone wrong between Nia and himself, he brooded. When that empty-headed Lucy had made advances. He gave a huge sigh, wishing he could begin all over again, wondering how he was to overcome Nia's refusal to see him.

He had tried to visit her three times since that first call. Once the maid said Miss Nia was not at home, on the second Martha had appeared and echoed her previous sentiments. The third time he went directly round to the stables and found Nia at work with her father and the horses. But to his chagrin, when she saw him she ran off, leaving him hurt and vulnerable.

Liam had approached him.

'I'm sorry, Madoc. It appears she has no wish to see you.'

'I can see that. But I need to talk to her to get a few things straight. If she would speak to me, explain her reasons, that's all. Then perhaps I can rectify matters.'

Liam nodded, studying Madoc's face.

'I can see your problem, man.' He shook his head and Madoc thought he seemed sympathetic. 'Women are hard to fathom sometimes.'

'They are,' Madoc agreed fervently.

Liam fiddled with the rope attached to the horse he was training and said quietly:

'I don't know what happened on the beach...?' He glanced at Madoc.

'I swear I told you the truth, Liam.'

'I am wondering if she is embarrassed ... after what she said to me that night.'

'I don't know, but I love her, Liam. You—' He snapped off his words, wondering if it sounded as if he were pleading.

But his hopes soared when Liam said quietly:

'I wouldn't give up, if I were you.' As Madoc's face lit up, he continued: 'But don't tell my good lady I told you that.'

'I'm grateful to you for telling me, Liam. You've given me hope, if nothing else.'

'I only want my daughter's happiness . . . and I think that lies with you, Madoc. I'll see what I can manage,' said Liam enigmatically.

But I still haven't seen her. Madoc sighed.

CHAPTER TWENTY-FOUR

M ADOC was awake before it was light and lay staring at the ceiling, his mind for once on the coming fight instead of on Nia. Today was the test! And more than once had he cursed himself for issuing that challenge to Bull. Anticipation of the physical hurt he was obliged to receive did not worry him unduly, but the niggling idea that he could lose the fight he found intolerable. For Bull to come out on top would be unthinkable.

Everybody was right; he must have been mad. After all, the man was a professional fighter, it was his vocation in life as much as it was Madoc's to be a seaman. Well, too late to worry now; he must just do the best he could. He could never have let that monster get away unchallenged after what he did to Tom.

He threw back the bedclothes and padded over to the window, looking out at the dawn on the sea beyond. It was a dark autumn day; the ocean was unsettled, restless and brooding, an all-over grey, with not a gleam of sunlight to brighten its surface. It mirrored his own mood exactly.

I think I'll go for a swim, he decided, *maybe that will clear away the cobwebs.*

After washing and dressing he carried his riding boots as he went down to the kitchen, so as not to disturb the household. The sleepy scullery-maid was stoking up the sulphurous fire, her mobcap all awry, and she jumped as he entered the kitchen, making no sound in his stockinged feet.

'G' morning, sir.' She bobbed a curtsy.

Madoc returned her greeting and took an earthenware teapot from the pantry. He put a teaspoonful of tea into it, from the large china caddy. As he lifted the blackened kettle from the trivet over the fire the skivvy recognized what he was doing.

'There's no need to be making your own tea, Mr Madoc. I'll do it for you,' she said.

'I can manage quite well, thank you, Gwynedd,' he said, pouring water on to the tea. He sank on to a chair near the big scrubbed wooden table, and waited for the tea to steep, his thoughts still on the coming fight.

Madoc and his father were aware that the methods he had been practising were illegal – kicking was forbidden by the new rules. But so too was bare-knuckle fighting, along with butting, gouging and hitting below the waist – methods which Bull regularly employed, as Madoc and David had seen when they attended a fight. These methods were supposed to get the fight stopped.

'If Bull can break the rules, so can I,' Madoc had asserted, when he and his father discussed it. 'As far as I can see, it is every man to his own methods. At least it will only be two of us in the ring, not a gang of his cronies.'

'Hmm.' David was still unhappy about him fighting at all, as Madoc well knew.

'Has word got around much more?' Madoc had asked him, after Robert was so disapproving at the office.

'Seems like. Quite a few people have asked me about it . . . though I feigned ignorance. You will be pleased to hear that a number of people are betting on you.'

Madoc gave a hollow laugh.

'Wagering I shall lose, I suppose?'

'No. To win.'

'I'll have to make sure I don't let them down then.'

Madoc came back from his swim refreshed and swung his leg over to dismount when he noticed Nia's horse in the stable yard. His blood gave a sudden surge, his stomach tightening with anticipation.

'Is Miss Nia here?' he asked a sleepy Trevor as he flung his reins at him.

'Yes, Mr Madoc. She—' Madoc didn't wait to hear the rest as he raced across to the house. A maid looked up at him as he dashed through the servants' quarters.

'Miss Nia is waiting for you in the drawing—' a voice began.

He hurried on before she could finish speaking and burst into the drawing room, pulling up abruptly as he found Nia pacing around the room.

'Good morning, Nia.'

'Madoc.' She came over, dark eyes huge in an unnaturally pale face. 'Please tell me it's not true.'

His heart plummeting, he regarded her bleakly. Was news of the fight the only reason she had come? He was desperate to take her in his arms, but didn't dare in case he frightened her off again.

'Madoc. Have you really challenged Bull?'

'Does it matter to you?' His voice was curt.

'It's because of Tom, isn't it?' When he didn't answer she added: 'Bull could kill you.'

'Nonsense. I'm no weakling, I can hold my own in a fight. Anyway, I've grown a bit since the last time I fought him.' His spirits rose a little at the concern on her face.

'I don't care. Please don't do it.' She reached out, touching his face. 'Is that why you're growing a beard? Oh! It's soft,' she said with surprise. His face was thickly covered with a heavy black stubble as, telling everyone he had decided to grow a beard, he had not shaved for over a week in case he nicked himself with his razor. A blow could open up even a slight cut.

Laughter rumbled through him.

'What did you expect it to be like? A yard-brush?'

She didn't join in his mirth.

'I don't want you to be hurt, Madoc.'

He caught her hand as she withdrew it from his face, lifted it to his lips and kissed it. He found it was cold and trembling. He put his arms around her, drawing her close against him, and with a little sigh she put her head on his chest. Elated, he felt her heart beating against him.

'Nia. Why wouldn't you see me? I've been going nearly insane.' When she didn't look at him or answer he continued: 'I love you more than my life, Nia. I can't bear it without you. Will you marry me, please?'

She raised her head then, eyes gleaming like jet. Then her face puckered.

'Don't you want to marry me?' Uncertain again, his body stiffened. 'You don't love me?'

'Of course I do, you big idiot.' She rubbed the back of her hand across her eyes. 'I've always loved you.'

'But you don't want to marry me?'

'But I do! I do! More than anything in the world. But I thought. . . .' Her voice trembled as she spoke, coming out in a whispered gasp. 'I thought . . . you didn't . . . want to marry me. Because I'm half-gypsy.'

'God, Nia.' His voice was ragged as he hugged her, rubbing his face in her hair, catching strands of it against his whiskers. 'Don't ever say such a thing. Not ever. I wouldn't change one single thing about you.'

He bent his head and kissed her, gently at first, then more urgently as she reached up eagerly, standing on her toes, tangling her hands in his unruly damp hair, pulling his head down, kissing him back, her lips hungry for his. Breathless, they drew apart, staring at one another. He laughed, throwing his head back, his teeth flashing white against the black stubble, his eyes glowing aquamarine with happiness.

'I can't believe it. At last! I've been going mad with longing for you.'

'But Lucy? I thought you loved Lucy.'

'Lucy? How could I love that affected, simpering woman? As soon as I met you again I knew there had never been anyone else. Not ever. I love you, wanted you. Only you. I knew I'd love you for ever . . . but you didn't seem to want me.'

'I did, desperately. But I needed to be sure of your feelings before I let you see mine.'

'And I felt the same. I thought you were rejecting me in no uncertain terms. How stupid we've been.'

'Then, on the night of the party, I thought I had finally lost you to Lucy.'

'You should have known better.'

'But what about that night on the beach?' She pulled back out of his arms, rigid, doubtful again, searching his face. 'Why did you say you couldn't marry me?'

'I thought you and Rob loved each other. That I was going to ruin it for both of you. I was absolutely insane with jealousy every time I saw you with him.'

'I wanted to make you jealous,' she admitted.

'You managed that all right. And you thought I pulled away from you because. . . .' He shook his head with disbelief. 'No wonder you refused to see me. I didn't know what to do, what I had done, because after that night on the beach I thought you must love me. I knew we were meant to be together. I decided that no matter how much Rob loved you, he couldn't come into it. I wanted to ask you to marry me . . . but you kept sending me away!'

'I wanted to see you,' she admitted. 'But Mama was so adamant, I was afraid she was going to get another attack.'

'I was frantic. . . .'

'Is that why you challenged Bull? It is! I can see it on your face.'

'As long as I have you I can take on the world.' He laughed aloud again, gathering her back in his arms.

'No! I want to know about the fight. When is it?' He didn't reply so she repeated the question. 'You must tell me – please.'

'Today.'

'No! You can't! You mustn't go through with it.' When he shook his head she said: 'Please, Madoc! Cancel it! For my sake.'

He flinched. 'Nia! You can't ask me to call it off. You know I can't drop out of it now.'

'Will you call it off for me? Do you love me enough to do that?'

'God!' His arms fell away from her and he swallowed hard, going cold. He ran his hand through his hair. 'Everyone will think I'm afraid to face Bull and, even worse, *he*'ll think I am! You don't want that to happen, do you?'

'Nobody would ever accuse you of that.'

'Bull would.' He turned away, his stomach knotted at the thought of calling it off, of humiliating himself – even for Nia. He must make her understand how he felt. He straightened and turned back to her, held both her arms and transfixed her with a hard stare, his expression grim.

'Nia. If you truly mean to ask this of me, if you want me to call it off that badly . . . I will. . . .'

'Madoc, you . . .' Her strained expression had eased.

'Wait a moment, hear me out, Nia. I will not be happy about it, but I'll call it off. For you,' he said through gritted teeth. 'But you will have to live with the knowledge that I'll feel like a coward. And I will forever have to endure that humiliation. Is that what you are asking me to do?'

With a little cry she flung herself at him, shaking her head.

'No! I know you too well. I can't ask you to do it.'

He heaved a sigh of relief.

'Thank God for that.'

'But I am terrified you'll be hurt.' She stared at him, anguished. He grinned.

'I'm not mad about the idea either. But I've got a few tricks I can pull. My old man has been . . .'

'He knows about it? He never agrees?'

'He disapproves strongly. But, like you, he knew I couldn't back out once I'd challenged Bull.' He went on to tell her about the training he had been doing each morning.

'What about your hands?' She lifted them, examining them.

'Well, my hands are not exactly soft after all the years I've spent at sea. Harder than Bull's, I'd say.'

'I suppose so,' she agreed. 'But what about the burn? Did you have scars?'

'Yes, but there was hardly any on the back of my hand. And it didn't extend to my knuckles.'

She turned his hand over touching the scar on his palm.

'And what about this side?'

'That's all healed up as good as new,' he reassured her. 'It's quite a while since it happened.'

She bent her head and kissed his palm and he caught her to him again, pressing her firmly against the length of his body.

'If you only knew how much I love you,' he murmured, lowering his mouth to hers, his tongue exploring it in a stirring, sensual caress. He felt himself harden against her and would have pulled away, but she pressed closer, arching towards him as his fingers found her breast through her blouse, teased at her nipple.

'God, Nia,' he groaned. 'This is neither the time nor the place.'

There was a tap on the door and the maid entered as they leapt apart. Her knowing eyes flashed over them.

'Sorry. I didn't know you were in here, Mr Madoc,' Sîan smirked. 'I came to fetch the newspaper for Mr Robert.' She took her time crossing the room, her hips swaying provocatively in her dark, hooped skirt, the ribbons in her cap dancing as she tossed her head. She gave them an impudent grin as she left.

'The brazen little madam.' Nia was amused. 'She was making eyes at you.' Madoc laughed and she gasped. 'She's done it before hasn't she?'

'I believe I told you previously, I don't grab and kiss the maids. Even very pretty ones.'

It was Nia's turn to laugh.

'I suppose I'll have to get used to seeing women flashing their eyes at you. I hope Bull doesn't spoil your looks.'

She pressed herself against him again and he hugged her close.

'Make love to me! Now,' she whispered. 'Please.'

His mouth opened slightly and he sucked in a breath.

'Now? Are you sure?'

'Very sure.'

'We'll have to sneak up the stairs. Wait a second.' He looked through the door into the hall. 'Coast is clear. You go up first, I'll follow you.'

She nodded, eyes like stars, and he watched her race up the stairs holding up her skirt. He heard no voices, and once he was sure that she would have reached his room he followed her. He closed the door softly behind him and turned the key in the lock. She was standing looking at him, her chest heaving in great gasps of air.

'I have been waiting all my life for this moment, Madoc Morgan. I knew I would never marry if I couldn't have you. No one else could come anywhere near.'

'Nia. My precious love.' He took a step towards her, ripping open his shirt as he did, tearing off some of the buttons in his haste to take her in his arms. As his lips met hers he began undoing the buttons on her blouse, sliding it off her shoulders. Eagerly she pulled her arms out, shaking the garment from her, pushing herself against him. He tugged at the ribbons on her chemise, snapping them, so that her soft breasts fell out against his bare skin. He bent his head, kissing the valley between those sweet orbs, teasing and licking her nipples.

Nia felt shafts of delight stab through her, and an answering surge of desire throughout her whole body. She moaned as his tongue tantalized, arching herself against his hard body. Reaching for the ties on her waist she undid them, letting her skirt and underclothes fall around her ankles as he put his arms around her and lifted her on to the bed. She saw him impatiently pull off the rest of his clothes. He knelt alongside her, his tongue moving over her, stroking her, caressing her, sending her trembling into an ecstasy of yearning.

'Madoc!' she whispered. 'Please, Madoc. Please.'

As he lowered himself to the bed alongside her she saw his eyes on her, a swirling turquoise of passion, before he closed them, his tongue and lips seeking her breasts, her neck, her mouth. She was aware of the iron-hard muscles of his thighs and chest pressing her, his male hardness thrusting against her, his hands wandering over her body, her secret places. She opened her thighs to him but still he held back, his tongue probing and teasing her mouth until she quivered and smouldered. Then he came together with her, gently, softy, slowly. She dug her nails into his shoulders as there was a moment of sharp pain, then the smouldering fire burst into an explosive ecstasy, convulsing her body as she arched against him, screaming his name as he climaxed at the same moment.

Madoc kissed her gently, his lips soft, not demanding, then leaned up away from her on his elbows, looking down at her.

'I promise I will love you for ever,' he whispered. 'With my whole heart and soul. As long as I live.'

Madoc started as there was a tap on the door and someone tried the handle. 'Mr Madoc, sir. Do you want your clean towels?'

Madoc jumped off the bed, grinning as Nia thrust the pillow over her head to smother her laughter.

'Will you leave them outside, please Sîan,' he called.

'I bet she has been listening outside the door,' Nia giggled, her gaze travelling over his body, a smug expression on her face. 'But you're mine.'

'I surely am, thank God. I wonder if she told the family you were here?' His laughing eyes met hers. 'Your name will be mud this time, as well as mine.'

She put her face back to the pillow as she began laughing again.

'Nia. I am so happy I'd like rush in and tell the family right now. But we can't do that until I've spoken to your parents.'

'Yes we can. I am going to be your wife and I want everyone in the whole world to know.'

'But what if your mother won't allow me in to ask for your hand?' His mood was light-hearted, the fight forgotten.

'Idiot.' She jumped up and began reaching for her clothes. 'Let's go down and tell them now.'

In the back area of a coal yard on the Strand, four stout stakes had been hammered firmly into the ground and a square formed around them with two rounds of thick ropes. A buzz of conversation rose from the sizeable crowd assembled; tobacco smoke, mingled with the heavy smell of stale perspiration and unwashed clothes, hung strongly in the air. Two men were collecting money at the yard gate, another was taking wagers from people jostling around him. Others were touting their wares from trays: boxes of matches, pork-pies, twists of tobacco.

Stripped to a pair of trousers, his heaviest boots and with a hefty belt buckled around his waist, Madoc pushed his way through the crowd. As it parted to let him through he was aware of all the eyes on him, assessing him. Some were openly derisive, some approving, some encouraging, most frankly excited as they anticipated the brutality of the contest.

Pushing down the apprehension tightening his stomach, he assured himself he could control it, use it to help him. Deliberately he turned his mind on the 'greybeards', the towering waves of the Horn; if he could face and survive those he could survive the lesser might of Bull. He swaggered up to the ring, jutting his chin, mouth pursed aggressively, and vaulted effortlessly over the top rope landing, catlike, on his feet inside the ring.

Acknowledging the cheers at his entrance he grinned, holding his arms up in the air. As his second, his father had followed closely on his heels; his other second was Bryn Jones, from the *Gower Girl*. Tom, amongst others, had offered to be a second, but Madoc had declined as they all agreed that as a lawyer he was not it a position to take part in anything even marginally illegal.

He glanced around, finding friends from all walks of his life; his childhood, the village, the office, many shipmates – his eyes widened as they alighted on the boy in working-clothes standing at the ringside. He glared at him but the boy avoided eye contact.

'That's Nia,' Madoc whispered to his father. 'See. Over there, dressed as a boy. Get her out of here!'

His father sighed.

'There was no possible way we were going to prevent her coming, so we dressed her up as a youth.'

Madoc was appalled.

'I don't want her here.'

'Neither do I.' David shrugged. 'But she is as stubborn as your mother. Pity help any children you may have.' He gave a crooked grin.

As Madoc blew a frustrated breath there was a ragged cheer and Bull shambled his way through the crowd, a sneer on his face as he ducked awkwardly between the ropes.

'I'm gonna kill you, Morgan. You ready for it?' He lumbered threateningly towards Madoc.

Madoc, one arm draped nonchalantly across the ropes, threw him a grin, his eyes dancing.

'Quite ready . . . Bullock's Balls.' He deliberately goaded him with the childhood nickname which had always infuriated him. Madoc and his father had decided that it was a good idea to get Bull riled up, so he would be more likely to make mistakes, whereas Madoc needed to keep a cool head and consider what he was doing at all times.

Bull gave a roar of anger and lunged towards Madoc as the referee stepped in front of him, lifting a restraining arm.

'Not yet, Bull.' He bellowed to make himself heard above the suddenly heightened murmur from the interested crowd. 'To your corners, gents, and when I drop my hand come out fighting.'

Aware that he was becoming tense, Madoc consciously tried to relax, but as he stepped over to his corner, his eyes met Nia's under the youth's cap she wore, her hair stuffed inside.

'You shouldn't have come,' he protested quietly, looking away as he spoke.

She ducked her head down keeping her face out of sight from any curious scrutiny.

'Do you think people would be surprised if I reached over and gave you a kiss?' she whispered.

Madoc let out a loud hooting laugh. She was obviously trying to get him to unwind and succeeded admirably. He caught a few people looking at him, their expressions dumbfounded to see amusement on his face at a time like this; he grinned, waving to them.

The referee had been spouting something about Bull. Madoc turned his attention back to him just as he began:

'And his challenger is Madoc Morgan. I know some people are surprised to find a gentleman taking on Bull, but many of you will also know Madoc. They will know he's been a Cape Horner since he was a lad. A veteran of many trips, he is a hard man, and will be no walkover as far as Bull is concerned.'

There were a few jeers from Bull's cronies, but Madoc was surprised when a cheer rose from the crowd.

'...and each round will end when someone is knocked to the ground.' The referee raised his arm, '...so come out fighting.' He dropped his arm as his assistant knocked a metal spike against an old ship's bell.

Nia had been studying Madoc's impressive body. Broad shoulders, a powerful physique, hard and firm, with a sprinkling of dark hairs across his chest, it tapered neatly to his waist, well-defined muscles rippling with each movement. He is magnificent, she thought, distracted for a moment from her anxiety. *This incredible man is mine!*

The bell went and the crowd fell silent, Nia only realized that she had been holding her breath when it came out with a rush as Madoc left his corner. Trim and compact compared with Bull's ungainly bulk, Madoc danced around Bull on the balls of his feet, an impudent grin on his face as Bull kept swinging ponderous punches which Madoc dodged effortlessly.

'Come on, Bull,' Madoc taunted, laughing at him. 'You are supposed to hit me.'

'I'll kill ew,' Bull snarled. Lunging forward he surprised Madoc by stamping on to his foot, pinning him to the ground with his colossal weight, then he swung his fist. Madoc was unable to dodge the blow completely and Bull's knuckles connected with a firm crunch on Madoc's face, knocking his head back and splitting his lip. Nia smothered her cry with a hand over her mouth as Madoc reeled back with blood streaming down his face, he was shaking his head groggily as Bull punched him hard below the belt.

Horrified, she heard Madoc grunt as he doubled up on to his knees and Bull thudded another blow at his face. Madoc slumped to the ground and the bell sounded as Bull brought back his foot to kick him, but he was near a gathering of Madoc's shipmates and a hand came through the ropes and grabbed Bull's raised foot, sending him crashing over backwards. The referee skipped into the ring.

'First round, gentlemen. Thirty seconds to the next.'

David and Bryn dashed into the ring, heaving Madoc to his feet as Bull stumbled back on to his. They dumped Madoc on to a crate in his corner and Bryn threw a jug of water over him.

'Hold this under his nose.' Nia handed David a bottle. Madoc coughed, making a face, as Nia passed over a second bottle. 'Dab that on his mouth to stop it bleeding.'

As David complied, the bell sounded again and Madoc got to his feet, still looking dazed.

'Keep away from him, Madoc,' Nia heard his father mutter. 'Give yourself chance to recover.'

The scene around him still wavered as Madoc raised his hands in front of him, his open palms facing one another, moving them in the air in the way his father had taught him. He saw Bull watch them warily, wondering what he was doing, and Madoc kept well back out of reach of Bull's fists as he felt his strength returning. He won't pull the same trick a second time, Madoc thought. He was recovering as Bull came towards him, and Madoc danced back, neatly side-stepping his blows, this time making sure he kept his own feet clear of Bull's massive ones. Ducking under another swing, Madoc chopped the side of his hand across Bull's throat then immediately brought his foot up, delivering a vicious kick to his knee, all the considerable strength of his thigh muscles behind it. With a howl of surprise and anguish, Bull went down heavily on to the kicked knee and toppled over. The bell sounded again and Madoc went back to his corner.

'You all right?' his father asked.

'Yes. Got my wind back now.' He glanced at Nia and winked briefly and was rewarded by a tremulous smile. Madoc prodded the inside of his cut cheek with his tongue; one of his eyes was swelling rapidly and closing, making it difficult to see. David dabbed at it with some liquid, probably supplied by Nia. Glancing over at Bull, he could see his seconds winding a piece of linen tightly round his knee.

'You got him nicely with that kick.' David approved. 'I hope that worries him.'

'So do I, after what he did to Tom.'

'Hmm. I have a feeling you're going to get more than a little hurt too unless you keep out of his way.'

'Next round.'

Bull's face was vicious as he limped towards him.

'You won't get away with that.'

Madoc darted forward beneath Bull's swing, slamming a hard fist into his stomach, then brought another fist thudding at his face, sending him reeling back, blood pouring from his nose. Bull wiped his hand across his face, scowling when he saw the blood on his hand, and lumbered back towards Madoc, who managed a sharp kick to

Bull's ribs. As Madoc repeated the kick to the same spot Bull bellowed, trying to stumble back out of range, but Madoc danced after him, applying another kick to his bandaged knee. Bull's leg gave under him and he tumbled to the ground again.

Madoc went back to his corner feeling pleased with himself. 'That's two rounds he hasn't touched me,' he crowed.

'Don't get complacent,' David told him grimly. 'If he catches you off guard he could finish you with one punch.'

The next time Bull ploughed straight at Madoc, his fists swinging wildly. Madoc dodged back out of his way a few times without realizing how near the ropes he was getting. He backed into them and before he could slide sideways, Bull threw a punch. Madoc managed to move his head fast enough to evade the first blow but, unable to retreat, the second caught him, jolting his head back on his neck, sending stars rocketing through his head. As he felt himself sliding to his knees another hammer blow hit him. The stars went out as everything went black.

He came to with that vile stuff under his nose again and he tried to move his head away from it. A hand clamped his head to it, however, and he coughed and spluttered to full awareness.

'Take't away . . . feel sick,' he muttered, as bile rose in his throat.

Understanding, Bryn thrust a jug of water at him, holding it to his mouth, then he held a bucket for him to spit it into. Madoc, grateful to get rid of the bitter mixture of bile and blood filling his mouth, took a second gulp of water as the bell went again.

'Don't forget. Keep away from him,' David warned him again. 'And the ropes. Don't let him get you against the ropes.'

Madoc was swaying slightly as he rose to his feet, his eyes unfocused. It felt as if someone were hammering nails inside his head. Bull appeared to be swimming as he came towards him grinning, and Madoc blinked hard, forcing himself to concentrate.

Got to know what I'm doing. Get Bull mad. He managed to conjure up a leering grin at his opponent.

'Come on then, Bullock's Balls – no balls.' Madoc raised his voice, loud enough for some of the crowd to hear and was rewarded by a ripple of amusement.

Bull gave a bellow of fury and lurched towards him, wildly swinging his fists. Madoc brought his leg up, catching Bull hard in the ribs. This time, however, Bull grabbed and held his foot, but as he tried to push Madoc over, Madoc reached behind him and grasped the ropes, taking his full weight with his powerful seaman's arms. Jumping his other foot off the ground he managed to kick Bull in the temple. As Bull wavered, releasing Madoc's leg, Madoc applied a second kick, then dropped lightly on to his feet. He swung a punch as Bull swayed forward, connecting first with a solid blow from his fist, following through with a second blow with the bony part of his elbow. The last blow jarred, sending pins and needles shuddering down his forearm to his fingers. He became aware of the crowd roaring as, shaking his arm and working his fingers, he stood back, watching Bull slumped to the ground.

Bull never moved as the bell sounded and his seconds rushed forward, having great difficulty in dragging his huge bulk across the dusty ground to his corner. Hastily they threw water over him, slapping his face, calling him, even holding his nose. One of them yanked at his arms, trying to get him to sit up, but he was still unconscious as the bell sounded again.

The referee went over to his corner and bent down to look at him. He came back to the centre and there was a huge bellow of agreement from the crowd as he held up Madoc's arm. Madoc could hardly hear what the referee said as he announced him the winner, and everyone rushed into the ring, shaking his hand and slapping him on the back. Grinning, aching, cut, bruised, dirty, smeared all over with blood and coal dust from the ground, Madoc searched for Nia amongst the crowd. Finding her, he pushed his way through to her, caught her hand and turned to face the crowd.

'I want you all to meet the woman I am going to marry,' he yelled as he pulled off her cap allowing her glorious hair to tumble down around her. Everyone gave a roar of approval, then a second one as she stood on her toes and kissed him lightly on his split mouth.

The crowd parted as Madoc made his way over to Bull, now standing amongst his cronies, and Bull scowled as Madoc glared at him. In a loud voice Madoc bellowed:

'Bull! I want everyone here today to know I am warning you and your cronies. Never, any one of you, try to touch a member of my family or any of my friends again.' Then he added through his teeth: 'I know who you are.' He stared at each of them in turn, then turned on his heel and walked away.

Nia pushed up close to him and he draped an arm around her

shoulders as she put hers around his waist.

'Are you all right?' She frowned, her eyes examining his battered face and body.

His swollen lips managed a grin.

'Never been better. Let's go home and plan a wedding.'